TORCH

A HENRY HOLT MYSTERY

OTHER BOOKS IN THE CARVER SERIES
BY JOHN LUTZ

Spark

Hot

Bloodfire

Flame

Kiss

Scorcher

Tropical Heat

TORCH

JOHN LUTZ

HENRY HOLT AND COMPANY
NEW YORK

Henry Holt and Company, Inc.
Publishers since 1866
115 West 18th Street
New York, New York 10011
Henry Holt® is a registered
trademark of Henry Holt and Company, Inc.

Published in Canada by Fitzhenry & Whiteside Ltd.,
195 Allstate Parkway, Markham, Ontario L3R 4T8.

Library of Congress Cataloging-in-Publication Data
Lutz, John.
Torch / John Lutz. — 1st ed.
p.   cm. — (A Henry Holt mystery)
1. Carver, Fred (Fictitious character)—Fiction.   2. Private
investigators—Florida—Fiction.   I. Title
PS3562.U854T67   1994   93-28431
813'.54—dc20   CIP

ISBN 0-8050-2610-X

Henry Holt books are available for special promotions and premiums. For details contact: Director, Special Markets.

First Edition—1994

DESIGNED BY LUCY ALBANESE

Printed in the United States of America
All first editions are printed on acid-free paper.∞

1   3   5   7   9   10   8   6   4   2

FOR SOPHIA
BY ANY OTHER NAME

*"If I should love you,
what business is it
of yours?"*

—GOETHE

TORCH

A HENRY HOLT MYSTERY

1

CARVER SAID, "You can trust me."

Donna stared at him across the table and said, "I know I'm not trustworthy, so why should I think you are?"

"Because Beth recommended me, and you can trust her. She's honest to the point of cruelty."

Donna Winship smiled. She was attractive when she smiled, but still not the sort to inspire men to fight. Her features were made more delicate by the middle-aged lines etched in them, like fine cracks in bone china. She had dyed blond hair cut shoulder-length and with a wisp of bangs; brown eyes like those of a frightened animal run to ground, gazing out from behind the bangs as if they were foliage meant to conceal her from hunters. Maybe that was the way she felt. She had a plump and pleasing figure beneath a business suit tailored to make her look crisply efficient, which was probably impossible. Carver guessed she was in her late thirties, but he knew he might be off five years either way. She looked like one of those average, not *un*attractive women used in commercials for weight control programs or tanning salons, the type the composite female TV watcher could identify with, just as the advertisers had schemed. You couldn't trust advertisers.

"I'm sorry I doubted you," she said. "The past month or so has made me suspicious of everyone."

"Beth said you wouldn't feel that way without good reason." Beth had also said Donna seemed to be under horrendous stress.

Donna nudged the olive below the ice cubes in her martini and took a sip. Her hand was steady enough. "Beth's a sweetheart."

"I noticed."

After a night of especially exhausting lovemaking, Beth had convinced Carver that he should meet with her friend Donna. Donna was having problems and didn't want to go to Carver's office, didn't want anyone to know she'd consulted a private investigator.

Carver had hesitated, so Beth had gone about persuading him as only she could persuade. He'd pretended to be hesitant as long as possible, then finally agreed to meet Donna Winship that evening at the Happy Lobster on the coast highway and get the story from her. Beth had thanked him in her own special way.

Carver smiled. It was something, the way people used each other. It kept him in business.

The Happy Lobster had semi-private tables with pink table-cloths and a wide, curved window that looked out over the vast blue-green Atlantic, mesmerizing diners with its shifting, rolling planes of shadowed and glimmering depths. There were a few high clouds today of the sort that taunted the uninitiated with the promise of rain this time of year on the east coast of Florida. Dusk was beginning to settle in. The sky met the sea in a haze that obscured the horizon and that at sunset would darken and close like the fold of an envelope.

They were only meeting for drinks and conversation, but Carver had gotten a restaurant table so they'd have more privacy than the lounge provided. When Donna had walked in, he'd recognized her immediately from Beth's description and the blue dress she'd said she'd be wearing. Beth must have described him well, too, because Donna had put on a strained smile and made her way directly across the restaurant toward him. She had a nice, fluid walk; several male diners interrupted their chewing and glanced after her.

There followed fifteen minutes of drink sipping and tentative verbal fencing, much of it self-deprecating on Donna's part.

Feeling he had her confidence at last, Carver said, "Why do you say you're not trustworthy?"

Donna raised her dark eyebrows in surprise. They were barely visible beneath the dyed, wispy bangs. "Beth didn't tell you?"

"No. She thought you should. We're starting from scratch."

She gazed out at the endless Atlantic, then back at Carver, decision in her eyes. There was no sound for a while except the murmur of conversation among the other diners, the muted clinking of flatwear against china. The sea breaking on the beach below couldn't be heard through the thick glass. "I'm a married woman, Mr. Carver, the mother of a four-year-old daughter."

She seemed to expect Carver to comment on that. He said, "That's not a bad situation." For an instant he thought of his own daughter, living in St. Louis with his former wife in a world not meant to contain him.

"And I'm seeing another man."

"Why?"

"I no longer love my husband, and he no longer loves me. Mark made it clear months ago that our marriage was going to end."

"Another woman?"

"I suspect so, but I'm not sure. He simply became distant, refused to communicate. It's still that way."

"Is he abusive?"

"Only verbally, when he bothers to talk to me." She took a long pull of her martini and placed the glass back on its improbable lobster-shaped cork coaster. "We've become locked in a kind of war of nerves, if you know what I mean."

"I know," Carver said. "All happy marriages are different; unhappy marriages are alike."

She looked back at the sea and thought about that. He doubted if she believed it. There was something about her expression. The sea had depths; she had depths.

"Mark stopped giving me money," she said, still looking at the sea, "so two months ago I arranged for day care for Megan—our daughter—and got a job as a receptionist at an insurance company. I knew where the marriage was headed and wanted to provide for our future."

"Yours and Megan's."

"Exactly. No matter what Mark does."

Pieces were beginning to fall into place for Carver, but he said nothing, letting Donna talk.

She produced a lacy white handkerchief from somewhere and began wringing it between small, shapely hands with pink-enameled nails. "I'm not sure if Mark knows about Enrico and me. I'm not sure he'd care if he did know, except that despite our marital problems, he's very possessive of anything that belongs to him, including his wife. And despite all the strain on our marriage, I'm still his wife."

"Enrico?"

"Enrico Thomas, the man I'm involved with. We met two months ago when he came into the office to see about insurance. He didn't have an appointment, so he had to wait for almost an hour, and we began talking. The next day he sent me flowers. The next day he called. The next day we met for lunch. We've been meeting ever since, and for more than lunch. Mark would consider that wrong, since I'm still a married woman. He's . . . very religious, a traditionalist. I don't think it's wrong; I think it's necessary." She sounded defensive. "Enrico gives me the air to breathe that Mark denies me. Can you understand that?"

"Sure. We all need oxygen to survive. But you're afraid Mark knows, or will find out."

"My husband's never laid a hand on me in anger, Mr. Carver, but he has with other people. He can be a violent man in a way few of his friends know about. His rage is old and deep in him and comes to the surface suddenly and unexpectedly. A few years ago I saw him beat up a man in an argument over who was first in line at a theater. Fifteen minutes later he was his usual calm self."

"Does Enrico know you're married?"

"I never told him I was, but I suspect he knows." A deep determination transformed her for a moment; her gentle eyes darkened and held the depths of the Atlantic, near as eternity on the other side of the window from martinis and lobster bisque. "I intend to keep seeing Enrico, Mr. Carver."

Carver rattled the ice in his glass. The waiter took it for a signal and looked inquisitive. Figuring what the hell, Carver held up two fingers, and the waiter nodded and glided away between the tables. "I'm not sure exactly why you want to hire me, Donna."

"I want you to follow me."

Carver considered. "You mean you want a bodyguard?"

"No, I simply want to be followed."

"What about the times when you meet Enrico?"

"Then, too."

"Usually," Carver said, "my clients want me to follow someone other than themselves."

"Then I guess I'm not your usual client." She fished in her straw purse and withdrew a dark blue checkbook. She scribbled in it with a white plastic ballpoint pen, tore out a check, and laid it on the table in front of Carver.

He read it upside down and saw that it was for a thousand dollars. He didn't reach for it, though. Not yet.

Made uneasy by his hesitation, she said, "Beth told me your fees. I can afford you. I cashed in an old life insurance policy."

"It isn't the money," he told her.

"It's always the money," she said sadly.

"Meaning what?"

"Money and love are always mixed together, like it's a law of nature. That's all I meant."

"I'd like to know more."

"There isn't any reason for that."

"I'd still like to know."

"I'm sorry."

"Maybe when you trust me more?"

"Maybe," she said.

If it weren't for Beth he might have politely refused the job, then stood up and left. Wisely if unprofitably turned his back on somebody else's money and love and trouble.

Donna scribbled again with the white plastic pen, this time on a cocktail napkin.

"Here are my home and office addresses and phone numbers," she said, and laid the folded napkin next to the check. She was obviously bothered when he made no move to reach for either. Carver on the fence, sensing trouble on both sides. "Beth assured me you'd help," she told him. And he heard something new in her voice for the first time: barely controlled terror.

She stood up suddenly, as if her nerves simply wouldn't allow her to sit there any longer, talking to a virtual stranger about the dark currents of her life. "*Will* you help?" she asked, as if this might be his last chance and hers.

He sighed, then picked up the napkin and check.

He said, "You won't even know I'm around."

With a relieved smile, she said, "Thank you. I'm leaving

now, but I'm going to meet Enrico at Riley's Clam Shop at ten o'clock tonight. Mark thinks I'm in Orlando, visiting my mother for the weekend."

"Where's Megan?"

"She's with my mother." With an abruptness that surprised Carver, her soft eyes brimmed with tears. "You don't think I like this, do you?" She seemed angry at him, as if he'd accused her of something. "It isn't easy being torn between two men, two worlds, with a daughter whose welfare I have to look out for."

"No one would like it," Carver said, still surprised by the sudden mood swing. Beth was right; her friend showed all the signs of being under tremendous stress. Something had gotten inside her skin and was pressuring.

"I'm a good mother."

"I never doubted it."

She sat back down, then clasped her hands tightly together and refrained from wiping away her tears, as if she didn't want to smear her mascara.

Carver reached across the table and gently touched the tense hands, trying to soothe her. "Take it easy. Things can always be made to improve."

She pulled her folded hands out from beneath his touch. "Sometimes they can never be made right again. Telling yourself otherwise is only naive and self-deceptive."

"If you love this Enrico, maybe he's your answer."

She shook her head. "I'd like to think so, but I'm not sure. I do love him, even though we haven't known each other long. But that only adds to the agony. I'm afraid I'm as much a traditionalist as my husband, Mr. Carver. The love I have for Enrico comes with a load of guilt. I mean, my God, I'm a married mother! I took my marriage vows seriously, even if Mark didn't, and now I'm the one who broke those vows."

"Marriage vows don't give a husband the right to mistreat or neglect a wife, Donna. And believe me, you're being too rough on yourself. You're not the first woman to have an extramarital affair. And you wouldn't be the first to have a good reason for one." He gave her what he hoped was a reassuring smile. "My former wife had good reason."

She looked at him curiously. "Did you mistreat her?"

"Not intentionally, but I backed her to the wall all the same, and the strain on our marriage made her look to another man for what she needed. After a while, I quit blaming her." He wasn't being completely honest, but he figured now was the time for a benign lie.

Calmer now, the moisture in her eyes almost back to normal, Donna got off a shaky smile and said, "Maybe you're right."

"I know I'm right."

She clutched her straw purse and stood up again. She seemed calmer. "Do you know where Riley's Clam Shop is?"

"Uh-huh. Driven past it. It's that place on Vista that looks like it's built out of driftwood."

She nodded. "Enrico and I meet there often."

"Meet him there tonight as planned, then," Carver said. "Don't look around for me. Don't even think about me."

She gave him a glance from beneath the bangs, a shy smile. "What Beth said about you is right."

"Oh? What would that be?"

"That you're a good man but it doesn't stick out all over you."

Carver said, "Until recently, Beth led the kind of life that didn't put her in contact with many good men."

Still smiling, Donna chewed her lower lip for a few seconds, then said, "Thanks, Mr. Carver," and turned and strode from the restaurant. The same men who'd stared at her when she entered watched her leave. A few women watched her, too, with what looked like curiosity. Maybe she was clouding up to cry again. Or barely suppressing a scream. She was a woman very near to an emotional explosion, Carver thought, and at times it showed.

After she'd gone, the waiter arrived with fresh drinks. Carver sat sipping his and watching the ice melt in hers.

About ten minutes had passed when he heard the shriek of rubber on concrete and a crash that shook the building.

2

IN THE corner of his vision Carver saw several gulls, wings flashing white against the darkening sky, take flight toward the open ocean. There was a hush, then a burst of activity and voices from the lounge, near the restaurant's entrance. The diners at the tables near the windows looking out on the highway had parted curtains and were straining to see something to the north. Carver got his cane from where it was propped on the chair next to his and levered himself to his feet. He could see people from the lounge streaming out the door now, and he followed after them.

There was still plenty of light left in the evening. And heat. He felt the hot gravel of the parking lot sear into the thin soles of his moccasins as he made his way toward the highway along with most of the people who'd been in the restaurant. Two men nearby were wearing white uniforms and tall white chef's caps. Someone tripped over Carver's cane, sending its tip dragging through the gravel, mumbled an apology and then hurried on ahead.

On the broad highway, near the mouth of the lot's driveway, dual strips of burned rubber blackened the concrete. Carver saw that they ran about a hundred yards along the highway, then, beyond the restaurant, veered across the yellow line and the adjacent lane.

In the tall grass beyond the shoulder, several hundred feet past the restaurant, a tractor-trailer lay on its side like a wounded dinosaur. It was obvious that the driver had slammed on the brakes and then skidded until the truck had hit the soft gravel shoulder. Probably it had jackknifed before overturning. The out-of-square trailer's doors had sprung open, spilling wooden crates of oranges onto the highway. Oranges dotted the foliage near the truck, and hundreds of them had rolled onto the highway.

Distant sirens were warbling in the humid air, and miles down the straight, flat highway vehicles were pulled to the side and red and blue lights flashed. Carver moved to the front of the gaping crowd from the restaurant. He could see the tractor now, a shiny blue Kenworth, lying on its side at a sharp angle to the trailer, its wheels and underside exposed in a way oddly obscene. A husky man in Levi's and a faded red tee shirt was seated nearby in the grass, a stunned expression on his bearded face. Half a dozen people were clustered around him. He didn't seem to be aware of them, or to be seriously hurt.

There was another knot of people just to the right of the driveway, none of them speaking. Carver set the tip of his cane on firm concrete and limped over to see what they were staring at.

Something in him knew even before he saw the woman sprawled on the gravel shoulder. Dread jogged his memory and he glanced toward the parking lot to see again a barely noticed gray LeBaron convertible with its door hanging open, a straw purse visible on the front seat.

". . . thought I saw her earlier in the restaurant," a woman's quavering voice said as Carver found an opening in the crowd and pushed his way to where he'd have a clear view.

He'd seen the woman earlier in the restaurant, too.

Donna Winship lay on her side with one arm pinned beneath her body, the other flung above her head as if she were making a dramatic gesture. Her modest blue dress was torn and bloody and worked by the rolling of her body up around her hips, revealing lacerated legs and ripped panty hose that hung like strips of flesh. Maybe some of it was strips of flesh. She was shoeless, and one of the panty hose feet was loose and yanked to form a point about six inches beyond her toes, as if she'd tugged it that way as she'd begun to undress. Her wildly tumbled hair concealed most of her face, but Carver could see that beneath the cuts and dirt her expression was peaceful.

A highway patrol car reached the jackknifed trailer first, followed within seconds by another that arrived from the opposite direction and cut across the grassy median.

One of the troopers began setting out flares along the highway while the other talked to the truck driver, who now had his legs drawn up and his face resting on his knees. Someone pointed toward the people around Donna Winship, and the trooper looked grim and began jogging toward the newly discovered accident victim.

People moved aside, but when the trooper, a young guy with a deep tan and close-cut black hair, got to within twenty feet of Donna he saw that she was obviously dead. He came the rest of the way at a walk. Behind him, more emergency vehicles were arriving, including an ambulance. Two attendants were talking to the truck driver now, bending over him with their hands on their knees.

The young trooper knelt down and looked at Donna but didn't touch her, then he straightened up and hitched a thumb in his belt. He looked suddenly older, and sad and tired. His job was a weight.

"Anyone know who she is?" he asked.

Carver said he did. He took a few steps forward and leaned on his cane. The trooper looked him up and down, then politely asked him to accompany him to the patrol car. Carver walked alongside him, glancing out to sea, thinking of the peaceful expression on Donna's face and for some reason remembering the gulls that had taken wing immediately after the accident. The trooper who'd laid out the flares approached, nodded with an unfathomable look at his colleague, then continued past them on his way to make sure no one disturbed the body.

A PLAINCLOTHES cop from the Sheriff's Department joined Carver and the trooper in the car, introducing himself as Sergeant Dave Belquest. He sat in the back and laid a tiny tape recorder on the top of the front seat-back, near Carver. He was a beefy man of about fifty, stuffed into a wrinkled and perspiration-stained light gray suit. He had bushy gray eyebrows, gray tufts of hair protruding from his ears and nostrils. As soon as he'd entered the car, the interior smelled strongly of stale tobacco. Carver smoked an occasional after-dinner cigar himself and hoped he never smelled like that.

Carver acknowledged that he was aware the conversation was being taped, then gave them his statement. He described everything that had occurred between himself and Donna Winship inside the Happy Lobster. Everything other than her affair with Enrico Thomas; this was, after all, Beth's friend, and he owed her something for her thousand dollars. Ethics had gotten him into trouble before, and he knew they might this time, too. But the daughter, Megan, had lost her mother and deserved a memory unblemished by Carver.

"You say she left the restaurant about ten minutes before you heard the crash?" Belquest asked in a hoarse, death-wish smoker's voice. The tobacco stench came at Carver even stronger, like a warning.

"That'd be my guess," Carver said. Beside him, the trooper was jotting things on a leather-bound notepad.

"Any more guesses?" Belquest asked.

"I think she was driving the gray LeBaron convertible in the parking lot. Its door is hanging open, and what looks like the purse she had in the restaurant is on the front seat."

Belquest's right hand moved to the pack of cigarettes in his breast pocket and touched them. Withdrew. He wanted to light up but knew he couldn't in the close confines of the patrol car. It was almost as warm in there as outside; the engine was idling but the trooper must not have set the air conditioner on high. "The parking valet said the victim sat in her car for a while, then got out and walked over to the highway. He thought she might be having car trouble and was going to flag down someone to give her a ride to a station. He noticed she'd left her car door open, and he was walking over to close it before seeing if he could help her, when he heard the truck's brakes. Didn't even see her get hit, is what he said. He was watching the truck skid down the highway, then hit the shoulder and turn over."

"You'd think if she had car trouble, she would have come back in the restaurant and phoned. Or maybe asked me for a lift."

"I'd think that," Belquest said. "But the valet didn't. He's a sixteen-year-old kid and was probably thinking of girls or surfing or the new Paula Abdul record." He sounded irritated.

"What's the truck driver say?" Carver asked.

"That she stepped out in front of the truck. Looked to him like it was on purpose." Belquest's right hand feinted toward his cigarettes again, then rested on the back of the front seat near the recorder. Nicotine had him in too tight a grip to let go easily. "You think she was in that kind of a mood when she left the restaurant?"

Carver thought about that. What kind of a mood was it that

prompted someone to step deliberately in front of twenty tons of truck?

"You said she was tense," Belquest pointed out. "Was she that tense, do you think?"

"There's no way to be sure," Carver said, "but she might have been. She had plenty of reason."

Belquest looked out the car window at Donna's body being loaded into a second ambulance that had arrived after the first had carted away the driver for examination and possible treatment. Two tow trucks were parked near the overturned truck now, their drivers standing and apparently discussing how to right the behemoth. Traffic was moving again, crushing oranges, waved on by the first trooper on the scene.

"People do things on impulse," Belquest said. "Suicides don't always seem in the mood when they commit the act. I knew a cop once, just got married, got a promotion, then ate his gun. Seemed happy only an hour before, on his way to living out the American dream."

Carver said, "Something must have changed for him. He found himself in some other country and some other dream."

"Odd she'd hire you to follow her," Belquest said. "Didn't that make you curious?"

"Sure. I tried to get her to tell me her reason, but she refused."

"How come you'd accept a case like that?"

"Donna Winship was a friend of a friend who was worried about her."

"Good friend?"

"To both of us."

"What's this good friend's name?"

Carver gave him Beth Jackson's name, then the address he wanted to give him.

"That's your address," Belquest said.

"I told you she was a good friend."

Belquest thanked him for his statement but didn't seem quite satisfied. He switched the tape to rewind, and Carver thought he was about to ask him some questions off the record.

Instead he said, "Jesus! Damned things are killing me by inches, but I gotta have a smoke!" He flung open the car door and climbed out into the greater heat, his hand already fumbling at his pocket that held the cigarettes.

Carver thought about the gulls again, like fragments of a soul taking to heaven.

3

RILEY'S CLAM SHOP was as much a bar as a restaurant, so it was doing a boisterous and profitable business at ten that night. Carver parked his ancient Olds convertible at the far end of the lot, near a row of gracefully bent palm trees. He had the car's top down, and the deep bass beat of the music wafting from Riley's was loud enough for him to feel it in the pit of his stomach.

The restaurant was on Vista Road, about five blocks from the ocean. On the coast, Vista ended at Magellan, about half a mile north of where Carver's office was located, on the same street. Riley's looked as if it were built out of odd pieces of driftwood that had washed up on the beach; there was a time not so long ago when that kind of cutesy architecture was popular in coastal Florida, especially in tourist areas. Keeping to the nautical theme, a pierlike plank walkway led to the entrance, flanked by subdued lights concealed in dense and flowery shrubbery. On the gray-weathered wood above the door was mounted what looked like a real anchor.

Several men and two women were lounging outside the entrance, near what appeared to be a ship's watch bell and a large, spoked wooden wheel that might have been used to steer a Spanish galleon. The women wore tight jeans and loose blouses. Some of the men wore casual slacks and sport shirts, some had on jackets and ties. One of the men, wearing a jacket and brightly flowered tie, was doing an animated dance in time to the music, trying to impress the women, who looked bored. The taller of the two women, a slender brunette, crossed her arms and turned away as if trying to put the whole thing out of her mind.

Carver climbed out of the car and crossed the moonlit lot, the shadows of the breeze-tossed palm trees dancing at his feet. The brunette with her arms crossed glanced at him, then leaned with her shoulder against the thick post supporting the ship's bell. She smiled, uncrossed her arms, and gave the spoked wooden wheel a turn, as if it were a wheel on a TV game show allowing her to choose a vowel. Carver doubted if she'd ever been to sea.

Inside the restaurant the music was deafening, provided by a five-piece all-female band featuring a shiny and complicated electric keyboard. Carver sat at the bar and lip-synched to the bartender that he wanted a draft beer.

He sat sipping his beer from its frosted mug and trying not to listen to the music for a few minutes, looking over the crowded restaurant. All the tables were occupied by at least two people. There were half a dozen or so men seated or standing at the long bar who might be by themselves. A sign over the door advertised that there would be a bikini contest next Friday, Jello wrestling the Friday after that. Carver saw no reason why the two events shouldn't be combined.

Carrying his beer, he went outside and across wooden planks to a public phone he'd noticed mounted on a corner of the building. The brunette near the ship's bell smiled at him again.

He was about to phone Beth, so he didn't smile back, but he raised his stein in a kind of salute to her and all womanhood.

Beth wasn't in her apartment, so he called his beach cottage five miles up the coast highway. She had a key and came and went pretty much as she pleased. Which was most of the time. He'd given Belquest the cottage as her address because she'd be easier to reach there, and he'd know about it sooner rather than later. It was only when she had a work overload, as she had now, and had to hole up to meet a deadline, that she spent nights in her closetlike efficiency miles from the beach.

She answered on the second ring and said, "Where you been, lover?"

"How'd you know it was me?"

"I been waiting long enough for you, Fred, it doesn't matter much anymore if it's you."

"I thought you'd be at your apartment tonight."

"No, I finished the polluted fish story. You talk to Donna?"

So Beth didn't know, hadn't caught the information on the news.

"Fred?"

He set the beer mug on the shelf above the tattered phone directory. "I've got some bad news about Donna," he said. And he told her what had happened.

She was quiet for a long time. Then, "Christ, Fred! You think she really killed herself by stepping in front of a speeding semi?"

"It looks that way. She might have been in that kind of mood, the way she was acting in the restaurant."

"What about Megan? Her little girl." Beth sounded as if she might be about to cry. Not like her at all; she treated tears as if they were acid that might sear her cheeks to the bone.

"She's with Donna's mother. The mother, the husband, they probably know by now."

"Lord! What do you suppose they'll tell Megan?"

"I don't know. I'm not sure what I'd tell a four-year-old kid in this situation. Or how soon."

"Fred, before Donna left the restaurant, did she tell you what was bothering her? Why she wanted to talk to you?"

"Yes and no." He told Beth about Donna paying him to follow her.

"And she wouldn't tell you why?"

"No."

"It's not Donna at all, this stepping-out-on-her-husband business. She's not the type, though we both know almost everybody can be."

"Almost everybody," Carver said. "My impression was the husband pushed her into it. Did you ever meet him?"

"Couple of times. He seemed nice enough. Donna said he had a temper, though never with her. They seemed happy together. That was a few years ago, though. Things can change."

"Can and do," Carver said, thinking of his own life.

"What are you gonna do now, Fred?"

"Follow somebody else. That's part of why I called you."

He gave Beth the phone number of Riley's Clam Shop and asked her to wait a few minutes, then call and ask for Enrico Thomas.

When he went back inside, he saw that his place at the bar had been taken. He stood near the door, beneath the bikini and Jello sign, idly sipping his beer and studying the men at the bar who didn't appear to be with someone or were in a waiting attitude. There was a big man in a plaid sport jacket, looked like a high-pressure salesman. An athletic type in a pullover shirt—Carver could picture him as Donna's secret lover. A man about Carver's age, bald on top like Carver, was seated near the far end of the bar, staring morosely into his beer as if he might have been stood up. Could be the guy who'd swept Donna off her feet and into infidelity, Carver thought. Or maybe he was flattering himself because of his resemblance to the man.

The phone rang, and the bartender, a wiry little gray-haired man in a white shirt and checked vest, hurried over to answer it.

He cupped his hand over the mouthpiece and shouted, "Enrico Thomas?" Looking up and down the bar. "Enrico Thomas here?"

A few of the men glanced at him, but no one wanted the call.

"Go see if there's an Enrico Thomas out at one of the tables," the bartender shouted to a blond waitress, and set the phone next to the beer taps. Carver could hear the waitress's high, cutting voice calling Thomas's name.

From nearby a voice shouted, "Hey! Over here! I'm Enrico Thomas."

The bartender pointed to the phone, and the man who'd spoken moved toward it.

He'd just come out of the restroom, a slight man with dark hair and eyebrows and mustache. He was wearing gray pleated slacks and a black sport coat, white shirt, no tie. He was very well groomed, wore his clothes well, and he crossed the room toward the phone with the fluid economy of a nifty lightweight boxer or dancer.

Carver saw rather than heard him say hello, then yes, then look puzzled and place the receiver back down on the bar. Beth had gotten him to confirm he was Enrico Thomas, then hung up as instructed.

Thomas looked all around the bar, then walked to the wide arch separating it from the main restaurant and gazed around, standing for a moment up on his toes for a better view. Gleaming Italian loafers flat on the floor again, he glanced at his watch. Carver shot a look at the beer-ad clock behind the bar—illuminated, flat-bellied surfers sitting around a campfire and boozing it up with beautiful girls who looked about sixteen. Ten-twenty. He took a sip of beer, watching the small, neat man rub his chin over and over and rock slightly on the balls of his feet. He acted as if he was waiting for someone, all right, getting impatient. Someone who was fifteen minutes late and would never be on time again.

Thomas found a spot to stand near the end of the bar and ordered a drink that looked like bourbon and water. He stood there sipping it slowly, talking to no one, switching his gaze back and forth from the ball game on the TV above the bar to the door. Somebody on TV hit a home run, but Thomas seemed disinterested.

At exactly 10:35, looking slightly agitated, he dropped a couple of bills on the bar and walked past Carver, out the door.

Carver waited a few seconds, then followed. As he made his way to the Olds, he saw Thomas getting into a red Corvette convertible. Carver lowered himself into the Olds and got it started just in time to follow the Corvette from the lot.

He made a note of the license plate on Thomas's car, then stayed well back from it. Within minutes they were outside the Del Moray city limits, traveling south along the coast highway. Then Thomas cut west to 95, drove south to the Bee Line Expressway and headed west again, toward Orlando.

The Olds's huge prehistoric engine was made for gas guzzling and highway speed. Carver had no trouble keeping the Corvette in sight. He sat in the rush of warm wind and noise, feeling the vibration of road and engine running through the car, along the backs of his thighs, knowing it would be late tonight before he'd see Beth.

ENRICO THOMAS slowed the Corvette on Belt Street in Orlando and cruised along at about thirty. Then the low-slung car's brakelights flared as it made a sharp right turn into a low garage alongside a two-story beige apartment building with cracked stucco, ornate rusty iron balconies, and thick vines crawling wild up its north side. The garage door had either been open, or Thomas had signaled an automatic opener as he approached. The glow from the sodium streetlight on the corner tinted everything, including the blooms on the vines, a sickly orange color.

Carver pulled the Olds to the curb on the opposite side of the street and watched Thomas emerge from the shadows of the garage. He appeared to point inside the garage's dark interior, and the garage's overhead door slowly lowered until it met the ground. Thomas then locked the door with a key before walking toward the apartment entrance. A car like the Corvette would be stolen every other day in this neighborhood unless its owner took precautions.

Carver could call his friend, Orlando police lieutenant Alfonso Desoto, and probably get Thomas's precise address from the Corvette's license number, but he was here and wanted to make the trip bear fruit as soon as possible.

Letting the Olds's engine idle, he took his foot off the brake and the big car crept along the curb until it was almost directly opposite the apartment building. All of the building's windows facing the street were visible from here.

Within a minute or two after Thomas had entered the building, lights winked on in the second-floor-west corner unit.

Carver switched off the softly rumbling engine, climbed out of the car, and crossed the street.

The blossoms on the vines had a perfumed scent that carried on the warm night air, but the building's vestibule smelled oddly of fresh paint and stale urine. There were crumpled, paint-spattered newspapers on the dirty tile floor. Carver saw that graffiti had been recently painted over on the wall above the bank of tarnished brass mailboxes. That "Miranda loves" someone or something was still visible through the new, thin coat of blue paint. Carver figured what Miranda would really love would be to move out of the building.

He saw her name right away in the slot above one of the

mailboxes: Miranda Perez. There were eight units in the building. Carver checked the mailbox slots for Thomas's name but didn't see it. The upper west corner unit appeared to be occupied by someone named Carl Gretch—at least Gretch got his mail there.

"What the fuck you doing?"

The voice made Carver jump.

He gripped his cane tightly just below the crook, ready to use it as a weapon.

"Who the fuck are you?" the voice said.

Carver peered up the dark stairwell and saw Enrico Thomas poised halfway down the steps to the vestibule, leaning forward and glaring at him. In his right hand was a knife with a long, thin blade that reflected what little light there was in the dim building.

"I'm looking for Miranda Perez," Carver said.

"Don't play stupid; I saw you at Riley's Clam Shop, saw you following me in that big tub of shit you drive. All the way here from Del Moray."

"I drove here to see Miranda," Carver said. "She loves me."

"Loves everybody with a few dollars to spend, but I doubt she and you ever met. Like I asked before, what the fuck do you want?"

There was nervousness in Thomas's voice now. Carver wasn't playing his part the way Thomas had imagined, didn't seem scared enough. Well, Carver knew he was scared. On the other hand, there was something about the way the almost girlishly thin man on the stairs held the knife—too tightly, too near the glint of the blade. He obviously wasn't an experienced knife fighter. Carver decided to run a bluff.

"I'm leaving," he said. "I might even call the cops."

"You're not going till you say why you followed me."

"Sure I am. I pretty much go where I please, and a scrawny little player like you doesn't bother me much."

"Fucking gimp, I got a mind to saw off your good leg if you don't start talking."

Carver turned to face Thomas directly, balancing himself and lifting the cane. "Close quarters here. You really want to use that blade?"

"Just try me."

"If you come down those stairs with that knife," Carver said, "there's no going back for you. I'm going to take it away from you and feed it to you sideways. I'm going to enjoy doing it."

Thomas hadn't expected this, aggression from a cripple, a cane brandished as a weapon. Carver was in his forties with a stiff left leg, but his upper body was lean and powerful. And though he was average size, he was still larger and more muscular than Thomas.

Sensing the balance shift, Carver moved slightly toward Thomas. The knife extended, Thomas backed several steps up the flight of stairs. He looked a bit startled, as if his legs had moved on their own.

Carver said, "Going down or up?"

"You say you know Miranda," Thomas said, almost whining, "but I bet she wouldn't have anything to do with a fucking cripple like you for any amount of money."

"Well, you ask her when you see her. We're crazy in love with each other. But you're changing the subject. You coming down here with that knife?"

Time stopped in the bubble of events. Thomas licked his lips. Carver had assumed he was Latin, but up close, even in the dim light, he didn't look Latin at all, despite the dark hair and mustache.

"Please come down here," Carver said.

That did it. Thomas wasn't the type to be told what to do, even if a "please" happened to be attached. Deftly folding the knife closed, he retreated another few steps, moving backward up the stairs easily, nimbly, still facing Carver. "I know what you look like," he said, almost spitting the angry words. "Don't you forget that." He backed up two more steps, into the shadows of the landing.

"And I know what you look like," Carver told him. "Like a million other guys who know that down deep they don't have what they need."

He edged to the street door, then pushed it open and moved outside. As he limped away, he listened for the door to sweep open behind him, for Thomas's rushing footsteps.

But no one emerged from the building.

Carver returned to the Olds and lowered himself into the warm vinyl upholstery.

As he put the transmission lever in drive and pulled away from the curb, he saw Enrico Thomas in the second-floor-west apartment. He'd struck an absurdly dramatic pose, standing squarely at the window like an anorexic, miniaturized colossus with fists on hips, watching Carver as kings on balconies gaze down on subjects about to be ill-used.

Carver thought, A dangerous man with a knife.

He was shaking badly as he drove away.

4

THE LIGHTS were burning in his modest but private beach cottage when Carver parked the Olds next to Beth's car. Her car was a LeBaron convertible, like Donna Winship's, only white rather than gray, the sort used in droves by car rental companies in Florida and then sold by local dealers. The similarities in the women's cars was enough of a reminder of life's impermanence that Carver was eager to get inside the cottage and talk with Beth, touch her, in appreciation of her continued if fragile existence. Of his own.

Beth, a tall black woman with the look of a tribal queen turned fashion model, was seated on the sofa by the lamp, barefoot and wearing Carver's faded blue terrycloth robe. When he came through the door, she set aside the three or four sheets of white paper she'd been reading. She was a journalist for *Burrow*, a small and gutsy local weekly newspaper that sent its reporters where angels feared to tread. Beth liked that.

"Get what you wanted?" she asked. The lamp starkly side-lighted her strong features, her prominent cheekbones and forehead. She was a woman who'd seen far too much for most people, but not for her. She'd fought her way out from under, starting with the Chicago slum of her girlhood, and would keep fighting. Everything about her told you that, from her regal, undefeated bearing to the bite of her words when she was angry and the directness of her gaze as she assessed the world. Her eyes were different tonight, though; she'd been crying.

It was cooler inside the cottage, but still too warm. Carver crossed the plank floor to the small kitchen area, opened the refrigerator and got out a cold Budweiser. "I know where Enrico Thomas lives—if that's his name." He went to the couch and sat down next to Beth. She snatched away the article she'd been working on before he sat on it.

He was going to kiss her, but her arm was around his neck and she was kissing him. She smelled of scented soap and shampoo. She leaned away, smiling, but with her eyes still sad.

He said, "I appreciate you."

"Works both ways, Fred."

He told her about following Thomas from Riley's Clam Shop into Orlando, the confrontation inside the building, the different name above the apartment's mailbox.

"Where's that leave you?" she asked.

"Waiting until morning. Then I'll call Desoto and see if he'll run the Corvette's license plate number." He glanced at the papers she'd placed next to the lamp on the table. They were marked with red felt-tip pen where she'd been revising. She was being careful with this article; often she sent in her story to the *Burrow* office using the modem in her computer. "I thought you were finished with the pollution story."

"I am. This is something else. I've been working on it for a while and should be able to wrap it up soon."

"What's it about?" he asked, nodding toward the papers.

"A mail-order company that sends overpriced junk merchandise to grieving widows and pretends the husband ordered it just before his death. Bastards!" She sat back and crossed her improbably long legs, parting the robe high up her bare thigh. "Fred, I'm sitting here wondering if things would have worked out the same way today if I hadn't arranged for you and Donna to meet."

"They wouldn't have worked out exactly the same," he told her, "but the end result probably would have been the same. Your friend wasn't holding up well under the strain of a disintegrating marriage, and like you said, she wasn't the type to have an affair. Despite the glowing account of her relationship with Enrico Thomas, I suspect he only made things worse for her."

What he didn't say was that he'd been wondering the same thing as Beth: If he and Donna Winship hadn't met and talked, would she still be alive? Not that he considered himself responsible for her impulse to destroy herself, but undeniably, if the kaleidoscope of fate had been turned a few degrees either way, things might be different. He told himself that life was a risk for everyone every second and he bore no blame, but how could he really know? Had he said something seemingly innocent to trigger the plunge of spirit that had prompted a desperate woman to take her last and fatal step?

Beth gently lifted the cold beer can from his hand and took a sip, then touched the rounded damp side of the can to her forehead as if trying to relieve a headache.

"There's the matter of the thousand-dollar retainer she gave me," Carver said.

Beth lowered the can but didn't hand it back to him. "What about it?"

"Donna Winship hired me to follow her, and obviously that's impossible now."

"You followed that Enrico Thomas character."

"To satisfy my own curiosity, not as part of why she hired me."

"So the nature of the job has changed."

"There is no client, Beth, so no job."

"Well, you can't very well return the money if Donna's dead."

"I won't cash her check," Carver said, "but it'll be entered in her checkbook, so her husband will know about it. I'm going to have to talk to him, return the check to him."

"Don't do that, Fred. The way Donna talked, the guy turned away from her and tuned her out completely. Believe me, she wouldn't want you to return the retainer."

"If I simply hold the check, he'll eventually contact me with his own questions."

She looked thoughtful, then resigned. "I suppose that's true. And if you do cash it, he can get you for fraud. Judging from how Donna came to think of him, he probably would."

"So I'll drop by and give him the check," Carver said. "I'll let him think she hired me to follow him, checking to see if he was having an affair."

"Are you doing Enrico Thomas a favor?"

"Doing Megan Winship a favor. There's no reason she or anybody else has to know about Thomas and her mother."

Beth took another sip of beer then gave him back the can. "Some world, huh? A person steps outside the lines, maybe only once, and there can be a multitude of victims."

"That's why I'm returning the check to Mark Winship."

"Maybe I can get this company I'm writing about to send him a thousand dollars worth of crappy merchandise along with a bill addressed to Donna."

Carver laughed. He finished the small amount of beer left in the can, then got his cane from where it was propped against the cushions and stood up. On the way to the bathroom he tossed the empty can into the kitchen wastebasket. It made a satisfying clatter in the bottom of the metal basket, as if signaling the end of a miserable day.

As he was rinsing out his mouth after brushing his teeth, he noticed the reflected Carver in the mirror looked exhausted, older than his forty-odd years. Certainly older than he'd looked this morning, and than he hoped he'd look tomorrow. The scar at the right corner of his mouth was dragging on his lips, giving him an especially sardonic expression. He was bald except for a fringe of thick gray curly hair that grew well down the back of his neck. His catlike blue eyes, tilted up at the corners in his tan face, were bloodshot and eerie-looking from fatigue; no wonder Thomas had been afraid of him despite the knife. When he twisted the faucet handle to stop the flow of water, muscles danced in his corded arms and across his bare, tan chest. His upper body was hard and powerful from his therapeutic morning swims in the sea and from dragging himself around with the cane. One of the few advantages of having a locked and ruined knee.

When he returned to the cottage's main room, he saw that Beth had gone to bed. He turned off the light and joined her in the screened-off sleeping area.

She was awake, waiting for him in the humid darkness. Nude, as she always slept. He felt the warm length of her lean body, then the wetness of tears as she moved her head onto his pillow and her cheek brushed his. One of her firm breasts, surprisingly large for such an otherwise slender woman, pressed against his ribs. The sound of the surf playing itself out on the beach drifted in through the open window like urgent, incomprehensible whispering, as if the sea knew something profound it would share if only its ancient language could be understood. Had human beings ever understood it? Beth flung a long leg across Carver and sighed.

He remembered what she'd once told him in her blunt and incisive manner: Sometimes women needed to be fucked, sometimes they needed to be held, sometimes they needed both. Though it sounded a bit like something from *The Playboy Philosophy*, he figured she was probably right.

Without having to be told, he knew this was a night for holding, then for sleep and whatever absolution it might bring.

5

CARVER SWAM out to sea to the point where he could watch
other early morning risers walking the curved shoreline, some
of them with their heads lowered, combing the beach for shells.
The sun was still low and the ocean was cool. He stroked parallel
to the shore for a while, feeling that the strength of his arms, his
endurance, could power him forever, even though he knew better.
In the water, kicking from the hips, his powerful upper body
working in rhythm with his legs, he was as physically capable as
any man and more capable than most. He loved his morning swims,
so much so that at times he wondered if evolution might be working
on him in reverse, luring him back to the sea.

He turned over and floated on his back for a while, gazing
up at a cloudless sky going from gray to blue. The sun felt warm
and heavy on his upper chest and face. The only sounds were
the massive slide of the ocean and the occasional cry of a gull,
like that of a woeful, desperate woman. He rode gentle swells
that would become higher then flatten out before crashing onto
the beach. As he rose on one of the swells to its peak, he glanced

in at his cottage, a small, flat-roofed structure nestled where the beach curved to form a thin crescent of sand. The Olds sat by itself near a grouping of date palms beside the cottage; Beth had risen earlier and left to pursue her story for *Burrow*. He raised a wrist and glanced at his waterproof watch. Almost eight o'clock. Desoto would be at his desk in police headquarters on Hughey in Orlando.

Carver rolled over on his stomach and began swimming at an angle toward the beach, using the momentum of the waves to hasten his crawl stroke. Within a few minutes he was near enough to feel the backwash of the surf, and to see his cane jutting like a beacon from the sand near his white towel.

Next came the part he didn't like. He waited for a particularly large and powerful wave, then stroked hard and rode it in as far as possible onto the beach, using the great momentum of the ocean to help him ashore. He lay still then, holding his ground as wet sand and shells around and beneath him moved again toward the sea in the backwash of the surf.

No matter how well this method worked, he still had to crawl several yards to the cane and his towel on dry sand. This morning was no exception, and he was glad as he often was that the stretch of beach in front of his cottage was almost completely private because of the curve of the shoreline.

In a sitting position, he dried off with the towel as best he could, then used the cane for support as he stood up. He draped the towel around the back of his neck, then set out for the cottage, careful where he placed the cane in the soft sand.

After showering and dressing, he poured a cup of coffee from the pot Beth had left on the burner of the Braun brewer, leaned on the breakfast counter near the phone, and called Desoto.

He got through to the lieutenant right away and filled him in on what had happened, and why he wanted the Corvette's license plate number run through the Motor Vehicles Department.

For a few minutes Desoto said nothing, and all Carver heard

on the line was a soft Latin melody he was sure came from the portable Sony that sat on the windowsill behind Desoto's desk. Guitars, he thought. Desoto loved slow guitar music.

Then Desoto said, "A terrible way for a woman to go, *amigo*, stepping in front of a speeding truck." Desoto truly loved women, the entire sex, and it pained him to see or hear about a woman in the kind of agony that had prodded Donna Winship to her death. "Are you thinking it might not have been suicide?"

"No, I think she killed herself," Carver said.

"And you also think that by saying something else in the restaurant, treating her differently in perhaps some small matter, you might have prevented her death."

"Yes, but I know that's a stupid way to think."

"It is. The world is always much simpler in retrospect. But if you're satisfied the woman's death was suicide, what's your interest now?"

"I feel I owe her something."

"Because you do feel remotely responsible for her death?"

"Maybe. And because she was Beth's friend. And because when I went to Riley's Clam Shop to get a look at Enrico Thomas just to satisfy my curiosity and to try to get some hint as to why Donna wanted herself followed, Thomas turned out to be worth learning more about."

"And what will you do with the information?"

"Nothing, probably. He's a dangerous sleazeball, but that isn't illegal. I'm driving over to return Donna's retainer to her husband this morning, then I should be out of whatever it is I'm in."

"So this is merely more of your curiosity satisfying, hey?"

"Sure."

"Well, I think it's your dog-with-a-rag obsession. Once you get a lock on something that seems to tug back, you can't turn loose."

Carver felt a twinge of anger. "You're constantly calling me obsessive."

"Only an observation, my friend."

"Well, you're obsessive about it."

"Only because you are constant in your obsessiveness and your impatience to get to whatever it is you're seeking. It's a problem for you, but it makes you good at what you do."

"Are you going to run the Corvette's license number?"

"Of course. I'll phone you back as soon as I have any information."

"How long will it take?"

"See, *amigo*: impatience. I'll probably get back to you within the hour."

Carver thanked him and hung up.

Obsessive. Desoto called him that, Beth called him that— only she didn't seem to mind.

Carver wondered why they couldn't simply think of him as determined.

He knew he was determined.

ONLY HALF an hour had passed before Desoto called.

"Red ninety-two Corvette belongs to one Carl Gretch," he said, and gave Carver the address of the apartment on Belt Street in Orlando.

"Anything on Gretch?"

"No outstandings. But I checked further. He did a stretch in Raiford five years ago for burglary."

"That it?"

"It is for the wages of sin; he's no longer on parole. He's a thirty-two-year-old male Caucasian, blue and black, five-foot-five and a hundred thirty-five pounds. Not a good size for penitentiary life."

"The right size for Enrico Thomas, though. Know anything about the burglary?"

"No. Might have been youthful indiscretion, boys being boys."

"I doubt it," Carver said, ignoring Desoto's sarcasm. "If it was a one-time thing, the judge probably would have allowed probation."

"All it means, though, is that your late client was seeing a guy with a record. It happens."

"Guy with a record with a knife."

"Hmm."

"I'm still curious," Carver said.

"Still obsessed. Are you going to keep poking around?"

"No," Carver said. "Whatever Donna Winship was mixed up in, it's over. For her, anyway. For me, too."

"Yes. Concentrate on living clients," Desoto said. "They're far more profitable."

Carver thanked him for the help and advice, then broke the connection but didn't hang up. He dialed the home number Donna Winship had given him. He wanted to make sure Mark Winship was there before driving to see him to return Donna's check, tell his benign lies, then walk away from the Winship tragedy and let it play out on its own.

No answer.

Carver hung up the phone, then looked in the directory for Mark Winship's address. Found it within seconds: 333 Blue Heron Road. On the moneyed side of town, farther from Carver's cottage in decimal points than in miles. He decided to drive into Del Moray and drop by the Winship home even though he'd gotten no answer to his call, in the hope that the grieving widower would be there but didn't want to speak on the phone. If Winship wasn't home, Carver would drive to the office, do paperwork, and try to contact him later, maybe catch him this evening on the way back to the cottage.

There was, after all, no rush about returning Donna's check.

THE WINSHIP house was one of the smaller ones on Blue Heron, but still expensive. The Del Moray paper's account of Donna's death had mentioned that her husband was a financial consultant; apparently he'd done well with his own investments.

The house was a low, contemporary structure of white bricks. The roof was all planes and angles, and the corner of the house nearest the driveway was floor-to-ceiling glass behind which drapes were closed to keep the sun out. There was no car in the driveway, but the garage door was closed. A tall sugar oak grew near the garage, and a walk led around through a colorful garden that looked as if it followed the property line into the backyard.

Carver got out of the Olds and walked onto the porch. Standing in the shade of the roof's overhang, he pressed the door button and heard bells chime faintly inside. They played four notes of a song he didn't recognize.

No one came to the door.

He pushed the button and heard the abbreviated tune again, waited a few minutes, then hobbled down off the porch and walked to the garage door. It was one of those overhead doors with a small window at eye level in each section. The windows were dirty, but Carver leaned close to one, rubbed it in a circular motion with the heel of his hand, then peered inside.

Two cars were parked in the dim garage, Donna's gray convertible and a green Jaguar sedan. The Jag was doubtless Mark's, so unless the family had a third car he might very well be home. Possibly he was outside and hadn't heard the door chimes. It was worth checking on, anyway.

Carver followed the stepping-stone walk that led through the garden. Azaleas bordered the walk on the garage side. Beyond them long-stalked dahlias swayed in the faint warm breeze. Low ground cover bearing tiny white blooms spread to the garage's back corner and around, where a small white iron bench posed pristinely beneath an oleander tree bearing clusters of pink flowers.

When Carver walked beyond the bench, he saw Mark Winship immediately. He was seated in a large wooden glider in the shade of an arched trellis bursting with red roses, an open book in his lap, his head bowed in concentration.

Carver set the tip of his cane on sunbaked lawn and limped toward him. Clouds of tiny insects rose around his feet and the cane with each step. Some of them found their way inside his pants cuffs, tickling his ankles.

When he got closer, he saw that Mark Winship was wearing glasses with tortoiseshell frames, resting somewhat crookedly halfway down his nose, and that the book in his lap was a Bible.

When he got closer still, he noticed the small silver revolver in Winship's right hand.

Then the blue-black hole in his temple.

6

CARVER SETTLED into the chair facing Lieutenant William McGregor's desk at Del Moray police headquarters. The office was sparse, with a curling tile floor that was supposed to look like wood parquet, dented black file cabinets, and, on a table alongside the desk, what looked like a combination fax, answering machine, phone, clock, police band radio, and coffee maker. The walls were a shade darker than institutional green only because they hadn't been painted in decades. But the office did have a window, looking out on the parking lot; McGregor was moving up in the department. His problem was that he tended to move down as often as up. It had to do with his character.

"So, look who found a dead body," he said, grinning and lowering his six-foot-six frame into the chair behind the desk. He was a thin man but coiled and powerful, with a face to match his character. Long features, prognathous jaw, squinty little mean blue eyes, lank blond hair that hung Hitler-style over his forehead. Between his yellowed front teeth there was a wide space that he constantly probed with his tongue, as if trying to imitate a lizard. Come to think of it, Carver mused, it wasn't an imitation at all.

"Was there a suicide note?" Carver asked.

"You know there was a note, asshole, because you read it before calling the police." The tongue probed and flicked. "Know why I think that?"

"Sure. Because *you* would have read it."

"You betcha! It's good we understand each other."

Carver understood McGregor, all right. He was unprincipled, uncouth, untrustworthy, and a number of other un's. And ambitious and self-serving. Most of all ambitious and self-serving. He'd even considered taking a run at getting elected mayor of Del Moray at one time; for the graft and free pussy, he'd told Carver. But Carver had known too much about him and put a stop to that. McGregor had never forgiven him. Never would.

"The note I didn't read didn't say much," Carver said. He'd found it stuck between the pages of the Bible in Mark Winship's lap, and had indeed read it before phoning the Del Moray police. In what was presumably Mark Winship's handwriting it said simply, *I die by my own hand, with grief and regret*, and was signed, *Mark Winship*. "Was it written with the pen in his shirt pocket?"

"You mean you didn't match ink colors?" McGregor asked.

Carver smiled. The ink color of note and pen had matched.

"If it wasn't that this guy committed suicide," McGregor said, "I'd find a way to hang a murder charge on you."

Which meant the gun in Winship's hand had fired the death bullet, and paraffin tests indicated the dead man had squeezed the trigger.

The pink tip of McGregor's tongue peeked out between his widely spaced front teeth like an evil little internal serpent. "The interesting thing is what probably drove him to kill himself. His wife got herself run over by a truck yesterday. Stupid cunt stepped right out in front of it, and *splat*! Or so the story goes."

"So he was grieving over his dead wife," Carver said, "and

the strain got to him." He never shared knowledge with McGregor unless it was absolutely necessary. McGregor saw knowledge as power and seldom failed to use it in the most heinous way. It was too late for power to corrupt McGregor, but he could certainly corrupt power.

"The thing is"—the tongue probed obscenely—"the wife was having a drink with you just before she ran out on the highway and tried to hug a speeding semi. That makes me curious."

"Why?"

"Because you're involved, fuck-face. And because the double suicide of a Del Moray couple with an address in my jurisdiction suggests that there's more to the story than an unhappy marriage gone wild. The department makes assessments for promotion in two months, and I'm being considered. Next step is captain, then chief, and don't think it isn't a possibility. I don't want anything making waves in my jurisdiction, messing up my chances. For now, it'd be best for me, and for you, if there was nothing evil going down."

"So something evil might move up," Carver said.

"You betcha."

"At least you're honest about it."

"I'm not honest about anything!" McGregor sounded genuinely offended. "All I am is legal."

"And not even all the time."

McGregor aimed his jut-jawed, lewd grin at Carver. "If I gotta swim in this ocean, I'm gonna be a shark. That bother you, guppy?"

"Only when you enjoy it."

"Well, then be bothered, 'cause I always fucking enjoy it. I've adapted, just like Darwin said always happens with the strong, and you haven't. We both know the world is shit—difference is, you kid yourself there's something better than shit, while I don't. In fact, I gotta admit I love to roll in it."

"It's rubbed off," Carver observed.

Still grinning, McGregor picked up a sharp pencil and made a little jabbing motion in the direction of Carver's heart. Kidding, but there was malice in his eyes. "What'd you and the late Donna Winship talk about yesterday?"

"Nothing important. Weather, sports . . ."

"Tell me straight, Carver, or I'm gonna make sport of you."

"You sound as if you're investigating a double murder. Is there some doubt that either of the Winships was a suicide?"

"Sorry, that's police business."

"Is this conversation police business?"

"It ain't social. Not with a pus-bag like you."

"Then there must be something big happening under your nose, and you don't understand it so you're upset and taking it out on me. I guess I should call my lawyer."

McGregor stared at him with a look that could melt titanium.

"Do I get my phone call?" Carver asked.

Slowly McGregor unfolded his long body until he was standing at full height behind the desk, looming over Carver. "What you get, fuck-face, is outa this office. Now."

Carver waited a few deliberate seconds. Saving face, as it were. Then he leaned on his cane and stood up.

"That's better," McGregor said with satisfaction. "It'd be wise of you to be on your best behavior for a while. And don't think I won't be watching you and your dark-meat cunt."

Carver didn't answer. He knew McGregor was trying to provoke a show of rage. McGregor fed on that kind of thing. He lived to jerk people's strings, to make any kind of unpleasant impact in their lives. It was his charming way of communicating.

At the door, Carver paused and turned around, his blood racing but his expression calm.

"You finally got yourself a window," he said, looking around the drab green room, "but this sure isn't the office of a guy who'll ever be chief."

McGregor said something to him as he left and closed the

door behind him, but it made little sense to Carver even if it was intensely personal. It was language you seldom heard even at the movies.

THAT AFTERNOON Beth said, "McGregor's the worst kind of cop there is. Corrupt and admits it, so he stays on the safe side of the line while he's messing up other people's lives."

"He doesn't admit it to everyone," Carver said, "only the people he's sure already know."

"That has to be a growing number."

"But it hasn't grown large enough yet. It probably never will. He'll see to that. Survival of the fittest, he'd call it. Cops like McGregor retire secretly wealthy."

"And unbothered by conscience."

"But he'll probably be haunted by the opportunities he missed," Carver said. "That can be worse than a conscience for a guy like McGregor."

They were seated on stools at the breakfast counter in Carver's beach cottage, eating tuna-salad sandwiches and drinking beer. Neither of them much liked to cook; this was a typical meal when they ate in. Carver had been home for a while, seated on the porch with his good leg propped on the rail and watching the sea, thinking. Beth had been out scrounging up facts about her wayward mail-order company, and had returned fifteen minutes ago for lunch and to use her word processor.

"So don't get involved with McGregor," she said. "I don't want him messing around in our lives."

Carver removed the top slice of rye from his sandwich and added mayonnaise. Better. He chewed tuna salad, swallowed and took a sip of Budweiser. Then he swiveled slightly on his stool so he could look past the silhouetted planters with their dangling vines, hanging by chains in the wide window. The ocean was choppy today and seemed to rise toward the horizon so that it was higher than the roof of the cottage. It appeared vast and ominous. Far out near the horizon, a large ship sat seemingly motionless in the haze. An oil tanker, Carver thought.

"Fred?"

"McGregor and I agree on a few things," he said.

"I'm sorry to hear that."

"The Winship suicides don't feel right."

"Hell, no, they don't! Does a pair of suicides ever feel right?"

"I mean, there's a lot more to them than what's on the surface."

"Why should you care?"

"I don't know, but I do care."

"That's just one of the ways you're not like McGregor," she said around a bite of sandwich. "But there's nothing in it for you if you keep poking around, using up your time."

"You know better."

"Sure. I meant monetarily. 'Course, that thousand-dollar check might still cash without any trouble, especially if you get to the bank on time. And you've done some investigating and put your ass on the line, kind of earned it." She licked mayonnaise from a long, red-nailed finger and smiled. "Think of that, lover."

He had his pension and had made a few sound investments, had most of what he wanted. The essentials, anyway. He didn't need the thousand dollars. And it was Megan Winship's money now. He downed the last of his beer and said, "Fuck the money."

Beth laughed from somewhere down deep. "That's my Fred! Dumb but I love him."

Carver figured "dumb" was better than "obsessive." Maybe.

He got down off the stool, leaving his cane and using the counter and stove for support while he got another beer from the refrigerator.

Working the pull-tab, feeling cold foam run between his thumb and forefinger, he said, "Talk to me about Donna Winship."

THE APARTMENT building Carl Gretch lived in looked even more depressing in the harsh morning light. Like the man himself, probably.

Carver had driven into Orlando to be parked on Belt Street across from the building by eight o'clock, on the off chance Gretch-Thomas was an early riser. He didn't want to miss connections with the knife-wielding Romeo.

He sat behind the Olds's steering wheel for a moment with the engine idling, gazing at the dirty beige stucco building with its rust-pitted iron balconies. Pigeon droppings, invisible under the streetlight two nights ago, looked like candle drippings on the surface of the wall not covered by vines. The vines, with their brilliant red tubular blossoms, were the only good thing about the place, possibly the only good thing in the neighborhood.

The old car might overheat if he sat there much longer with the engine running and the air conditioner plugging away, so Carver switched off the ignition. Even at eight o'clock, oppressive heat began to push into the car almost immediately. The sun was determined to punish Florida again today.

Carver was about to climb out of the car when he saw a man emerge from the apartment building.

Not Gretch, though.

This was an older, gray-haired man, powerfully built but slightly stooped, wearing a baggy white tee shirt and even baggier jeans. His flesh and his clothes hung loosely on his frame, but muscle danced beneath the slack skin of his arms. Carver watched him plod stiffly to the flat-roofed garage where Gretch had parked the red Corvette night before last.

The old man drew a ring of keys from a pocket of the baggy jeans and unlocked and opened the door next to Gretch's. He went into that section of the dilapidated four-car garage and a few minutes later came out dragging a large green rubber trash can and a long-handled push broom. He set the can upright, leaned the broom against the garage wall, then used his keys to open Gretch's garage door.

There was no car in the garage.

The old man got the broom and entered the garage, still with the same rigid, plodding walk, as if he'd never been in a hurry in his life. A few seconds later he moved back out onto the sidewalk, grabbed the trash can by its rim, and slid it inside out of sight. It made a hollow, scraping sound as it was dragged over the concrete.

Carver climbed out of the Olds and crossed the street toward the long garage. As he got closer, he could see the man's white tee shirt in the shadows, moving like a disembodied ghost as he methodically swept the floor.

Dust was drifting out of the garage as Carver stood in the open doorway and leaned with both hands on his cane, listening to the relentless scratching of stiff bristles on rough concrete.

He said, "I'm looking for Carl Gretch."

The sounds of sweeping ceased, and the old man shuffled

into the light, holding the broom before him as if it were a flag he might carry into battle. He was well into his seventies, with liver spots on his flaccid skin. He was even thinner up close, with bony shoulders and knobby elbows, but plenty of muscle still clung to his bones, and the hand gripping the wooden broom handle was gnarled and powerful. His face seemed to be trying to collapse in on itself with age, brow lined and low over deep-set searching eyes, chin on a trajectory to meet nose. "You a friend or relative?" he asked.

Carver said he was neither.

The old man made a hacking sound, then turned and spat off to the side. "So's the landlord lookin' for Gretch," he said. "Bastard didn't bother payin' his back rent afore he moved out yesterday."

"You mean he left without notice?"

"Sure. That ain't unusual in this building. But Billy Peekner still don't look kindly on people leavin' when they owe the last three months' rent. Give a character like Gretch a break by carryin' him that long, it's a sure thing he's gonna sting you. I told Billy that, but he was too mush-hearted to listen."

"Billy's the landlord?"

"Yeah. Shouldn't be, though. Billy's got too much kindness in him to own and manage a place like this. He oughta be runnin' a soup kitchen, or workin' for the U.S. mint givin' out money." The old man's gaze flicked to Carver's cane, back up to his face. "You a bill collector?"

Carver said, "Not exactly."

"Too bad. Billy mighta gave you the job of trackin' down Gretch and gettin' him to pay up on the rent besides whatever other bad debts he's got. Fella like Gretch, I know he's gotta owe plenty of people all over town. Probably the way he paid for that fancy car of his."

"Ever hear of Enrico Thomas?" Carver asked.

"Nope. Why?"

"It's a name Gretch has used."

"Not surprisin'. He's the type that'd use different names. What are you, a cop?"

"A private one."

"Like that Spenser on TV?"

"As opposed to Columbo," Carver said. "I get the impression you and Gretch didn't get along very well."

"Nope, we didn't. My name's Ed Hodgkins. I manage the place for Billy, and Gretch was always givin' me a fit about everything from leaky faucets to burned-out light bulbs. He's a perfectionist about everything except payin' his bills on time."

"Does Billy live on the premises?"

"Billy? Hell, no! He's born to money. He ain't about to live in a dump like this."

"Do you mind if I go up and have a look at Gretch's apartment?"

Hodgkins smiled at Carver and raised a white, bushy eyebrow. "You workin' for somebody Gretch owes?"

"Owes and can't pay," Carver said.

"You look plenty fit despite the cane. Private cops like you, do they ever get physically persuasive with deadbeats like Gretch? You know, make them wanna pay what they owe for fear of more interest buildin' up?"

Carver knew what the old man was thinking, so he decided to let him think it. He leaned on his cane and said nothing.

"Uh-*huh*!" Hodgkins said, grinning. "Well, an experience such as that'd be just what a character like Gretch might need. You give me your name and I'll call you if he turns up here again or I hear anything about him."

Carver gave him his plain white business card with only his name, address and phone number.

Hodgkins squinted at it. "From Del Moray, huh. I got relatives over there. Cousin Charmaine and an Aunt Della."

"I don't think we ever met," Carver said.

Hodgkins glared at him. "You humorin' me, young fella?"

Carver laughed. "Yeah, I guess I am. Sorry."

Hodgkin's seemed mollified by the admission and apology. He shoved a gnarled hand into one of the jeans pockets and pulled out the ring of keys again. They jingled as he worked one of the keys off the ring and handed it to Carver. "My hunch is, you're exactly the kinda fella I'd like to see catch up with Gretch. His apartment's number 2-W, last one on the second floor west."

Carver thanked him, then said, "By the way, did Gretch put out any trash before he left?"

"Sure did. Lots of it."

Carver brightened. He might be able to get a lead on Gretch by poking through what he'd thrown away.

"Already been picked up, though. Early this mornin'. It was in ripped up plastic bags. You wouldn't believe the stench. Smelled to high heaven."

Carver said, "I'm not sure if I'm disappointed."

"Just lock up behind you and bring the key back to me soon as you're done," Hodgkins said.

Carver said he would, but Hodgkins didn't hear him. He was already back inside the garage, scraping tracks in the dirty concrete floor with the push broom.

When Carver reached the building entrance, he glanced back and saw thick clouds of dust rolling from the dim garage out into the sunlight. Hodgkins working up a storm.

GRETCH'S APARTMENT was furnished in Salvation Army decor. A hodgepodge of scarred and threadbare furniture in the never-never land between new and collectible sat on a mottled blue shag rug that had probably been there since the seventies and never cleaned. The place was neat but dusty; Carver wondered what might be hiding in the long nap of the carpet as he crossed the room toward the kitchen.

Hodgkins had been busy there. All the cabinet doors were open, and dishes and pans were stacked in the sink, still wet from washing. The gray and white tiled floor was swept if not waxed, and the sharp smell of insecticide was heavy in the air.

Carver moved on toward the bedroom, glancing in the bathroom to see that Hodgkins had been busy there, too. Where they weren't chipped or yellowed, the old white porcelain fixtures gleamed. The same insecticide scent was present here, but not nearly as strong as in the kitchen. Carver was gaining respect for Hodgkins, who must have been on the job since six or seven o'clock this morning to have accomplished so much.

The double bed in Gretch's bedroom was stripped to the mattress, which, surprisingly, looked almost new. The dresser drawers were empty, and the closet rod held only wire hangers. A black palmetto bug, surprised by the light when Carver opened the closet door, scurried to a corner and flattened itself to squeeze into a crack in the back wall. Apparently it hadn't heard about the insecticide in the kitchen and bathroom and thought the place was still safe.

There was a stack of mail-order catalogs on the closet floor, in the back corner opposite the one where the palmetto bug had made its temporary escape. They were men's clothing catalogs, mostly. Carver examined them and found nothing unusual. All of the order forms were still inside. Apparently Gretch received them then tossed them in his closet in case he wanted to order something later. Then, like most people, ignored them. Most of the catalogs were outdated.

Carver saw that the bottom wooden shelf in the closet was empty except for the plastic cap to a spray can. The top shelf was higher than eye level. He ran his hand along its rough wood surface, being careful not to pick up a splinter. Then his groping fingers came in contact with something flat and smooth. Paper. A magazine. He gripped it and pulled it down.

It was pornography. A bondage magazine featuring women

bound with ropes, leather, or tape in various uncomfortable positions. Carver tossed it back up on the shelf, moved his hand around up there some more, and felt what he knew immediately were photographs.

The subjects, Carver wasn't surprised to find, were women. Not bound this time, but in sexy, smiling and apparently willing poses, some of them modest even though nude or almost nude. They were of three women, and many of the poses were similar. Most of the photos were of a skinny blond who, while attractive, appeared to be pushing fifty. Or maybe she was only forty and had lived faster than time. In a few of the photos she was wearing a silky red nightgown parted to reveal her breasts. All of the photographs were in color and were 35-millimeter, not from instant cameras. None of the shots had been taken in Gretch's apartment; the backgrounds were sort of generic, like motel decor. Though the photos weren't graphically lewd, they weren't the sort that could be sent to a standard commercial developer; if Gretch had taken the photographs, he had to have developed and printed them himself, or had someone he could trust do it for him.

Carver was relieved not to find Donna Winship among the photos' subjects. He kept one shot of each woman, then put the rest back where he'd found them.

When he returned the key to Hodgkins outside the garage, he said, "Did Gretch ever bring women up to his place?"

"I never seen it," Hodgkins said, leaning on his broom, "but that's not to say he never did. He looked like a goddamned lounge lizard, and he had that car always looked and sounded like a high-speed jukebox. Certain type woman goes for that stuff. Young ones, mostly, that ain't been burned yet."

As Carver drove away, he thought about the blond woman in the photographs.

Not so young. But maybe never been burned.

8

DESOTO WAS in his office, on the phone. When he saw Carver, he waved for him to sit down in the hard wooden chair near the desk. Carver closed the door and sat.

"Find him, just find him, hey?" Desoto was saying into the phone. That was pretty much Desoto's life, Carver thought. His own, too. Find him. Or her. This time, for Carver, it was Carl Gretch.

Desoto continued to exhort whoever was on the other end of the connection to find whomever was being sought. The expression on his handsome Latin features was one of bemusement; he wasn't as upset as he must seem to whoever was listening on the other end of the line. He was elegantly dressed, as usual—pleated gray slacks, white shirt, lemon yellow tie, gold ring, wristwatch and cufflinks flashing as he paced and talked into the phone. A dandy with a badge. Carver saw the gray suit coat that matched the pants draped on a shaped wooden hanger slung over a brass hook on the wall. Clothes and women were Desoto's passions. And Latin music, like the guitar solo leaking from the

Sony behind his desk now. A slow song with a relentless, tragic beat, like life itself.

"This job is a sad thing sometimes," Desoto said, hanging up the phone. He sat down behind his desk and adjusted his cuffs, flashing gold and sending chimeras of reflected light dancing across the office walls. "A child dies from internal injuries and the father disappears." He shook his head. "No one will escape punishment on this one, *amigo*, not the guilty or the innocent."

Carver said, "Carl Gretch."

"One of the world's guilty, it would seem."

"He's disappeared, too. Moved out of his furnished apartment in a hurry."

Desoto tilted back his head as if tired, closing his eyes for a moment and taking in the sad guitar. "People like Gretch are always moving. Doing harm, then moving, then doing harm again. It's in their very nature."

Carver wished there were some way to jolt Desoto out of his blue philosophical mood. He said, "Mark Winship shot himself in the head yesterday." Well, that probably wouldn't help.

"I heard," Desoto said, still seeming to concentrate on the music. "What about the little girl? Melissa?"

"Megan. She's with her grandmother."

Desoto nodded and looked at Carver. "You think Gretch is connected to the mother and father's suicides?"

"Indirectly."

"Are the Del Moray police satisfied the father's death *was* suicide?"

"They're satisfied because they want to be." Carver heard the distaste in his own voice.

Desoto smiled, his perfect teeth flashing white in his tan complexion. "You've been visited by McGregor?"

"'Fraid so. We had a long talk after I discovered Mark Winship's corpse."

"You had a chance to look at Winship's body. Do you think it was suicide?"

"Yes. Probably."

"Then why do you want Gretch?"

"There's more to this than what's floating on top for everyone to see. Two people dead. Suicide, legally. But if they were pushed into it, somehow made so desperate that death was the only way out, I call it murder."

"Ah, now you're rewriting the law."

"Yes."

"Something a policeman can't do."

"I'm not exactly a policeman."

"Not exactly. At times, not even remotely."

"Mark Winship might well have killed himself out of remorse over what happened to Donna. But I need to know why she stepped in front of that truck. Need to do something about it."

Desoto's handsome white smile was fleeting, his brown eyes somber. "More unwritten law, hey?"

"Sometimes the written law isn't enough. McGregor is aiming for a promotion and doesn't want any waves made in his jurisdiction. He's not interested in the law, or in justice. Mark Winship could have been shot twenty times and McGregor would still call it suicide."

"*You* called it suicide," McGregor pointed out.

"Yes, but I'm looking into it further. McGregor won't."

"And he won't appreciate you doing his job."

"That's why I'm talking to you," Carver said.

Desoto said nothing. The guitar solo was over now and a woman was singing a slow Spanish lament that had to be about lost love.

"McGregor's going to throw up roadblocks whenever possible," Carver said. "I might need you to help me by doing some things he won't."

"Such as?"

"Letting me know if Carl Gretch's name turns up in police business."

"A friend's not supposed to help a friend do something foolish and dangerous."

"I'm not asking to drive while drunk," Carver said. "I only need a little information now and then."

Desoto leaned back in his chair and laced his fingers behind his head. The office was warm but his shirt was dry. Carver couldn't remember ever seeing him perspire. The Spanish woman launched into a crescendo of sound and drama, muted by the Sony's low volume. Desoto said, "McGregor has the instincts of a snake."

"Does that mean you want to help me on this?"

"It means I want to hurt McGregor. It isn't right he should be promoted rather than tortured and executed."

"Whatever your reasons," Carver said, "thanks." He reached into his pocket and drew out a folded sheet of yellow legal paper. "There's something else," he said, laying the paper on the desk.

"I thought there would be."

"This is a partial list Beth made up of the Winships' friends and acquaintances. Can you check out the names, see if anything of interest crops up?"

Desoto unfolded the sheet of lined paper and studied it. "I don't see any known drug kingpins or mass-murderers on here."

"According to Beth, there wouldn't be. The Winships were your average middle-class couple for years, then they had marital problems and were headed for divorce."

"That's your average middle-class couple," Desoto said.

Carver planted his cane and shifted his weight over it so he could stand up from his chair.

"Where are you off to now, *amigo?*" Desoto asked, refolding the list of names more crisply and neatly than it had been when Carver had laid it on the desk.

"I'm going to talk to some of the people on my copy of that list."

Desoto tapped the folded edge of the list on his desk. It made a sharp, ticking sound. "Our arrangement works both ways, my friend. If you find out anything interesting, I'd like to know."

"Instead of McGregor?"

Desoto shrugged. "I didn't say that."

Carver said, "I didn't ask it." He lifted his cane for a moment in a parting gesture. "Thanks for your help and understanding."

"We're all in the justice business," Desoto said.

"Not McGregor," Carver said, limping from the office into the chaos and order of police headquarters.

9

ACCORDING TO Beth, Donna Winship had little outside life other than aerobic workouts, which was where Beth had met her, and tennis lessons at the Del Moray Country Club. The first name on Beth's list of Donna's friends and acquaintances was Ellen Pfitzer, also a club member.

The Del Moray Country Club was on the ocean, just north of the marina. It was a complex of low buildings made of pale cast concrete with lots of tinted glass and with blue-shingled roofs that were the exact color of the sea on a sunny day. The grounds were neat and green, especially around the largest building, a clubhouse containing a restaurant and lounge and windows looking out on the swimming pool and tennis courts, and beyond them the ocean. On the wide sand beach was a pavilion with a thatched roof that lent shade to a bar and a dozen round tables with high-backed wicker chairs. To the right of the pavilion, closer to the water, were white lounge chairs and wide blue umbrellas with white fringe. There was a scattering of sunbathers on the beach, men in trunks and loose-fitting shirts, women in one-piece suits, a few younger ones in bikinis. A few older ones almost in bikinis. Their actions were slow and deliberate, as if they'd become drunk from the sun.

Carver had visited the place several times last year with a wealthy client who thought his daughter might be engaged to a fortune hunter. He'd been right, but the marriage had taken place anyway, and for now, anyway, daughter and fortune hunter were living happily in Miami, maybe even in love with each other.

Before driving here, Carver had phoned Ellen Pfitzer, and she'd agreed to meet him in the club lounge for a drink and to discuss Donna's death. He was fifteen minutes early, so he chose a table by the window and ordered a Dewar's and water, then sat watching a mixed doubles match in the nearest court. The woman at the far end of the court was a leggy redhead in a white and blue tennis outfit with a skimpy skirt. The other woman was a short blond, sturdily built, in a plain white outfit, who played with single-minded ferocity but was obviously the least accomplished of the four players. Both men were much younger and much smoother on the court, and seemed to be playing with some reserve. Carver guessed they were the women's instructors. He wondered if either of the women was Ellen Pfitzer.

The short blond hit a forehand rocket, yelling with effort, but it was long and the redhead stood smugly, holding her racket back with both hands and watching the ball drop behind the line.

It must have been game point. The redhead's partner gave her a big grin and a hug, then they and the other man walked off toward the part of the clubhouse containing lockers, saunas and exercise equipment. The blond woman backhanded sweat from her forehead and trudged toward the clubhouse. Despite her stockiness she had a graceful walk, the muscles in her firm, tan legs rippling with each step. Large breasts bounced slightly beneath her white pullover shirt. She had a figure made more for pinup calendars than for tennis. Her head was bowed and she was gazing at the ground in concentration as she passed from sight.

She must have stopped to freshen up. Ten minutes passed before she entered the lounge and stood looking around, ignoring the speculative glances of some of the men at the bar. She saw Carver, saw the cane where he'd leaned it against the table, and came toward him.

She had an open, friendly face with blue eyes and a slightly turned-up nose, and she was even shorter than she'd appeared on the court, probably under five feet.

"Ellen Pfitzer?" Carver asked.

She nodded, and he introduced himself and motioned for her to sit down.

When she was settled, the waiter appeared and she ordered a Tom Collins. Needed to cool off after the hotly contested tennis match in the sun.

"I was watching you play," Carver said.

She smiled. "So what did you think?"

"That it was too hot for that kind of thing."

"I only play because it's great exercise and burns a lot of calories. I'm always fighting to keep my figure."

"You're winning," Carver said.

She gave him another wide grin and took a long pull on the drink the waiter had placed in front of her. She lowered the glass and said, "Ah!" the way actors say it in TV commercials. Carver waited for her to sell him something.

"Donna's funeral was this morning," she said.

"I know. I didn't go. I have a thing about funerals. They seem superfluous."

"They are, of course," Ellen said. "There weren't many people there. Donna's mother and daughter, a few of the people from the insurance company where Donna worked. I was a pallbearer, along with your friend Beth. The mortuary supplied most of the others."

Carver hadn't talked to Beth since early that morning. He wondered if there would be many mourners at Mark Winship's funeral. "Did you know Donna's husband?" he asked.

"We met a few times, but I wouldn't say I knew him. Donna talked about him a lot, though. They were unhappy lately, but I guess that's no secret."

"She say why they were unhappy?"

Ellen took another sip of her drink, just nibbling at the ice this time, while her blue eyes sized up Carver as if he were a tennis opponent. She placed the glass back on its coaster. "I talked about you with Beth after the funeral. In a sense, I guess you're still working for Donna."

"In a sense. I want to know the reason for what happened."

"You're the kind of guy who can't let go. That's what Beth said."

Great, Carver thought. More of that obsessive talk.

"Donna confided in me several months ago that she and Mark were having problems," Ellen said. "Then, about a month ago, she told me she was having an affair."

"Did she say who she was involved with?"

"She said it was nobody I knew, and she just referred to him as 'Enrico' every now and then. I think she wanted me to know it wasn't anyone at the club, any of the tennis pros. That kind of thing happens a lot around here, you know, but Donna wasn't the type."

"What type was she?"

Ellen ran a blunt, unpainted fingernail up and down her tall glass and thought for a few seconds before answering. "She was a nice woman. I know 'nice' is a word used too frequently, but in Donna's case it applies. She was friendly toward everyone, but also a little shy. This is a fairly exclusive club—I'd even say snotty. Donna and Mark were members only because of Mark's affiliation with people through his investment counseling. He seldom came here at all. Donna was aware she didn't travel in the same circles as a lot of the members and didn't seek out people. She didn't mind not associating with some of the snobs around here. She was actually the homebody type and was content until her marriage started to go bad." A serious light entered Ellen's blue eyes and she leaned toward Carver earnestly. "I'll tell you what type she *wasn't*. She wasn't the type to have an extramarital affair. I don't know exactly what Mark Winship did, but the marriage must have been hopeless for Donna to get mixed up with another man."

"Do you remember what she said about Enrico?"

"She said she was happy only when she was with him, and it was positively eerie how compatible they were, how they loved and hated the same things. You know the phase, when endorphins take the place of reason. She said it almost made her believe in fate or astrology. If it helps you any, I'm sure she was totally hooked on this guy. I wish I'd met him."

"Be glad you didn't."

Her eyes widened over the rim of her glass. "Have *you* met him?"

"Briefly," Carver said. "We didn't get along."

"Maybe you caught him at a bad time."

"If I did, he reacted badly. He threatened me with a knife."

Ellen shook her head. "Well, Donna wouldn't be the first woman to gravitate toward the wrong man when her marriage was breaking up. Her husband was right for her at one time, when she was thinking straight, but under the strain, with things coming unglued, she might have been temporarily attracted to someone who was more or less his opposite."

That sounded pretty good to Carver. He was becoming impressed by Ellen Pfitzer.

"But suicide," Ellen said. She shook her head no as if she'd been asked to throw a tennis match. "That wasn't like Donna, either."

"Had she acted strange lately?"

"She was nervous and depressed, but I wouldn't describe her as suicidal."

"It was an impulsive thing," Carver said.

Ellen scowled. "Probably thanks to Enrico."

"Do you remember anything in particular Donna said about her husband?"

"She mentioned that he'd withdrawn from her, that he'd become cold. She said he acted as if the marriage was already ended and he was just marking time until the divorce. Exactly what you'd expect to hear about a marriage on the rocks, when one of the partners has given up completely."

"Did he turn cool toward her for a reason?"

"None that she knew. She told me she asked him what was wrong. Begged him to tell her. All he'd say was that he was unhappy. He'd refuse to be specific. They hadn't really talked about a divorce yet. When she asked him if he wanted one, he wouldn't give her an honest answer. She thought he was stalling, even though he seemed to have made up his mind she was no longer going to be a part of his life. He'd dismissed her from his existence. She told me she felt like a ghost when she was in the house with him."

Carver looked out the window at the sunbathers on the beach. Beyond the pavilion's thatched roof, he could see a few of the luxury cruisers docked at the club's private marina, their white hulls bobbing in the gentle, sheltered water, their navigational antennae and painted brightwork gleaming in the sun. Everything and everyone at the club was bright and clean and rich.

"Was Donna a good tennis player?" Carver asked.

"Not really. She was too timid, didn't seem to mind if she lost. Yet for some reason she'd occasionally become ferocious and go to the net more than anyone. She'd still lose, but you had to watch out or she'd take your head off with one of her forehands."

He showed Beth's list to Ellen. "Who else should I talk to on here?"

She pointed to the name beneath her own, then sat back. "To tell you the truth," she said, "I think I knew Donna as well as anyone. We shared . . . you know, women's confidences."

"What about the name below yours? Beverly Denton?"

"Yeah, Donna mentioned her. I think she's a friend of Mark's, really. The three of them used to spend time together, but Donna said she and Beverly never saw each other anymore, what with the way Mark had been acting. I doubt if she'd be of much help."

"What about the possibility of Mark and Beverly having been romantically involved?"

"Anything's possible. But I think Donna told me not long ago that Beverly was engaged to some guy who refurbishes yachts." Ellen brushed back a strand of blond hair that had fallen over one eye; it had to bother her playing tennis. "Anyway, like I said, Donna and I shared confidences. If she'd thought Mark and Beverly had a thing going, she'd have told me."

Wishing Donna had shared even more confidences with Ellen, Carver thanked her and stood up.

She glanced at his cane. "That a temporary thing?"

"As temporary as I am."

"Well, there are worse things in life than a stiff leg. You seem to do okay for yourself."

"I haven't curled into a ball and cried for a long time."

"Me, either. Not since last night." She smiled in a way that suggested she wouldn't mind if he sat back down.

He laid one of his business cards on the table. "If you hear anything more about Enrico Thomas," he said, "call me and let me know."

"So that's his last name. Thomas."

"No," Carver said, "I was getting to that. His real name is Carl Gretch, and he seems to have disappeared."

Ellen looked surprised. "Donna was going with a guy who used an alias?"

"And a knife," Carver said. "See, she didn't share as many confidences with you as you thought."

"It makes me wonder," Ellen said, sounding a little mystified, "what else she didn't tell me."

As Carver left the rarefied, moneyed atmosphere of the club lounge, he tried to imagine Carl Gretch there and couldn't.

What had nice Donna Winship been thinking?

10

CARVER SAT at a table in the shade of a tilted umbrella and ate a taco. After leaving the country club, he realized he hadn't had lunch and was hungry, so he drove to a taco stand he liked near the public marina, on Magellan about half a mile from his office. It was a pleasant place to think and get indigestion.

He leaned over the table as he bit into the brittle taco shell, careful not to drip sauce on his shirt or pants. It relaxed him to sit and watch the boats bobbing at their moorings or putting in or out of the marina. As he wiped grease from his fingers and leaned back in his plastic chair, a large sailboat with its canvas down glided on alternate motor power parallel to the shore, then altered course to head toward open water. He sipped his Busch beer and watched its sails being hoisted when it was farther from shore.

It was late enough for him to be the only customer other than two young girls perched on stools at the stand's counter. He figured no one would be bothered by smoke, so he finished his beer, then fired up a Swisher Sweet cigar. He liked to smoke the small, slender cigars sometimes after meals. A substitute for dessert.

He watched shreds of smoke drift away on the sea breeze and thought that what he knew about the deaths of Donna and Mark Winship had about the same substance and permanence.

By the time the cigar was half gone, the sun had moved enough so that the tilt of the umbrella was wrong and allowed sunlight to lance beneath it and glint off the smooth white table. Carver's eyes began to ache.

There was an outside public phone near the stand, so he snubbed out what was left of the cigar in a square glass ashtray on the table and got up and deposited his empty beer can, wadded napkin, and the crumpled paper that had held the taco in a trash can. Some of the hot red sauce from the wrapper got on the edge of his hand and he licked it off, then went to the phone.

The two girls at the counter glanced at him, then looked away with obvious disinterest. He was too old for them, in another universe. Or maybe it was the cane. He wasn't sure which he hoped it was. The old guy laboriously scraping a grill stared at him from behind the counter as if he thought Carver might want another taco, then returned to his work when he saw that Carver was moving toward the phone.

The plastic and metal of the phone shelter was hot from the sun. Carver leaned on it for support, hooked his cane over a steel lip, and inserted most of the change he'd received when he'd bought lunch. He called his office, waited for the answering machine to kick in, then punched out his personal code on the phone's keypad to signal the machine to play his messages. Four of them, according to the machine's electronic brain:

The garage where he had the Olds serviced called to say he couldn't bring the car in for an oil change as scheduled and should phone for another appointment. There were a couple of hang-ups. Then Hodgkins, the manager of the building where Carl Gretch had lived, was on the machine telling Carver that

Gretch had returned to the apartment. The time on the message was 1:05, an hour ago.

Carver replaced the receiver and made his way through the scattering of tables and umbrellas to where the Olds was parked with its canvas top down. He lowered himself into the hot vinyl upholstery behind the steering wheel, got the engine started, and drove fast for Orlando and the apartment on Belt Street.

THE DOOR to Gretch's apartment was closed and locked. Carver rapped on the checked enameled wood with his cane. Waited and listened. No answer and no sound from inside.

He went back down to the first floor and the apartment door lettered MANAGER and knocked.

Hodgkins opened the door almost immediately. He was wearing the same baggy jeans he'd had on when Carver had last seen him, but he'd changed from his white tee shirt into a crisp blue and gray plaid sport shirt that still had creases in it from being folded when it was bought. He smelled like stale pipe tobacco with an underlying scent of bourbon.

"Figured you'd be here in a hurry," he said, "but it wasn't fast enough. Gretch was only in his place about fifteen or twenty minutes. When I stopped him on his way downstairs and asked him about the rent he owed, he acted like he was in a big hurry, said I should fuck off. Them were his exact words. Then he was past me and out the door and into that fancy car of his. Left twenty bucks' worth of tire on the street screechin' outa here."

"Was he carrying anything when he came downstairs?" Carver asked.

"No, not as I can recall."

"Mind if I go up and have another look around his place?"

"Not in the slightest."

Hodgkins shuffled out of sight for a minute with his stiff-jointed gait, then returned and handed Carver a key attached with string to a metal-rimmed cardboard tag with *2-W* lettered on it in black ink. Carver thanked him and climbed back up the stairs, clumping on the wooden steps with his cane.

Gretch's apartment looked exactly as it had this morning, but it was warmer and stuffier. Hodgkins had turned off the air-conditioning in the unit. Carver studied the mismatched furniture, but none of it seemed to have been moved. A bead of sweat ran down his ribs as he limped into the bedroom and saw that the bed was still stripped down.

Everything looked the same here, too. He opened the closet's sliding louvered door and felt around on the top shelf. The porn magazine and the photos he'd returned there were now gone. They must be what had drawn Gretch back to the apartment. More specifically, it would be the photographs he wanted. Black-mail material, maybe.

No, Carver thought, the photos weren't lewd or compromising enough for that, and they were of women posed by themselves. The most the subjects could be accused of was posing for what looked like amateurish attempts at the kind of mild pinup shots still seen on calendars in garages and small-town barbershops.

"Hello."

The voice was soft and throaty and might have belonged to a woman.

But when Carver turned around he saw a man standing just inside the bedroom door. He was Oriental and diminutive, maybe not even five feet tall, wiry beneath his loose-fitting gray slacks and long-sleeved white shirt. His hair was black and combed severely to the side, and his features were smooth and dainty, with the kind of toothy, cheery grin that had made stereotypes of a generation of Oriental actors. He was wearing light and supple tan leather shoes that might have passed for house slippers. He made absolutely no sound as he strode a few smooth steps toward Carver. It occurred to Carver that the man might have followed him up the stairs one step behind and he wouldn't have known it.

Something about the tight, controlled way the small man moved alerted Carver, but too late. The man's almost dainty right hand made a quick, elegant gesture, drawing Carver's gaze as one of the small slippered feet flicked out and kicked the cane from his hand. The man's other hand was against Carver's chest, then he was three feet away and grinning down at Carver, who was lying on his back where he'd fallen on the floor. Carver had never seen anyone move so smoothly so fast.

"Maybe we should talk," Carver said, raising himself on one elbow and noticing that his cane was too far away to grab.

The man kicked him in the ribs, almost casually, but so quickly that Carver couldn't block the flashing foot or clutch it so he could pull the man down on his level. The smile stayed firm as a mask on the man's face.

"Easy!" Carver groaned through his pain. "We're both Bruce Lee fans."

"Amateur shit," the tiny man said. He did a complete turn so quickly it appeared that film had jumped frames. Carver felt but didn't see the kick to his shoulder. His arm went numb as if it had been shocked with high voltage.

"I could splatter your brains on the wall just like a bullet had hit you," the man said. He had only a faint Oriental accent that Carver couldn't place. Everything he said sounded condescending. "I might mess up my shoes, though."

"Don't do that," Carver said. "They look expensive."

"They are made from the flesh of my enemies."

Carver didn't think the man was kidding. He lay still, figuring that was about the only defense he had. He didn't want to be kicked in his good leg; that might immobilize him to the point of panic.

The little man kicked his good leg. Carver tried with his uninjured arm to grab the blur that was a foot but failed.

"Have we met someplace before?" he grunted, forcing himself with great effort to lie still now, not thrash around and go into a blind rage of pain.

"You're Mr. Carver."

"Who are you?"

"I'm tonight's bad dream."

"Today's," Carver said, taking another kick to the arm. There wasn't much pain because the arm was already numb. The guy wasn't perfect.

"You're here to visit Mr. Gretch," the man said, "but he doesn't live here anymore. You and he aren't friends anyway, so you shouldn't try to locate him. There is no point."

"I only want to talk to him," Carver said.

"He doesn't want to listen. He's not a good listener. Are you a good listener?"

"I try."

"Mind your own business, or that of someone other than Mr. Gretch. Do you hear and comprehend?"

"Both those things."

The tiny man floated across the carpet and picked up Carver's cane. He twirled it as if he were a majorette leading a parade, then gripped it with both hands as if it were a sword and lashed the air with it in neat, symmetrical patterns. The last slash of the cane brought it straight down to rest lightly on Carver's Adam's apple.

Carver didn't move. He felt sweat break out on his face and turn cold. His stomach was jumping around with fear in a way he wouldn't have thought possible.

"You could be dead at this moment, Mr. Carver."

Carver didn't speak, only nodded.

The cane flashed up and away from his throat, and he closed his eyes, thinking it was about to descend with the same velocity and crush his larynx.

When he opened his eyes, the cane was lying near him and

the tiny man was standing near the door. Still smiling like a character in an old Charlie Chan movie, the man nodded, almost a bow, then was gone.

Carver rolled onto his side and waited for the pain to subside and at least some feeling to return to his arm and good leg. The fear he'd felt when he thought he might be killed with his cane was still in his stomach, making him nauseated.

Fifteen minutes passed before he trusted himself to grip the cane and stand up. He didn't move for a long time, because the room was tilting this way and that as if tossed on a wild sea. Everything hurt. He wondered if the quick little man had kicked him places he hadn't even been aware of at the time.

When the room was at last still, he slowly descended the stairs and returned the key to Hodgkins, who said he hadn't heard anyone on the stairs and had never seen a tiny Oriental man around the building.

"You mean like some kinda midget?" he asked, squinting at Carver as if suspecting some sort of joke.

"Almost a midget, but he packs a giant's wallop."

"Hmph! You find anything up there in the apartment?"

"Just that near-midget."

"Well, if I see him I'll sure phone you right away."

Carver got to the Olds and drove back to Del Moray, then up the coast road to his cottage. He wanted to submerge his aching body in a bathtub full of hot water before he got too stiff to move.

All the way along the coast, with the ocean on his right and gulls keeping pace briefly with the car and wheeling and screaming over the beach, he wondered if Gretch had noticed that three of his photographs were missing.

11

BECAUSE OF his bad leg, Carver usually showered instead of bathing. The tiny bathroom in the cottage was equipped with a small white fiberglass tub and shower stall. The tub was deep enough but not very long, which meant that when he sat in it he had to extend his stiff leg out at an uncomfortable angle over the curved edge into space. That was okay this time, since that leg was one of the few parts of him his attacker had ignored, probably following the maxim that if it ain't fixed, don't break it.

The hot water soothed his pain as he settled down as deep as possible in the tub. He wanted to avoid being so sore tomorrow that he'd be unable to get out of bed. He rested his head on the wall behind the tub and draped the hot, soaked washcloth over his face, thinking it had been one hellacious day.

Lying there healing with his eyes closed, he heard Beth say, "Kinda early for a bath."

He removed the washcloth and looked at her standing in the doorway. She was wearing yellow shorts and a black tee shirt lettered GUNS DON'T KILL PEOPLE. PEOPLE WITH GUNS KILL

PEOPLE. Her bare tanned legs looked impossibly long from Carver's low vantage point, and her heavy breasts stretched the shirt's fabric. She had on a yellow headband and bright red lipstick. It occurred to Carver that there was only one part of him that wasn't stiff, and she was about to change that. He altered the direction of his thoughts and told her why he was in the bathtub letting hot water work its magic.

When he was finished, she leaned her shoulder against the doorjamb and crossed her arms. She said, "I want in, Fred."

For a moment he thought she planned on getting into the tiny tub with him, then he realized what she meant. The Winslow deaths called to her on a personal as well as journalistic basis. Donna had been her friend, and Beth had set up the meeting with Carver just before her death. That someone had tried to frighten Carver off the case in Gretch's apartment meant that there was something to hide. Jeff Smith, her editor at *Burrow*, would be interested.

"You gonna keep me involved and informed?" she asked. Her expression was grave, her strongly boned face like something cast in bronze in a lost age.

Carver didn't like the thought of the tiny Oriental destruction machine focusing on Beth. He knew she wouldn't see it that way. She was physically tough herself and proficient in martial arts and probably figured she'd be a match for the little man. People who were into martial arts thought that way. Cockiness was part of the way they psyched themselves into knowing they could break wood or bricks with flesh and bone, psyched themselves into thinking it was important in the first place. He covered his face again with the washcloth.

"Fred?"

"You're in," he said from beneath the rag, knowing he had no choice.

He felt her kiss his forehead through the thick, soaked material.

"You had supper?" she asked.

"Just a couple of Tylenols."

"Hungry?"

"No."

"I'll cook us up some hamburgers anyway, then we'll eat while you fill me in on everything about the Winship case."

Fifteen minutes later, when the water had cooled and the scent of frying beef was prodding his appetite, he decided it was time to struggle out of the bathtub.

HE WASN'T as sore as he thought he'd be the next morning, but he didn't so much as consider his usual therapeutic swim in the ocean. The clock by the bed read 9:05. Beth was already gone. Despite Carver's reservations, they'd agreed last night that she would stake out Gretch's apartment to see if he or the Oriental man showed up again. If one of them did appear, Carver had given her strict instructions not to approach him but to very discreetly follow.

Carver sat up on the edge of the mattress and reached for his cane. With each breath, his side ached where he'd been kicked in the ribs. His good leg and his right arm were sore but functional. The involuntary groan he heard when he forced himself to stand up was his own but sounded like someone else's. Someone who should have sense enough to stay in bed.

He got dressed gingerly, careful not to extend his reach too far, easing into his pants and socks, then his leather moccasins. He went to the dresser and completely removed the top drawer. Taped to the back of the drawer was his .32 Colt semiautomatic. He slipped the gun's shoulder holster over his bare torso, then checked the clip and action and slid the gun into the holster. Then he put on a loose-fitting silk shirt with a tropical bird pattern and examined himself in the mirror. The looseness and wild print of the colorful material made the bulk of the gun barely noticeable.

When he phoned Burnair and Crosley Investments, where Mark Winship had been a financial consultant, and asked to speak with Beverly Denton he was told that Miz Denton hadn't arrived for work. Instead of leaving a message, he drove to a restaurant down on the coast highway and had a breakfast of scrambled eggs, jellied toast, and black coffee. Then he sat at one of the unoccupied tables outside and smoked a Swisher Sweet while he read the *Del Moray Gazette-Dispatch*. The motels along the beach were complaining that oil drifting in from the big tankers offshore was getting to be a major problem. There were no murders or other major crimes reported, only the oil; smooth sailing for McGregor.

By the time he'd returned to the cottage, a little past ten, Beverly Denton was at her desk at Burnair and Crosley. She agreed on the phone to talk with Carver about Donna Winship's death but didn't want to discuss it in the office. She suggested they meet in the small park across the street from Burnair and Crosley, where she often had lunch and relaxed. She'd be wearing a green dress with black shoes, she said. Carver told her he walked with a cane and would be the most handsome man in the park. She agreed to meet him anyway.

THE PARK was only about half a square block, a flat, grassy area where concrete benches were arranged in the shade of palm trees. In the center of the park was a twenty-foot-tall steel sculpture made up of a series of sleek, shiny panels rising like parallel knife blades tapered to different points. Carver wasn't sure what it was supposed to represent, but he liked it. Maybe it had been created to complement the building across the street that housed Burnair and Crosley, which was also made up of shiny, parallel panels of steel and tinted glass, only with elevators and offices inside.

Beverly Denton was easy enough to find. It was only 11:30 and the park was almost unoccupied except for two preteen boys climbing around on a jungle gym at the far end. She was sitting on one of the concrete benches and gazing out at the traffic passing on Atlantic Drive.

As Carver approached her he saw curiosity become decision in her eyes, which were dark brown like her short-cropped, boyish hair. She had lean features made to look even thinner by large gold hoop earrings. When she stood up and smoothed the skirt of her green dress, he noted that she was slender but shapely, a trim, neat woman who looked worried.

"Mr. Carver?"

He said he was and suggested they sit down on the bench, which they did, at opposite ends and angled to face each other. Like a couple of shy teenagers who'd just been introduced by a best friend. Beverly crossed her legs so tightly they seemed welded together. Her body language suggested that even if he was the most handsome man in the park, she didn't care; she wasn't in the mood.

He tried his smile on her, which he knew made his fierce features surprisingly amiable. She didn't seem reassured. He said, "You were a friend of Donna Winship." Telling her, not asking.

"I was a friend to both Donna and Mark," she said in a soft, steady voice, "but I wouldn't say a close friend of either." She stared for a moment at her short, red fingernails. "What's your interest in the Winships?"

"Donna thought something might be wrong in her life and hired me to investigate. I'm still investigating."

"Why?"

He decided to give her the short answer and not mention that he had been the last person to talk to Donna, that he had been

|76|

her last hope and might have said something that confirmed her despair and prompted her sudden impulse to end her life, that now he wanted to make up for it to assuage a guilt that maybe he shouldn't feel but most definitely did.

"Because I was paid," he said.

That seemed to satisfy her; coin of the realm was her job. She said, "Mark and I worked together. There across the street." She tilted her head in the direction of Burnair and Crosley. One of the hoop earrings caught the sun. "Mark was a financial consultant, as I am. When his client list became too large, he referred business to me. We became friends, and that's how I met Donna."

"What was your opinion of her?"

"She was nice."

The same word Ellen Pfitzer had used to describe Donna Winship. "Can you be more specific?"

Beverly raised her hands in a faint, futile gesture. "They seemed happily married."

"I'm told they weren't so happy the past several months."

"That could be. When I became engaged to Warren I didn't see them much anymore. The four of us went out for dinner a few times, but Warren and Mark didn't really hit it off, so we drifted apart."

"Warren's the fella who refurbishes yachts?"

She smiled. "You *are* an investigator."

"What about Mark? I assume you liked him."

"He was nice, too."

Carver looked out at the traffic, becoming aware that exhaust fumes were heavy in the park. "Nice, huh? Beverly, you could have told me this on the phone. Why did you agree to a face-to-face meeting?"

"Because it doesn't seem logical to me that the Winships killed themselves. I guess I can't quite believe it." She gnawed her lower lip and squirmed slightly on the hard bench.

Carver waited, knowing there was more. A squirrel chattered nearby, then scampered up the trunk of the nearest palm tree.

"What about you?" she asked. "Do you think they were really both suicides?"

"There isn't much doubt," he said, "but there's some."

"How often does that happen, a husband and wife committing suicide only a day apart?"

"I don't know," Carver said. "They don't keep statistics."

"There had to be a hell of a reason for it," Beverly said. "That's why I thought it'd be a good idea if we talked, because I feel their deaths *should* be investigated, and the police won't do it since officially they were suicides." She let out a long breath. "The last five or six months, Mark Winship was involved with another Burnair and Crosley employee, a woman named Maggie Rourke."

"He told you that?"

"No. He didn't have to. Maggie confided it to me about two months ago when she realized I'd noticed how they acted together when they thought they were alone one day in a file room. I figured it was none of my business, and Warren and I never saw the Winships again, so I didn't mention it to Mark or anyone else."

"Except for me, now."

"Because the Winships are dead, and that should be looked into."

"Tell me about Maggie Rourke. Something other than that she's nice."

Beverly smiled. "Okay, I'll try to be more insightful. Maggie's a financial consultant, too. She's in her early thirties and divorced, a focused career woman. It kind of surprised me that she'd let herself become involved with someone at work. But once she did tell me and I knew for sure, I began watching the two of them together, how they exchanged glances, fond touches. They acted like a couple too much in love to hide it.

The thing is, after Donna died, Mark surely would have talked to Maggie. That means she might know something important."

Carver thought she might indeed. "Is Maggie at work now?"

"No. After Mark's death she took her vacation time, I'm sure so she could mourn him in private. She left an address and phone number where she could be reached, though. She said it was a beach cottage south of town off the coast highway." Beverly felt around in her large black leather purse and withdrew a folded sheet of white paper. Carver could see the sharp impressions of typing on the side folded in. "The address and number are on here," she said, handing the paper to him. "Do me a favor and don't mention where you got them."

"I don't know where this will lead," he said. "At some point I might have to mention it."

"Well, if it comes to that, so be it. I'm not doing anything wrong." She stared at him as if for confirmation.

"You're doing something right," Carver assured her, and tucked the paper into his shirt pocket.

As he exited the sunny park, leaving Beverly to her thoughts, he watched the kids hanging by their knees on the jungle gym and wished he could play free that way just one more time.

12

THE FIRST thing Carver noticed about Maggie Rourke was that she was knockdown beautiful. It was the second, third, and fourth thing he noticed, too. It was hard to get around the way she looked and think of her in politically correct terms.

She was on the beach, beyond a small wooden cottage built on thick piering and with a cantilevered screened-in porch. There was an outcropping of rock to her left, and the beach tapered off to rough pebble and sea oat to her right, so she was more or less alone except for occasional glimpses of swimmers or sunbathers beyond the rock. She lay on her back like an offering, in a lounge chair adjusted almost to horizontal, a folded white towel for a pillow and backdrop for her thick and tousled long auburn hair. Her tanned body was slender and flawless in a white string bikini. As Carver approached, the goddess peeled off her sunglasses and peered up at him. Her eyes were gray and curious and maybe the slightest bit afraid.

She said, "Are you a friend of Mac's?"

"Who's Mac?" Carver asked.

"The man who owns this place."

"He a friend of yours?"

"Uh-huh."

Carver told her who he was and that he wanted to talk to her about the Winships.

"I don't see much point in that," she said. "They're both gone."

He stood quietly in the sun, leaning with both hands on the crook of his cane, making it obvious he wasn't going anywhere, so they might as well chat. The breeze off the sea felt cool on his perspiring back, the sun felt uncomfortably hot on his bald pate.

She replaced her sunglasses and settled her head back onto the folded towel. "I didn't know Donna at all."

"It was Mark I wanted to talk about," he told her.

"I knew him," she said, the blank dark glasses aimed straight up at the sky.

Carver said, "My understanding is that you and Mark were lovers."

"I suppose there's no reason now to deny it. We were in love, and now that's all ended. Mark's marriage was breaking up."

"Because of you?"

"Before he met me. Otherwise . . ."

"Otherwise what?"

She laughed without humor. "I was going to say that if he was happily married I wouldn't have allowed us to become so involved, but I'm not sure that's true. We probably would have fallen in love anyway. It was one of those elemental things that overwhelm people."

"It's a wonder anyone stays married," Carver said.

"Are you being sarcastic?"

"No, it was an honest observation. I'm divorced, myself."

"The whole world is divorced."

A gull swooped in low over the beach, then changed direction and flew out of sight beyond the outcropping of rock. It screamed as it passed from view.

Maggie said, "Mark was going to leave his wife for me."

"You're sure?"

She nodded, reaching down and finding a brown plastic squeeze bottle of sun block. "That's what he told me, and I believed him." She squirted the oily white substance into her left palm and began slowly rubbing it into the firm flesh of her stomach and thighs.

Watching her, Carver said, "I find it difficult to believe that a man with you to live for would commit suicide."

She dropped the bottle back to the sand. "Donna caused it. Donna had him all fucked up." Her voice was controlled but angry. She drew a deep breath and then very slowly released it.

"But Donna was dead."

"Yeah. Leaving poor Mark with enough guilt piled on him that he broke under it. He wasn't strong that way. He couldn't take it so he decided to . . . well, he decided not to endure it."

"Is that your take on what happened?"

"What other way is there to see it? Goddamned Donna stepped in front of a truck because she knew she was losing her husband. Mark was already under the strain of a marriage that was unraveling like a cheap sweater, with Donna blaming him for everything. Naturally, in the shock of what happened, he thought he was responsible for her death."

"Did he tell you that?"

"Yes. On the phone. I tried to talk sense into him but he wasn't listening. What she did, why I'm *sure* she did it, really got to him, just the way she planned it." She shifted on the lounge and made a helpless little gesture with a clenched fist, swiping at the warm air tentatively, as if afraid it might strike back harder. "I should have gone to him. It might have made a difference."

"There's enough misplaced guilt going around," Carver told

her. "Don't add to it." He thought she might be crying beneath the dark glasses, but all he could see in their lenses were reflections of clouds. "How long have you been with Burnair and Crosley?" he asked, trying to get her mind off guilt and recrimination.

"About six months."

"Is that where you and Mark met?"

"Yeah, it was a typical office romance. A cliché. We tried to hide it from everyone, but they saw through us even if they didn't say anything. They all knew Mark was married, and that put a damper on talk around the office, at least in front of us. But no matter how discreet you are, love between two people shows and generates gossip. Look how easy it was for you to find out about us."

"Did Donna know?"

"Mark didn't think so. And he didn't think anyone at the office knew. He simply wouldn't let himself see it in their faces."

"Did Mark know about Donna?"

Maggie sat up on the lounge and crossed her legs, facing Carver. She removed her sunglasses again. Her eyes fixed on his, and he could understand how Mark Winship had fallen. "Did he know what about Donna?" she asked.

"That she was involved with another man."

Maggie stared at Carver for a while, then threw back her head and gave a half laugh, half cry. A gull cried down near the sea, as if in answer. "You're sure about that?" Maggie asked.

"She told me so."

"Jesus! If only Mark had known!"

"Are you positive he didn't know?"

"Don't you think he would have told me?" She bowed her head slightly now, causing her auburn hair to fall forward and conceal most of her face. The sun glistened on her oiled, golden shoulders. "It would have taken so much burden off him if he'd known. He really cared about not hurting Donna. So did I,

| 83 |

really. Neither of us wanted to cause pain, we simply wanted each other."

The tragic geometry of love, Carver thought. He said, "Do you know, or did Mark ever mention, a man named Enrico Thomas?"

"No."

"What about Carl Gretch?"

"Not him, either. Was Donna involved with one of them?"

"They're the same man," Carver said.

Now Maggie raised her head and stared at him. "What is he, some kind of con artist?"

"I think so, but I'm not sure which kind."

"Getting mixed up with somebody like that sure doesn't sound like Donna Winship. She was . . . well, plain vanilla, if you know what I mean."

"She was vulnerable," Carver said. "Mark was withdrawing from her, and along came Gretch. Men like that can sense weakness in a woman, and they know how to close in on it."

"God, I wish Mark had known!" she said softly.

"It might not have made any difference."

"I hate that fucking word—'might'!"

Carver was getting miserably hot, standing there in the sun. Sweat was stinging the corners of his eyes. "I don't like that word either. It's part of the reason I do this kind of work." He handed Maggie his business card and said, "Will you call me if you hear or remember anything about Mark or Donna? Maybe something Mark might have said?"

She accepted the card, leaving sun block on his hand where their fingers brushed. "Sure. Why not?"

He thanked her for her time, then left her to continue grieving in the sun. It had to be hell, carrying so much sorrow for someone you couldn't admit having loved. The sidelong glances and gossip would continue for her, and to confront them head-on would only make matters worse.

Narrow wooden steps led up to firmer but still sandy soil. Carver was glad to be off the soft beach with his cane. He walked around to the front of the cottage where his car was parked. It was a secluded and shady spot, concealed from the road by shrubbery and a row of wind-bent palm trees and paved with white powdered rock that had become packed and hard as concrete beneath years of rain and the compression of tires. A three- or four-year-old black Nissan Stanza was parked in the shade. There was a red plastic rose taped to its antenna, making it easier to locate in parking lots. Carver was headed toward the Olds, looking forward to starting the engine and setting the air conditioner on high, when he caught movement in the corner of his vision.

He stopped walking and turned, leaning on his cane.

The little Oriental martial arts whizbang stepped out from the shade of the palms and smiled at him. He was wearing dark brown pleated slacks and an untucked white shirt that was laced up the front with rawhide rather than buttoned. He seemed relaxed, his arms and shoulders loose and his hands folded lightly in front of him.

He said, "Mr. Carver, you didn't heed my cautionary advice."

"I don't take advice well," Carver said. He was gripping his cane hard, knowing the little man would go for it first to put him on the ground.

"I could sense that about you from the beginning," the man said, edging toward Carver. "You possess admirable but danger-ous determination. It borders on obsessiveness, I'm sure. Even when you were at a terrible disadvantage in Gretch's apartment and agreeing to everything I suggested, I discerned a certain lack of sincerity in you. Would you be more sincere and truthful if I asked why you were talking to the woman on the beach?"

"No."

"Well, it doesn't matter. It's Mr. Gretch's life that you must stay out of, as I tried so hard to impress upon you without breaking any part of you or separating flesh from bone. So pain-ful." His tiny but muscular body took on a sudden tenseness and deadliness, and his hands unfolded and moved out in front of him. His knees flexed slightly so that he was in a slight crouch, and he began moving in on Carver. "Now the lesson must be more forcefully taught."

Carver quickly snatched the Colt from beneath his loose-fitting shirt and snapped the safety off, jacking a round into the chamber, then another, so the first round was ejected in the sunlight and the Oriental man would know the gun was loaded. "It's ready to fire," he said.

His tiny assailant stopped and stood very still. "But are *you* ready? I don't think so, and I'm an excellent judge of such qualities. It takes a certain uncommon willingness to shoot someone, Mr. Carver. I doubt if you possess that rare cal-lousness of soul"

Holding the gun steady, Carver said, "I possess it."

The man began walking smoothly and slowly in a circle around Carver. "People who can kill recognize the trait in oth-ers. I don't see it in you at all. No, you're not a killer, Mr. Carver. Few men are. They think they are, but when it comes time to muster the nerve to actually squeeze the trigger, they find they are too decent, too human. We don't kill our own so easily. We must first learn how to overcome certain inhibitions." He was walking faster. The circle, with Carver in its center, was becoming smaller. Carver set the tip of his cane and moved around it as an axis, always facing the tiny, dangerous man with the unfailing grin. Only about ten feet separated them now.

Carver said, "I suggest you don't come any nearer."

"I don't believe you've overcome your very human and decent inhibitions, Mr. Carver."

Carver shot him in the leg.

It wasn't easy. He remembered his pain and disbelief when

he'd been shot in the knee, and he moved his aim higher on the thigh. The gun wasn't as steady as it should have been.

The little man went down, his grin replaced by an expression of shock.

Seated on the hard ground, he ignored Carver and examined his bleeding thigh with what seemed a mild curiosity. Then with both hands and surprising ease, he ripped off part of the tail of his white shirt, knotted it, and wrapped it around the leg as a tourniquet to stem the bleeding. The brown pants were dark with blood. The wetness spread to below the knee as he struggled to his feet. There was a pattern of blood on the ground near his feet, more blood marring one of his supple brown shoes.

Carver couldn't believe it. The guy was really something. He was grinning again, bright as ever, and hobbling toward him. Toward the gun. A splinter of doubt pricked Carver. The little bastard might be right about him; he wasn't sure if he could squeeze the trigger again.

"I misjudged you," the tiny Oriental man said.

"You're doing it again," Carver told him, wondering if it was true.

The man stopped and stood unsteadily, his wounded leg trembling but still supporting weight. Carver leveled the gun at his heart. It was steady now.

Still smiling, the little man nodded as if in admiration. He shuffled backward, then turned and walked stiffly and proudly along the driveway and out of sight behind the shrubbery near the highway.

Carver had to be impressed. He was sure the bullet had missed bone and the injury was superficial, but a gunshot wound was a gunshot wound, and most men would be on the ground and screaming. This guy was walking around as if he'd suffered a charley horse.

The sound of a car starting reached Carver, and he caught

a flash of gleaming white metal as his assailant pulled out onto the highway and drove away.

The gun dangling in his free hand, Carver set his cane and made his way to the side of the cottage where he could see the beach.

Maggie Rourke lay on her stomach now on the lounge chair, her bikini strap unfastened so the tan on her back would be unbroken. She might have been sleeping. Apparently the breaking surf had concealed the sound of the shot.

Carver stood perspiring and watching her for a few minutes, then got into his car.

13

CARVER STOPPED at Sir Citrus, a roadside restaurant shaped like a huge orange, to phone Dave Belquest at the Sheriff's Department. The phone booths, near the back of the restaurant, were also shaped like oranges, only they had doors and orange-colored sound insulation inside. Carver left the door open so he wouldn't be stricken with claustrophobia and fed the orange phone change.

"I suspected you might call," Belquest said when Carver had identified himself. "I've been talking to people about you."

Carver didn't want to know what people had said. "Have you learned anything about the driver of the truck that killed Donna Winship?"

"Sure have. His name's Elvis Tarkenton and he lives in Alton, Illinois. No police record. Thirty-eight years old, married with four kids. He's been driving for the same freight line almost ten years and he's never had an accident."

"There's nothing at all to connect him with Donna Winship?"

"Not a thing other than that he ran over her. The man's a

churchgoing Midwesterner who was too shook up to drive after what happened. The freight line sent another driver to transfer cargo and finish his run, then his wife drove their car down from Illinois to take him home."

Carver didn't say anything for a while, watching a family being seated by a waitress in an orange uniform. Three blond boys and a small blond girl, all under ten, were arguing over who was going to sit by the orange-shaped window with the Disney character decals on it. The orange-clad waitress stood by looking bored; she'd heard the argument before.

"Carver?"

"Yeah?"

"Donna Winship wasn't murdered. That trucker isn't lying. And the parking valet didn't see anyone else around."

When Carver rested his bare elbow on the metal shelf beneath the phone it came away sticky. Someone must have spilled orange juice while using the phone. "What do you know about the valet?"

"That he's a nineteen-year-old kid working a summer job between college semesters. He's as likely to be a plant witness as he is to know where Hoffa's buried."

"I'm not interested in Hoffa."

"No? I'm surprised that one hasn't grabbed your attention and you haven't solved it. You know what the people I talked with said about you?"

The little blond girl got her way and sat by the window, smiling smugly.

"Carver? They said you were obsess—"

Carver hung up.

He crossed the orange tile floor and went out the door, thinking that it was possible in central Florida to get sick of citrus. They were obsessed with it here.

The little blond girl smiled at him through the window as

|90|

he lowered himself into the Olds to drive toward the Beeline Expressway and Orlando.

DESOTO LOOKED as harried as Carver had ever seen him. He'd actually loosened his tie knot.

Carver sat down in the chair facing Desoto's desk, and Desoto closed the office door, then walked around behind the desk and sat in the swivel chair. He slid the knot of his beige and yellow tie snug to his neck and explained that a woman had been found shot to death in a rented van behind a restaurant over on Orange Avenue. The van was full of suitcases that contained clothes for a man and woman and at least two small children.

"More domestic hell," Desoto said. "Sometimes I'm grateful to God that I never married."

"Suicide?" Carver asked.

"Yes, I see matrimony that way."

"I mean the woman in the van. Did she shoot herself?"

"Not likely. There were five bullet holes in her back." He shook his head, his dark eyes sad. "Such a beautiful woman. A young mother, no doubt. Vacationers from up north. We're searching for the husband." He sat up straighter and adjusted his cuffs. "But it's police business, and you should be thankful it's none of your concern. What *is* your concern today, my friend?"

"Another shooting." Carver told him about the encounter with the Oriental man and asked if Desoto had any idea as to the assailant's identity.

"I might have," he said. He asked Carver to wait, then got up and left the office. Carver knew he wasn't going far; he'd left his cream-colored suit coat draped neatly on its hanger.

Carver sat patiently without moving. The portable Sony on the windowsill was silent, and sounds from outside filtered into the office. People arguing, joking, laughing. Occasional footsteps in the hall outside. "I mean it," a woman said loudly somewhere outside the office. "It's true. I really mean it." Trying hard to be believed.

Ten minutes later Desoto returned with a mug book. His place had been marked by some fan-fold computer paper inserted between the pages. He laid the book on the desk where Carver could see it easily from where he sat, then opened it, withdrawing the computer printout and pointing to full-face and profile photographs of Carver's Oriental attacker.

The man's name was Beni Ho, and the photos were three years old, from when Ho had done brief prison time on an assault charge. His height was listed as five feet even, his weight 119.

"Him," Carver said. He tapped the photo with his forefinger.

Desoto leaned over Carver's shoulder. "You're sure this man did what you describe?"

"I'm sure."

"He isn't very big, *amigo*."

"Well, he's wiry."

Desoto handed the printout to Carver. Beni Ho had a long record of assaults and had done two prison stretches.

"There's no need for you to be ashamed," Desoto said. "This is a dangerous man, as several police departments would tell you."

Carver didn't recall saying he was ashamed of anything.

"Ho never uses a weapon," Desoto said. "That and his diminutive size have impressed jurors and prevented him from taking up more or less permanent residence behind the walls. But he doesn't need a weapon, apparently; he's said to possess every color martial arts belt and even some suspenders. He's injured several men severely, and rumor has it he's killed more than one. He jumped parole in Baton Rouge, Louisiana, six months ago. The Baton Rouge police say he's half Japanese, half Hawaiian, and all dynamite. An extremely lethal little package."

"What about Gretch?" Carver asked. "Anything else on him?"

"No. Gretch, from his record and what you've told me, isn't in Beni Ho's league." Desoto went back behind his desk. He switched on the Sony portable and tinkered with the dials but got only static. Apparently his favorite Spanish station was temporarily off the air. He turned off the radio and sat down, looking disconsolate. The beautiful, melancholy music was an important part of his days and his perspective.

"Maybe lightning struck the station's tower," Carver said.

"It hasn't rained in a week. Which of Beni Ho's legs did you shoot?"

"His right." Carver wondered what were the odds of a five-foot Oriental man checking into a hospital shot in the left leg and causing confusion.

"I'll run the routine check of medical clinics and hospitals," Desoto said, "and phone you if Ho seeks treatment. But from what you said, and what we know about him, he might be able to tough it out without hospitalization. He's a psychopath, and they sometimes have amazingly high pain thresholds."

"He was walking," Carver said, "when most men would have stayed on the ground."

Desoto smiled. "You admire him, hey?"

"The way I admired Hurricane Andrew." Carver moved the tip of his cane in a tight circular pattern on the floor. "What more do you have on Mark Winship's death?"

Desoto raised a dark eyebrow in puzzlement. "He's dead—what more is there? It was a suicide."

"Are you completely convinced? I think there are unanswered questions."

"They often are. People who commit suicide are usually more interested in getting out of this world than in any questions they might leave behind."

"I'm not so sure about that."

"But you're not suicidal. Not right now, anyway."

"I understand all the evidence points to suicide, but there's no way to completely rule out murder."

"True. But there's not nearly enough there to prompt an official homicide investigation." Desoto rubbed his chin with his thumb. "You really think Mark Winship was murdered?"

"I think it's possible."

"It feels like suicide. I wouldn't question it. I'm surprised you would."

"I didn't at first. But now I think there's a chance he was shot by someone else."

"A very slim chance, *amigo*. But no doubt enough of one for you to take for a ride. Who do you like as his killer?"

"What about Beni Ho?"

"He would have used his hands, then pushed Winship off a bridge or out a window to make it look like suicide. He's not a gun kind of guy. It's against his religion. Makes him feel less than a man. Machismo, face, whatever you want to call it—it's more important than life itself to a martial arts fanatic like Ho." Desoto talked as if, on a certain level, he understood and approved.

"What about Carl Gretch?"

"I couldn't rule him out. All we really know about him is that he doesn't like you. But it takes more than that to figure a man with a hole in his head and a gun in his hand was murdered."

"I've seen Maggie Rourke, the woman Mark Winship was involved with, and not many men would voluntarily leave her for the state of being dead. Not many men would leave her to step outside for a minute to pick up the paper. She's lovely and then some, the sort of woman whose beauty dominates her life and the lives of others."

"And that's what makes you suspect he was murdered? Because it strikes you as odd that he'd kill himself and leave a woman as beautiful as his lover?"

"Not entirely," Carver said. "It strikes me as odd that Maggie Rourke assumes he would."

Desoto cocked his head to the side and looked pensive.

Carver smiled. "I thought that was something you'd understand."

"I do," Desoto said, absently caressing a sleeve of his soft white oxford shirt, "but that doesn't change the evidence."

14

CARVER DROVE to Gretch's apartment to see if Beth was still there. He found her parked in her white LeBaron convertible half a block down from the building. Her head moved slightly as she checked his approach in the rearview mirror.

He parked the Olds behind her car, climbed out, and limped to the LeBaron. Invisible mosquitoes droned around him in the dusk, and he swatted one away from his eyes. Swatted at the faint, lilting buzzing, anyway.

The LeBaron's white canvas top was raised but the windows were rolled down. Despite the heat, Beth looked cool. She was seated motionless and unbothered; mosquitoes knew trouble when they saw it and stayed well clear of her.

She was reading something. Carver put his weight over his cane and leaned down to peer into the car.

She was studying a glossy mail-order catalog. Stacked next to her on the seat were more catalogs. He recognized them as the catalogs from the closet floor in Gretch's apartment.

"I already looked at those," he said. "There's nothing unusual about them. If they meant anything, Gretch wouldn't have left them behind."

"That's what Oliver North thought when he punched the delete button on his computer." Beth had this thing about Iran-Contra. She'd done a series of "Ends Don't Justify Means" articles for *Burrow*. Carver had seldom seen her work so hard on anything.

"Did Hodgkins let you into the apartment?" he asked.

"I never saw any Hodgkins. I let myself in without benefit of a key. Cheap-ass apartment locks. If I was a tenant there and got robbed, I'd sue."

Carver didn't bother pointing out the illegality of what she'd done. Or that ends didn't justify means, which he was sure would be the case in this instance. The catalogs were worthless, some of them dating back over a year.

"You're right about there being nothing in these," she said. "But what's *not* in them might turn out to be interesting."

"Nothing's been ordered from any of them," Carver told her. "The oldest ones were on the bottom of the stack. Gretch probably got them in the mail and put them in the closet out of the way in case he decided to order something later, then when the new catalogs came he did the same thing. Maybe he threw them away every couple of years. Lots of people treat catalogs that way. This is the age of mail-order. Send away for anything in any catalog, and a week later they all have your name and address on gummed labels."

He noticed then that she had a sheet of paper in her lap. There were columns of numbers on it. As he watched, she added another number and tossed the catalog she'd been reading on the floor on the passenger side with half a dozen others. *For After Eight* was lettered on its glossy cover, which featured a foppish-looking young guy and girl in what looked like Spandex tuxedos. They were grinning at each other as if just last night they'd discovered sex. Carver ignored the girl's figure and leaned closer and squinted at the columns of figures on the paper in Beth's lap.

"These are page numbers," Beth said. "Or, more precisely, the numbers of the pages that have been torn out of these catalogs. I'm going to get copies of the current catalogs and see what was on those pages."

"Maybe Gretch has a crush on one of the models and he's using the pages for pinups."

"Some of the pages are missing from men's clothing catalogs, or the menswear section of general catalogs."

"Still possible," Carver said. "It's unlikely, though, considering his relationship with Donna Winship. But Gretch wouldn't be the first bisexual gigolo."

Beth looked directly at him. She wasn't smiling.

"Okay," Carver said, "I won't deny it. You latched onto something I overlooked."

Now she smiled.

He leaned closer and kissed her cool cheek. "Thanks for the good work."

"You're improving, Fred. Growing as a human being."

He wasn't sure if she was kidding, so he said nothing. He was at least as smart as the mosquitoes.

He took over the stakeout for the rest of the evening, settling down in the Olds's sticky warm upholstery and watching the taillights of Beth's car draw closer together, then disappear in the dusk as she turned a corner. Maybe he should have made more of the catalogs. He had to admit that Beth might be right about the missing pages being significant. If that turned out to be the case, he'd go wherever her research led. He wasn't going to be recalcitrant about it.

Belt Street was quiet except for an occasional passing car. Carver could barely see the flow of heavier traffic on the major cross street three blocks down. As the evening deepened to blackness, the lights of the cross-traffic seemed to flow in steady bursts of red-tinted white streams each time the signal changed from red to green.

He and Beth were only going to keep a loose stakeout on Gretch's apartment; it would be almost impossible, and probably unproductive, for one of them to be in position all the time. Old Hodgkins would doubtless know if Gretch returned, and he'd call Carver.

Carver turned on the radio and tuned it to a Marlins game, heard immediately that the score was nine to one in favor of the New York Mets, and sat only half listening. The play-by-play man gave the scores around the league and mentioned the St. Louis Cardinals. St. Louis, where Carver's former wife, Laura, lived with their daughter, half a continent away from where Carver sat in the heat in an ancient convertible and watched a stucco apartment building darkening to join the shadows of the night.

At least he shouldn't have to worry about Beni Ho. The little man would have to take things slow for a while, maybe a long time if the bullet remained in his leg and he was forced to seek medical treatment from a doctor who'd follow the law and report a gunshot wound to the police.

But Carver knew that people like Beni Ho had their own medical plans with doctors who'd been compromised. Beni Ho, bionic little bastard that he was, might be limping after a limping Carver in no time. And there was always the possibility that Desoto was wrong about Ho's adherence to the martial arts' manly code. Ho might be hiding in the foliage right now, drawing a bead on Carver through an infrared scope mounted on a rifle.

Carver sat back and watched the apartment building through half-closed eyes, listening to the third inning and trying not to think about Beni Ho.

He was about as successful as the Marlins.

15

A SMILING Beni Ho crept toward Carver, who was teetering without his cane. When Carver turned to see if the cane was on the ground behind him, he saw that there was no ground. He was on the edge of an abyss that whistled and echoed with grief and loneliness. Ho stopped a few feet short of him, and with a wide, wide grin, extended a single, slender forefinger and nudged Carver into the abyss. As he plunged through blackness, wind or a scream whistling in his ears, he heard a voice say, "Stay away from that route if at all possible."

He realized he was no longer hurtling through blackness but was lying on his back on perspiration-soaked sheets, listening to the clock radio blare the morning traffic report.

Beth was beside him, sleeping through the back-up on Magellan, the accident on the Camille drawbridge, the nude jogger running with a dog on the coast highway. The clock radio was on her side of the bed.

"Beth!" he called fuzzily, still staring at the ceiling.

There was only the ranting of the radio. A disc jockey had

taken over from the guy in the traffic copter and was yammering almost faster than the ear could follow.

"Beth!"

"Whazzit, lover?"

"Turn that damned thing off!"

"'Zat?"

"The clock radio—hit the button!"

The deejay said, "Doin' the rock an' roll review to get *you* in the mood for the office *zoo*. We'll play while you're on your way for pay. We're gonna spin till you clock in. Music back through the years just for your ears!"

Stretched out on her stomach, her cheek mushed on her extended right arm, Beth opened her eyes sleepily and smiled at Carver.

Carver said, "Clock radio. Please!"

"Idea, Fred, is the device is s'pose to wake you up, get you vertical."

As Carver rolled onto his side and groped for his cane, he bumped it with his wrist and it clattered to the floor. Little Richard began to scream at him. He rolled onto his back again, bumping his bald pate on the wooden headboard. Ordinarily he liked Little Richard. But not at the moment. Not at the moment at all.

"Beth!"

She languidly reached out with a long arm, and silence dropped over the room like a blanket.

After a while she said, "I'll make coffee."

Carver said nothing. He found his cane, sat up with one leg on the floor, then swiveled around to slump on the edge of the mattress. He heard Beth, behind him, climb out of bed. The springs whined as she stood up. He sat staring at nothing, listening to her bare feet pad across the plank floor, hoping she'd get a splinter in a toe. She never had and didn't this time. Probably the woman could walk barefoot on hot coals. Pipes bonged and banged in the wall, and tap water ran for the coffee.

Too late on the stakeout last night, Carver told himself. It had been almost midnight when he'd driven away from Gretch's apartment. He'd observed little other than old Hodgkins standing as motionless as a statue for half an hour, holding a hose at his hip and watering the pathetic lawn. Like a fountain statue of a gunslinger. The great patience of the old often amazed Carver. It was something you noticed in Florida.

Drawing a deep breath, he stood up over his cane, steadied himself, and walked into the bathroom. He rinsed out his mouth, then splashed cold water on his face to wake up. Looked in the mirror. Looked quickly away. Then he went back out to his dresser, got out his red pair of swimming trunks, and sat down on the bed and eased into them.

"Coffee before or after?" Beth asked, when he was standing again and fastening the trunks' drawstring.

"After," he told her, and got a white towel from the bathroom and left the cabin.

The morning was cloudless but still cool. He hobbled toward the beach, walking with difficulty when he left the wooden steps and trod on sandy soil.

Near the surf line, he stuck his cane in the sand, dropped his towel beside it, and crawled backward into the surf. The water felt cold at first, waking him all the way. When a large swell roared in and burst onto the beach, he shoved himself seaward with both arms and let the wave's backwash carry him out to deeper water where he was floating free, then swimming.

He swam straight out from shore, using long, reaching strokes and breathing deeply and evenly. Then he treaded water for a while, looking back in at the cottage where Beth was brewing coffee, or maybe sitting at the table by now sipping it from her mug that was lettered with reproductions of newspapers' flubbed captions, such as *Police Help Dog Bite Victim* and *Prison Warden Says Inmates May Have 3 Guns*. Looking in at his life, really, and wondering why it had turned out as it had, what the mainspring was that powered its clockwork. But nobody ever really understood that one. Donna and Mark Winship hadn't understood. He thought of beautiful Maggie Rourke, grieving by the sea for her dead illicit romance that had been doomed from the beginning. Love could be such a disease, sometimes fatal. Sorrow swelled in his throat for Maggie, who was still suffering because she was the one still alive. People only thought they knew the reasons why they acted, while they kept on loving and hating and moving through life toward death and not understanding that, either.

He floated on his back for several minutes, staring now in the opposite direction, out to sea, focusing his gaze on a small patch of white sail. For a moment he felt an almost overwhelming impulse to swim toward it even though it was too far away to reach. Then he turned back toward the shore and the cottage and Beth.

He entered the cottage with his towel slung across his shoulders, his feet leaving wet prints on the floor. The scent of freshly perked coffee made him hungry. Beth was standing at the stove, wearing white panties and bra and spraying a frying pan with Pam. So she intended to prepare breakfast as well as coffee. Maybe she'd planned it that way from the moment she'd heard the blaring clock radio. Maybe. She was a difficult one to read. A surprising nest-feathering, domestic streak sometimes surfaced in her, like a sheen of something elemental from deep water. Though not often.

Carver wondered if she'd ever considered becoming a mother. They never talked about that.

He showered, dressed in light gray slacks, a black tee shirt and gray socks, black loafers. Beth was still standing at the stove when he came back. It was getting warm in the cottage. When she saw him, she walked over and switched on the air conditioner. His coffee was already poured and a plate of scrambled eggs, toast, and sausage links was on the breakfast counter. He sat on one of the high stools and sipped coffee. Beth disappeared behind the folding screen that partitioned off the cottage's sleeping area, then returned and sat across from him, wearing his blue terrycloth robe now. She was carrying her oversized mug with the newspaper captions on it. Carver could see *Man Minus Ear Waives Hearing*. Maybe this was the real news, that the world made no sense. Steam rose from the mug and caught the morning light like a prism, playing faint colors over the counter.

She said, "Anybody show at Gretch's apartment last night?"

He buttered a slice of toast and shook his head no. "What about the missing pages in the catalogs? They tell you anything?" He was sure they hadn't, or she would have told him by now.

"I'm still working at it," she said somewhat curtly. "So far, I've only been able to find two of the current catalogs. I'm driving in to Orlando today and visit a mail-order maniac I know, see if he can get me the other, older ones."

"What's on the missing pages you managed to match up?" he asked.

"Men's sport coats and accessories on one, beachwear on the other."

"Natty clothes, like a gigolo might wear?"

"Depends on how you view silk jackets with eelskin elbow patches."

"So maybe the missing pages contain items Gretch ordered from the catalogs."

"Except the order forms are intact in every catalog that was in his closet. And most of the catalogs look as if they've barely been leafed through. I think there's some connecting thread, and I'll know it when I see the other catalog pages."

"Maybe he's building a secret weapon out of tie clasps and sunglasses," Carver said.

"Maybe."

"More likely, he simply ran out of toilet paper now and then."

Beth lowered her coffee mug and looked thoughtful. It was an explanation she hadn't considered. She'd been raised desperately poor, and it was a possibility she might take quite seriously.

"Keep matching catalog pages," he said.

"I intend to."

"I'm going to give up on Gretch's apartment for a while and watch Maggie Rourke." He took a bite of toast and chewed while Beth gazed at him.

"Because she's fun to watch?" she asked.

He washed down the toast with a long pull of coffee that was still hot enough to burn the back of his throat. "Because, unlike Gretch, she can at least be found."

Beth turned her back on him and stood up. Leaving her mug sitting on the counter, she walked slowly over to the stove and lifted a sausage from the pan and began nibbling at it, still not looking at him.

Letting him know she didn't completely believe him.

He wasn't certain of the truth himself.

Nagging Wife Critical After Hammer Attack, he read on the mug.

16

CARVER DIDN'T bother to knock on the cottage door. He headed for the stepping-stone walkway around the north wall, leading to the beach. When he noticed the dark brown bloodstain on the ground where Beni Ho had bled, his stomach lurched and his grip on his cane tightened. Getting shot in the leg or anywhere else and surviving was also getting shot in the mind, and in a place that never quite healed.

The webbed aluminum lounge chair was still on the beach facing open sea, but beautiful Maggie Rourke wasn't gracing it today.

Carver returned to the front of the cottage and knocked on the door. He stood in the sun, waiting, listening to the faint tuneless music of brass wind chimes. He was going to tell Maggie about Beni Ho being shot in front of her cabin while she was working on her tan, see how she'd react. Then he'd say goodbye and leave, but he wouldn't go far. Just to where he could watch the cottage unseen. Maybe she'd go someplace, and he'd follow.

Either way, he'd see her again, look into those luminous gray eyes. Who knew what might be learned from that?

No one answered his knock.

He glanced around. The black Nissan Stanza that had been parked in the shade yesterday was nowhere in sight. He knocked again, louder, then tried the door.

It was locked.

He hobbled to a front window and peered inside. He could see through dimness to the sliding glass door that looked out on the ocean. The cottage appeared to be empty. He straightened up and watched a large bird that looked like a blue heron flap overhead toward the sea, gaining grace as it gained speed.

Carver got in the Olds, started the engine, and eased the big car over in the shady parking spot previously occupied by the black Stanza. He lowered the canvas top and sat in the faint sea breeze, waiting for Maggie to return. Probably she'd be back soon, he told himself. Maybe she'd run out for a loaf of bread or more sun block, or a good mystery novel in which to lose her grief.

She didn't return. Occasionally a car would approach out of sight on the coast highway and seem to slow as it neared her driveway, and Carver would reach for his cane leaning on the seat. Then the car would speed past.

When it was almost noon, and getting hotter by the second, he backhanded sweat from his forehead and climbed out of the Olds. Secluded as the cottage was, he didn't consider it much of a risk to see if he could slip the lock.

He went back over to the front door and tried to slide his Visa card between latch and doorjamb. When he'd succeeded, the door still didn't open. Apparently the deadbolt above the simple knob lock was holding it firm. He wasn't surprised. Failure was the usual result of the credit card technique. A set of lockpicks wasn't much more efficient unless in expert hands, and he wasn't an expert.

Carver gave up on the front door and went around to the back of the cottage and the sliding glass door overlooking the beach. He saw immediately that there was a sawed-off broomstick resting in its metal track, preventing it from sliding even an inch. The most effective way to lock a sliding glass door.

Leaving the exposed, ocean end of the cottage, he tried the two windows on the south wall to see if they were locked. The second one wasn't. He managed to slide the window open, then held gauzy lime-green curtains aside and leaned in.

He was looking at a bedroom with pale green walls and furnished with white wicker furniture. Even the ceiling fan was wicker. The bed wasn't, though. It was a white-enameled four-poster with a fringed canopy and sheer white curtains that draped gracefully to the floor to surround the mattress and act as mosquito netting.

Carver drew in his breath. Someone appeared to be sleeping behind the gauzy white material.

He leaned his cane carefully against the inside wall, then used his powerful arms to work his body far enough inside for him to touch the floor. Walking out away from the window with his arms, he dragged his body across the sill, using his good leg to break his fall so he dropped silently to his hands and good knee on the deep green carpet.

After waiting a few minutes, staring at the still figure in the bed, he levered himself to his feet with the cane. He stood still for a while, then moved quietly to the bed.

He edged closer and extended his free hand to move aside the diaphanous white curtain.

It took a few seconds for him to realize what he was looking at. Pillows and the white sheet had been arranged to make it appear there was someone lying on the bed. There was a hank of auburn hair visible on the one pillow that was resting crosswise on the bed, but there was simply no room for a head beneath the sheet that had been pulled halfway up the pillow.

Holding his breath, Carver clutched the sheet and slowly peeled it down toward the foot of the bed.

A rubber, flesh-colored doll about ten inches long was resting on the pillow. A child's doll. It had auburn hair like Maggie's, even had wide gray eyes like Maggie's. It looked as Maggie might have looked as a child. At a glance the doll seemed to be in one piece, but a closer look revealed that its limbs and head had been neatly severed and carefully placed within a quarter inch of the torso. Carver nudged it with a finger and it cried once, mechanically and pitifully.

There was something else about it. It was one of those anatomically correct dolls, and a long nail had been inserted in its vagina.

Carver backed away, leaving the doll as he'd found it, and moved to examine the rest of the cottage, bracing himself for what he might encounter.

He didn't find the doll's human counterpart, as he'd feared. He was the only human alive or otherwise in the place.

Now that his fear had left him, he realized it was hot in the cottage; none of the window units was running. He went back into the bedroom and examined the closet. Half a dozen simple but expensive dresses were draped on hangers. The dresser drawers contained panties, bras, folded blouses. There was a pair of well-worn Reebok jogging shoes in a corner near the dresser, white sweat socks balled nearby on the carpet.

He checked the bathroom next. The tub and walls of the shower stall were damp, and there was a mushy bar of soap near the drain. A turquoise towel on a brass rack was damp. A one-piece black swimming suit tied by its straps to another towel rack was dry. On the tub's edge was a green plastic bottle of shampoo without a cap.

When Carver opened the vanity drawers, he found an electric hair drier and bottles of makeup and nail polish, an emery board, a large red comb, and an unopened box of tampons. On the washbasin was a clear glass tumbler containing a red toothbrush and a tube of Colgate toothpaste. He ran a finger across the toothbrush's bristles and found they were soft and damp. He sniffed them and smelled toothpaste.

He went to the phone he'd noticed in the cottage's main room. It was a gimmick one that looked like a tennis shoe, complete with untied laces. He picked it up and pressed the heel to his ear. After Information gave him the number of Burnair and Crosley, he called it and asked to speak with Maggie Rourke.

He hadn't really expected her to be there and was slightly surprised when he was put on hold. The Muzak was Mozart. Class. How could anyone lose money at a place that played Mozart?

"I thought you were taking time off work," he said, when Maggie had come to the phone and abruptly stopped Mozart so commerce might commence.

She thought he might be a client. Carver told her he wasn't interested in commerce.

"Who is this?" Her voice had an edge to it. Fear?

"Fred Carver. Remember? We talked yesterday about Donna and Mark Winship. That's when you told me you were taking your vacation time."

"I remember. I changed my mind about using my vacation days. The solitude at the cottage was getting on my nerves, making me feel things more deeply. Things I didn't want to feel."

"What about the shooting?"

"Shooting?"

"Beni Ho, the Oriental man I asked you about yesterday, needed to be shot."

After a static-filled pause, she said, "That's a curious way to phrase it."

"He's a curious kind of guy."

"So are you. Who shot him?"

"I did," Carver said. "Outside your cottage. But only in the leg."

"I think I should call the police."

"I've already been to see them."

"What was this Ho person doing at the cottage? Did he follow you there?"

"Seems so."

"Why did you call me, Mr. Carver?"

That was a tough one. He wasn't exactly sure of the answer. "I wondered if anyone had told you about the shooting. You were sunbathing down on the beach and didn't hear it over the sound of the surf, and Ho and I both drove away afterward."

"If he could drive, you must not have hurt him very bad."

"Bad enough, only he was even badder. Didn't you notice the blood on the ground near where you park your car?"

"I noticed it. I assumed a cat or dog had caught and killed a small animal, maybe a squirrel. There are a lot of squirrels around there."

Carver considered asking about the dismembered doll on her bed, but she wouldn't like the idea of his nosing around inside the cottage. He said, "I think you and I should talk some more."

"I don't see why."

"A lot about the Winships is still up in the air."

"Since they're both dead, I don't understand why it should have to come down."

"Maybe I could explain."

She muffled the phone and said something indecipherable to someone in the office. Or maybe she was putting on the busy act. No more time for Carver. "Let me think about it," she said into the phone. "Call me some other time."

He settled for that and hung up the shoe that played Mozart.

· · ·

HE WAS parked in the Olds across the street from Burnair and Crosley at noon, near the park where he'd spoken with Beverly Denton. There was a chance Maggie would cross the street to have lunch with the squirrels and pigeons, or walk or drive to a restaurant where Carver could follow.

He raised the car's canvas top for what shade it provided and sat in the heat and suffered, waiting and watching the building.

She didn't emerge from the tower of reflecting planes until after two o'clock. By then the back of Carver's shirt and the seat of his pants were molded by perspiration to the Olds's vinyl upholstery. He wondered from time to time what it would be like to ply his trade in Minneapolis.

Maggie looked crisply businesslike and stylish in a pale blue skirt and blazer, a white blouse, and blue high heels. A black leather purse was slung by a strap across her shoulder. Gripped in her right hand and swinging at her side was a flat brown attaché case.

She strolled down to the corner, drawing men's admiring glances, then crossed the street and walked toward where he was parked. Her skirt clung to her thighs with each step, making it difficult for Carver to avert his gaze. Never had he been more appreciative of static cling.

She showed no inclination to enter the park. He was afraid she was going to approach the Olds, but instead she stopped and appeared to get into a car that was parked out of sight in front of a van half a dozen spaces away. Carver sat up straight and started the Olds's engine. Ahead of him, a shimmering haze of exhaust fumes drifted from in front of the van.

Seconds later, Maggie's black Stanza with the rose on its antenna pulled away from the curb to join the bright flow of traffic on Atlantic Drive, and Carver followed.

17

MAGGIE ROURKE drove north on Atlantic, then turned west on Gull, all the time sitting stiffly behind the wheel and seemingly staring straight ahead. She drove fast but not recklessly, and with a disdain for stop signs that had to garner her several moving violations per year. Maybe she knew somebody with more clout than ethics, so she didn't worry about traffic tickets. Maybe she knew McGregor.

She'd mentioned the cottage where she'd been staying belonged to someone else. Carver thought she might drive to her own address in Del Moray, but she was headed in another direction. Gull Avenue ran straight west away from the ocean, into the poorer part of town.

In a declining neighborhood near the Cuban section, Maggie pulled the Stanza to the curb lane and parked in the middle of the block.

It was a block lined with small shops, many of them bankrupt and boarded. Among those still in business were a tiny pharmacy whose door and windows were protected by heavy mesh curtains that could be lowered and locked at night, an occult bookstore, a barbershop that looked as if it might feature dog-eared back issues of *Hustler*, a plumbing supply shop, a tattoo parlor, and a lounge whose red neon sign, drab in daylight, proclaimed it to be S ELLIE'S.

Carver was surprised. This wasn't what he'd expected when classy and upscale Maggie had driven away from her well-paying job at Burnair and Crosley.

He was surprised again when she climbed from the Stanza, keeping her knees modestly together as the skirt of her business suit worked itself up, and after carefully locking her car, walked into S ELLIE'S.

Carver sat in the Olds and studied the place. It looked as if it occupied the entire ground floor of an aged four-story brick building. Curtains and yellowed shades indicated that there might be seedy apartments on the top three floors. Probably the lounge drew business from the warehouses of several small trucking companies Carver had noticed three or four blocks to the east. Even as he pondered this, two men in work clothes strolled down the street from that direction, talking animatedly with each other in what seemed to be a good-natured argument. One was tall and blond and was carrying a black lunchbox. The other was shorter and muscular and appeared to be Hispanic. They also entered S ELLIE'S.

After deciding the lounge was probably fairly large inside and he might be able to enter without being noticed by Maggie, Carver got out of the Olds. He didn't lock the door on the driver's side. That way if the Olds was stolen the thief might not slash the canvas top to gain access. That could prove expensive, if Carver got the car back. The minimal insurance he had wouldn't cover it. He crossed the street and saw the darkened outline of the missing letter on the neon sign, making it SHELLIE'S.

There was a small diamond-shaped window in the door. He peered inside. Half a dozen customers sat at the long bar, another half-dozen at small tables with hurricane lamp candle holders for centerpieces. A large-screen TV mounted high behind the bar was on, showing Rod Stewart hip-switching and spinning across a stage with a guitar, but no music seeped outside. Maggie was seated at the far end of the bar, drinking something tall and trying to ignore the portly little man on the stool next to her.

Carver moved back from the window in the door. This wasn't going to work. Shellie's was smaller and less crowded than he'd anticipated. He might be able to enter unnoticed by Maggie if it were nighttime, when there would undoubtedly be more customers and probably loud music and a haze of cigarette smoke. But now, in late afternoon, he decided he'd better stay outside.

He returned to the Olds, not liking the idea of sitting some more in the heat but knowing it was unavoidable if he wanted to do his job. And he took pride in his job. Almost everything else had been stripped from him when the holdup kid's bullet crashed into his knee. He had his work, and he did it no matter what else happened in his life. He wondered if that was being obsessive, or simply defining. Occupations did define people. He knew who and what he was, and what he had to do. At least most of the time. His was an occupation that hinged on certain constant aspects of human nature, not all of them admirable. That was oddly comforting in a high-tech age when job experience sometimes became obsolete even before it was completed.

He started the Olds, slipped the transmission lever to reverse, and backed down the street until he was almost a block away from Shellie's and from Maggie's parked car.

Trying to ignore the heat, he half listened to a call-in radio show about abortion and waited and watched and speculated.

Her co-workers and clients at Burnair and Crosley would be surprised to know this was where Maggie was spending her late lunch hour. If that indeed was what she was doing in a downscale dump like Shellie's, drinking her lunch. There was nothing about the place that suggested it served food, even if a customer might have the courage to eat there.

IT WAS almost four o'clock when Maggie emerged from Shellie's and walked, head down, toward the parked Stanza. Carver couldn't be sure, but he thought she was moving unsteadily and might be slightly drunk.

When she drove away, he followed.

The Stanza stayed in its proper lane, but it did weave once toward the curb. And it halted completely at the first stop sign on Gull, then accelerated slowly across the empty intersection. Maggie was driving very carefully, the way people did when they were drunk and trying to convince themselves and everyone else they were sober. He wondered if she was a secret alcoholic, and went to a place like Shellie's to drink so she wouldn't run into any of her straitlaced investment-world friends from Burnair and Crosley. If she was simply drinking to assuage her grief over Mark Winship's death, she probably would have done so somewhere else, or at home, not at Shellie's. Maggie seemed to be an experienced drinker.

She drove east toward the ocean until she connected with Magellan, then took it south to the coast highway. Obviously, she was finished working for the day.

Carver stayed well back from the black Stanza and listened to a clergyman and a female state representative argue about the French abortion pill. He knew where the car and the argument were going.

He continued past the driveway of Maggie's cottage after the Stanza had turned into it. Then he made a U-turn and parked on the shoulder behind some palms and decorative shrubbery dotted with tiny multicolored blossoms, where Beni Ho had been parked to watch the cottage when Carver had visited it the first time. He twisted the ignition key and switched off the engine and the radio.

The parking place didn't provide much of a view, actually. Carver could see the front of the cottage through the bushes, but not the door or the stepping-stone path to the rear of the place and the beach.

He decided to knock on the cottage door and try getting Maggie to talk with him while she was loosened with alcohol. She should be more cooperative and revealing thanks to her time spent in Shellie's. Besides, Carver had done enough sitting in the heat for one day.

Leaving the Olds parked where it was, he got out and walked along the road shoulder, then down the driveway to the cottage.

He rapped on the door with his cane and waited. There must have been a beehive somewhere close by; several honeybees droned past in the same general direction and made wide circles to disappear around the corner of the cottage. Worker bees knocking off for the day. A few of them buzzed close but didn't seem to pay much attention to Carver. They had more important business. It was time to check in with the queen.

The door opened and Maggie stood staring out at him. She was still wearing the blue skirt but not the blazer and was in stockinged feet. Carver's gaze started at her nylon-clad painted toenails and rose to her face. Her eyes were heavy-lidded and she looked mildly annoyed at being ogled. Used to it, though. A woman like her knew that some men's eyes traveled on their own.

Carver said, "You told me you might want to talk some more, said to come calling later."

She smiled at his pathetic attempt at subterfuge. "We both know I said 'call later,' not 'come calling.' "

He said, "Well, to tell you the truth, I phoned you again at work about an hour ago and they said you'd left for the day."

"So you thought you'd drive here and pester me in person?"

"I thought it might help both of us if we talked some more about Mark Winship."

"Not about Donna?"

"Donna, too."

Maggie ran her palms down her cheeks, dragging at the corners of her bleary eyes and distorting her features, the way kids do when they want to make a face. It amazed Carver that she was sexy even when she did that. What a temptation she must have been for Mark Winship. For any man who'd ever met her. She said, "I took a sleeping pill about an hour ago and it's kicking in, I'm afraid. We'll have to talk some other time, if at all."

Carver said, "Has anyone ever told you how beautiful you are when you're tired?"

"Countless times."

"Add my observation."

In a bored voice, she said, "Are you coming on to me, Mr. Carver?"

"No, I don't think so. Anyway, I suppose you'd say I'm spoken for." He smiled at her, making it reassuring, letting her know that sure, he found her attractive, but he wasn't going to be pushy about it, wasn't in the market.

She stared at him, gnawing hard on her lower lip. He wondered if alcohol had numbed the lip so she couldn't feel what she was doing.

Sensing she was weakening, he said, "Let's drive to a restaurant and get some coffee, put off that nap for a while. If you go to sleep now, you'll wake up at four A.M. and be tired all day tomorrow."

Wheels seemed to be turning inside her lovely head. Persuasive Carver. She was considering, all right. He was sure of it.

She said, "Fuck off, Mr. Carver," and slammed the door.

Carver stared at the blank surface of the door for a long moment, then placed the tip of his cane to the side and turned around. More bees droned past him, low to the ground, as if humiliated by the prospect of having to take crap from the queen.

He said, "I know how you feel," and followed the sun-washed driveway to where the Olds was parked on the gravel shoulder.

He wondered if Maggie had been in her bedroom before answering his knock. She'd given no sign of having found the dismembered doll on her bed.

As he drove away, he decided it might be a good idea to find out who owned the cottage.

18

A STOP at the county courthouse told Carver the cottage where Maggie was staying was deeded to Dredge Industries, Inc. He'd had a go at finding the company's address, but without luck. Dredge Industries had owned the property for three years.

It was a few minutes past seven when he pulled the Olds into the gravel lot of the Happy Lobster and turned his car over to the same young parking valet who'd been on duty the day of Donna Winship's death. If he recognized Carver, he showed no sign. He parked a lot of cars for a lot of people. Carver watched him leave the Olds in a space at the edge of the lot, near where Donna had died, then went inside to meet Beth for dinner.

She was seated at a table near the window, two tables down from where Carver had listened to and failed to help Donna. Her hair was tamed by a headband and her strong profile was silhouetted against the wide window and glimmering sea. He stood in the archway leading from bar to restaurant and admired her for a few seconds, then she saw him and smiled.

The restaurant was crowded, and several men stared at him with veiled surprise and envy as he made his way among the tables, kissed her, and sat down. Central Florida wasn't the easiest place for a white man and a black woman to be in love. It was an area where God and citrus and Mickey Mouse were sometimes worshiped to extremes. Maybe it had to do with the heat.

Three sun-browned, fortyish guys in shorts and identical gray tee shirts with alligators on their chests were still staring at Carver and Beth. They had a pitcher of beer at the table, and two of them were wearing caps lettered GATOR BAITER above the bills. There was hostility in their gazes, and the thin edge of envy Carver had seen in some of the other eyes that had followed him to the table.

Beth said, "Wonder what those swamp turkeys are thinking."

Carver thought about his bad leg, then Beth's two beautiful good ones showing beneath her light tan skirt, and said, "Probably they figure I must know some tricks."

Beth smiled. "You do, Fred, you do." She turned slightly and aimed her smile at the swamp turkeys, and they looked uncomfortable and concentrated on their drinking. Beth could be intimidating.

Then one of the men grinned and said something to a man at the next table, all the while looking at Beth. Carver knew what he was doing. He'd made a remark to the other man to fish for agreement on whatever he'd said about Beth. Bigots always sought, even sometimes demanded, confirmation of their beliefs. They needed that reassurance. But the man at the adjoining table simply turned away, as if he hadn't heard.

A pert blond waitress arrived and announced she was their server and rattled off a litany of specials, then asked if she could get them something to drink while they were making up their minds. Beth ordered a martini, Carver a scotch, rocks.

Carver made up his mind right away and set his lobster-shaped menu aside. Beth chewed the inside of her cheek and contemplated.

When she'd finally closed her menu, he told her about his afternoon following Maggie, and what little he'd discovered about ownership of the cottage.

Beth said, "Sounds like Maggie might have a drug problem."

"I only saw her drinking booze."

"Same thing, if you can't control it. Doesn't matter if it's booze, tobacco, or cornflakes—if it's got you instead of the other way around."

Carver didn't debate the point. Beth was sensitive on the subject. She saw no real difference between users of illicit recreational drugs and people who drank and smoked uncontrollably; she thought alcohol and tobacco were the latter's drugs of choice merely because they were legal and readily available. It was, to her way of thinking, an area where only the law defined morality, and with no real concern for the destruction of the addicts.

"A woman grieving the death of a lover might drink only to ease the pain, but she wouldn't do it in a dump like you described unless she was used to being there."

"That doesn't mean she's got a drinking problem," Carver said. "Maybe she likes unwashed guys with tattoos."

"That could be," Beth said.

He saw she was serious and didn't answer. The part of her past he didn't know about bothered him sometimes. It took effort to set it aside and leave it hers alone.

"This Dredge Industries might not be incorporated in Florida," she said. "If you want, I can find out more about it through *Burrow*."

"It might help," Carver said.

The waitress returned with their drinks and a broad smile. Beth ordered salad and lobster tail, Carver asked for the salmon steak special. The waitress seemed pleased, as if she'd sold him on the special, then sashayed away toward the kitchen.

Carver said, "Cheers," and sipped his drink and looked out the long curved window at the ocean, still rolling blue-green and vast, unchanged from when he'd sat looking at it and talking with Donna Winship, unchanged by thousands of years. Ships seemed to sit motionless in the haze of heat and distance out near the horizon, as if time were a slower process far out from land.

"You don't look cheerful," Beth said. "Did you and Donna sit at this table when you met here?"

"No. Two tables away."

Beth said, "Won't do you any good to dwell on it and muck around in a lot of sentimental bullshit, Fred. The past is the past. We live in the present and can try to do something about the future. That's all there is for any of us."

"You're cold."

"You know better."

He sighed and smiled at her. "Yeah, I do. What you are is realistic. And probably tougher than I am."

She raised her glass, not smiling. "I wouldn't argue either point."

Carver knew she was right about how futile and destructive it was to dwell on the irrevocable past, but she hadn't seen Donna Winship walk from the restaurant alive, then seen her minutes later mangled and dead on the pavement. That sort of thing made a vivid and lasting impression, and one that visited in dreams.

Beth put down her glass and bent sideways to reach something on the floor, causing one of her breasts to strain against her blouse. The move drew men's eyes like laser beams. She said, "Got something for you, lover."

He waited while she laid a yellow file folder on the table and opened it.

Inside were copies of catalog pages. They were fastened together with a paper clip and there was a yellow Post-it stuck to the top one with the date and name of the catalog scrawled on it. He assumed they were copies of the pages missing from the catalogs in Gretch's apartment.

"I found eight of the catalogs so I could see what was on the torn-out pages," she said. She turned the folder around so Carver could examine the pages right-side up.

He removed the paperclip and leafed through them. They were sharp copies, though not in color like the pages themselves. They all showed a series of male models wearing foppish clothes, from evening wear to bikini swim trunks.

"So whaddya think?" Beth asked from across the table. She placed the olive from her martini between her lips, sucked on it to enjoy the gin flavor, then deftly let it roll back on her tongue. Probably giving the Gator Baiters fits.

Carver said, "I think I wouldn't wear much of this stuff. Well, maybe the black leather jacket with the steel spikes running up the arms."

"You could bring it off," Beth said.

They were both aware that he sometimes dressed in a way not all that different from the catalog models. Wore dark pull-over shirts, dark slacks, and Italian loafers he didn't have to lace. No steel spikes, though.

He started to close the folder.

Beth said, "Look again."

He did.

This time he saw it immediately.

He examined each of the copies carefully. One of the models on every page was Carl Gretch. There he was in a European-cut sport coat, there in a striped silk shirt with a wild tie, there in an elaborate and probably wildly colorful kimono. In one shot he was seated at an outdoor table dining with a smiling blond woman with a spiked hairdo and a see-through top.

Carver straightened the copies and closed the folder, grinning. "Great work, Beth. I can check with the catalog publishers, get the photographers' names, then the name and address of the modeling agency that represents Gretch."

Beth tossed down the rest of her drink. "I already did that, Fred. It's the Walton Agency on Sunburst Avenue in west Del Moray."

Carver touched the back of her hand. "I'm proud of you."

She said, "Sometimes I'm proud of you, too, Fred."

19

THE WALTON AGENCY was a small, modern brick building angled on a narrow lot on a pretty good block of Sunburst. The bricks had been painted the dull brown color of an apple that surprises when you bite into it and find it rotten.

Carver entered the lobby through a tinted glass door, and found himself on plush beige carpeting. A middle-aged woman with unnaturally dark hair and troweled-on makeup sat at a marble-topped desk that had nothing on its surface but a complicated, many-lined white phone and an acrylic plaque that said *Verna* in graceful green script. On the wall behind her were dramatic color and black-and-white photographs of beautiful people. Years ago she might have been one of them. She was still hanging on by her long, painted nails. She smiled at Carver with lips the color of fresh blood. It was a wicked, guilty smile, as if she were a vegetarian caught being a carnivore.

He said, "You're one of the models, right?"

Verna's smile didn't seem to change physically, yet somehow it became more genuine. She had great-looking capped teeth.

"Once upon a time," she said in a husky voice that probably sounded sexy on the phone. He saw that behind the makeup she was pushing sixty, but you had to look closely to know it.

"Is Mr. Walton in?" Carver asked.

The smile stayed on the red lips but faded from her mascara'ed eyes. She dragged a large appointment book up from a shelf behind the desk and started to open it slowly, as if its leather cover were almost unbearably heavy.

"I don't have an appointment," Carver said, "but Mr. Walton will see me. It's about one of his clients."

"Are you looking for a model?" Verna asked.

"Yes. A man named Enrico Thomas."

She studied him for several seconds, as if trying to determine if he was one of the good guys. "Just a minute, please, Mr. . . . ?"

"Fred Carver," Carver said, smiling.

She got up from her chair and walked to the nearer of two oak doors, the one with VINCENT WALTON on it in black block letters. She still walked like a model, as if confidently and contemptuously striding along an invisible tightrope.

When she emerged from the office less than a minute later, she stood to the side and held the door open as an invitation for Carver to enter. He caught a whiff of strong perfume and sour breath as he slid past her.

THE PLUSH carpet in Walton's office was the same color as in the reception area, only foam-padded and twice as deep. Carver's cane sank into it as if it were cake.

Vincent Walton was standing behind his desk and smiling. He was a tall man with a long, handsome face and coarse dark hair with wings of gray combed straight back above his ears. He had a bristly, neatly trimmed mustache like a toothbrush that was also going gray. His eyes were genial but with a sparkle of the sort that suggested it was camouflage for what might be going on inside his head. His chalk-striped, double-breasted gray suit, pinched at the waist, looked like something from one of the catalogs in Gretch's closet.

He said, "You a photographer?"

"Detective." Carver decided to let Walton assume he was with the police.

"Private, I'll bet," Walton said, his gaze flicking to take in the cane.

Oh, well. "I'm trying to locate Carl Gretch."

"He's inherited some money, right?"

Carver was beginning to dislike Walton a lot. "He owes some people."

"Well, can't say I ever heard of him."

"How about Enrico Thomas?"

Walton laughed. "Him I know. Enrico's one of my models." He sat down in the brown leather swivel chair behind his desk. On the wall behind him were framed photographs of more of his clients. Carver looked but didn't see Gretch. "It's not unusual for a model to use a pseudonym, especially if it makes him seem more ethnic. Enrico hasn't been sent on a job for quite a while. It's been so long, in fact, that I no longer know how to reach him." He sat forward and rotated a large black knob that flipped cards in a huge Rolodex. "Last address I have on him is on McCrea Avenue. When I tried to call him about six months ago to go on a shoot, his phone had been disconnected. A letter I sent him came back to me, and I was told by the post office he'd moved and left no forwarding address."

"Was he in much demand as a model?"

"For a while, until he became difficult. Ethnic male models as well as female are in demand these days, and Enrico has great personality and attitude."

"Is that necessary in still photos?"

"Very much so. He carries himself with a kind of natural poise and arrogance that transfers well to film."

"How did he become difficult?" Carver asked.

"Temper. He'd get in arguments with the photographers, sometimes the other models, and upset the mood on sets. A couple of times he threatened people. Once with a knife. You don't last long in this business that way." Walton winked at Carver. "I bet that's why you're looking for him, right? He lost his temper and punched somebody, maybe cut them. Got his ass sued and lost."

"Something like that. Was he especially friendly with any of the other models?"

"Nope. Enrico sort of kept to himself. And this is a job. Most of my models barely know each other. They get called, they go on a shoot, they work hard while they're there, then they go home and wait for another call. You should see how a lot of them dress at home. You'd never guess they were models. Most of them can't afford the clothes they wear in front of the camera. Quite a few of them hold down other jobs."

"Did Enrico have another job?"

"Not that I know of. Until he ran into problems, he got enough work to make a living. Like I said, he's ethnic, and he's good at what he does when he isn't making trouble. The camera loves him."

"Was he a favorite of any particular photographer?"

"Hold on a minute." Walton stood up and walked to a black file cabinet and pulled open a drawer. He drew out a folder, opened it, and stood studying it for a few minutes. "Drew Kirk requested him several times. His studio's over on Sixth Street." He replaced the folder and slid the drawer shut on its smooth, noiseless tracks. He took a few steps toward his desk and stood still, making no move to sit back down.

Carver read the signal and stood up. He leaned on his cane and got one of his business cards from his pocket, handed it to Walton. "If Enrico gets in touch with you, I'd appreciate it if you'd call me."

"Why should I do that?" There was no hostility in Walton's

voice. It was a simple, logical question, the "What's in it for me?" asked by millions of businessmen every day. A guy like Walton wouldn't dream of *not* asking it.

"Money," Carver said.

Walton nodded. "Okay, I'll call."

Carver thanked him and started to wade through the carpet toward the door.

He stopped when he noticed the arrangement of photographs on the wall that had been behind him. They were all eight-by-ten head shots of male and female models. The second one from the left was of Maggie Rourke. She was wearing a low-cut something with puffed sleeves and smiling as if she'd just been pleasantly surprised by the photographer.

"Who's that woman?" Carver asked, moving closer and pointing with his cane at Maggie, almost touching it to the photograph.

"Margaret Rourke," Walton said without hesitation. "Maggie. She hasn't worked for me for quite a while. In fact, she no longer models. I sent her out on a couple of shoots for a swimwear catalog about ten months ago, then she quit the business and went into something else. I leave her photo up there because she looks so good."

"That's why she drew my eye," Carver said. "She should be in movies."

"Shouldn't they all," Walton said. "That's what most of them think, anyway. As if looks is all it takes."

Carver continued on toward the door.

Walking beside him, Walton said, "It's a shame Enrico can't get it together. He has the potential to be a top earner in this business."

"Potential is for last-place ball clubs."

"Yeah, I get your point," Walton said.

Carver doubted it.

He said goodbye to Verna on the way out and she favored him with one of her sly, carnivorous smiles.

20

DREW KIRK'S studio was on a residential block of Sixth Street and looked like a house. It was, in fact, a large house, white stucco with a red tile roof and enameled red iron balconies and shutters. It was old like the rest of the houses on the block, but unlike many of them it was well maintained and the lawn was green and had been recently mowed. Kirk probably lived upstairs, where lace curtains showed at the windows.

The only indication that the ground floor was a studio was a small black and white sign that read DREW KIRK, INC at the bottom of one of the beveled windows that flanked the front door. A smaller sign said ENTER, so Carver did.

He found himself in a large, cool foyer that held the faint chemical scent of developer. A wide blue-carpeted staircase curved to the second floor, but there was a blue velvet rope strung across it. An arrow on a sheet of thin white cardboard pointed to the left, where a door was lettered DREW KIRK, INC in the same bold black print as the sign in the window. To the right were two closed doors, richly grained wood with white porcelain knobs.

Carver pushed open the DREW KIRK door and found himself in a reception room with a polished hardwood floor, black file cabinets, a long red sofa and matching chair, and a large desk that held an Apple computer. The computer's screen was blank. There was no one behind the desk. The window looked out on the street; Carver could see the Olds squatting in the shade of a palm tree. The rust was barely evident from this distance.

Behind the desk was another door, and above it a green light and a red one, side by side like mismatched eyes. The green one was glowing, so Carver assumed it was okay to enter what must be the studio proper.

No one paid any attention to him when he opened the door and stepped into a surprisingly spacious studio littered with sets and equipment. The entire first floor of the house beyond the reception area had been made into one vast room broken only by supporting pillars and a walled-off corner that was probably the darkroom. At the far end of the room, a blond woman in a one-piece red swimming suit was standing in front of a pull-down backdrop of a beach with blue ocean and breeze-bent palm trees. A thin, intense-looking man wearing dark slacks and a white shirt with the sleeves rolled up above the elbows was standing beside a tripod-mounted camera, saying something to the model and signaling her with short, choppy hand motions to move this way and that. A younger man with shoulder-length brown hair was standing off to the side, near one of several brilliant lights also mounted on tripods. He had on a gray tee shirt and wide red suspenders that weren't necessary to hold up his tight, faded Levi's. There were two large white umbrellas situated on each side of the set, carefully angled to reflect softened light onto the subject, who was holding a wine bottle.

The suspendered assistant stared at Carver, making the intense-looking guy aware of his presence. He turned around, waved Carver over toward him, then went back to instructing the model, who fluffed her hair and glanced at Carver with disinterest.

". . . can't just look surprised, gotta put a little fear into your expression, Jane. Shock. And remember, there's just been an explosion."

Jane said, "Look at me! I'm all fucking wet."

"You're at the beach, baby," the intense guy said. He had to be Kirk. He was skinny enough to look unhealthy and resembled a young Sinatra except his face was badly pockmarked from long-ago acne.

The assistant grinned at Carver. He was in his twenties and already had terrible teeth. Carver saw now that he wore a silver skull-and-crossbones earring in his left ear. That and the long hair and the yellowed stump-toothed grin made him look like a pirate.

Carver leaned on his cane and watched. He noticed that the bottle in the model's hand had a champagne label, and a cork stuck on a thin wire that extended straight up from it was bouncing around about two feet above the neck. A clear plastic hose ran from the side of the bottle over to near the assistant with the earring. Carver noticed the model was standing in a shallow metal tray about five feet square. A hose ran from the tray over to a drain. Carver was spellbound.

The pirate switched on a large floor fan and the model's blond hair took on the desired windblown look, a strand of it trailing seductively across her face.

"Good. Just that way," Drew Kirk said. "Drop your arm a little more so it hides the hose. Okay, good. Perfect. Remember—shock, fear, all the while smiling."

The woman glanced at him curiously.

Kirk flitted around with a light meter, then crouched behind the camera. "Hit it, Wilbur!"

Wilbur the pirate turned a handle over at the sink and water rushed through the clear plastic hose. A little compressor kicked in and churned it up with air. Wilbur ran to the compressor and punched a button.

Air-foamed water burst from the neck of the bottle in a mini-geyser that made the cork on the end of the wire dance. It was impossible to see the wire in the rush of water. Water kept fizzing out of the bottle to meet the bobbing, suspended cork. The model kept smiling. The camera kept clicking and whirring. In the photo, it would appear that the woman had just popped the cork on the bottle and foaming champagne was gushing out, propelling the cork before it.

"'Atta baby!" Kirk yelled. "Don't hide the label with your fingers. Good." *Click, whirrr. Click, whirrr.* "Good, good, good. More shock!" The blond widened her eyes over her dazzling white smile. *Click, whirrr. Click, whirrr. Click, whirrr.*

"Good, good. Perfect! Got it, Wilbur," Kirk said, straightening up from peering through the camera.

Wilbur turned off the compressor and the fan, then the spigot at the sink, and the only sound was water draining from the tray where the model stood ankle deep in mock champagne.

"I'm all fucking wet!" she pointed out again.

"You did a great job, Jane," Kirk told her.

"Right on, babe," Wilbur concurred. "We all did a great job."

The model stepped out of the water and wrapped herself in a white terrycloth robe, then walked toward the room Carver had assumed was a darkroom. Wilbur began disassembling the set.

Kirk grinned at Carver and said, "Sorry to make you wait, but we were in the middle of a shoot."

"That's okay," Carver said, "it was interesting. I'll change my brand of champagne."

"The company's gearing up for a big promotion."

"I meant to a brand different from that one," Carver said,

tilting his head toward the bottle. "That one will always taste like water to me now."

Kirk grinned again. He looked amazingly like a pockmarked Sinatra when he did that.

Carver told him who he was, where he'd gotten his name, what he wanted.

Kirk rubbed his chin. "If Walton sent you over here, it must be all right."

Carver didn't tell him that Walton hadn't exactly sent him. He said, "Walton told me you use one of his models a lot. Enrico Thomas."

"I did at one time. But Enrico hasn't been around for quite a while. Last time I requested him, Walton told me he wasn't available."

"Enrico ever give you any problems?"

Kirk raised his eyebrows. "Me? Naw! I know what you're talking about, though. I heard some stuff about Enrico." He turned toward the busy Wilbur. "Hey, Wilbur, Enrico ever give you any trouble?"

"Not me," Wilbur said, coiling a cable.

"Do you have an address or phone number on him that might be different from Walton's?"

"I don't have that kinda info on any of the models. We deal direct through the agency. That's how this business works. Walton wouldn't like it if we started cutting deals on the side with his employees. Not that we'd do such a thing."

"Never ever," Wilbur said.

"Enrico ever say anything that might lead you to know what he did when he wasn't modeling, where he hung out?"

"No. Not as I can recall."

"Nightlinks," Wilbur said.

Kirk and Carver stared at him.

He stood there with the coiled cable and repeated, "Nightlinks. I don't know what it is, but I remember Enrico mentioning to one of the other models about working at Nightlinks."

"Walton told me Enrico didn't work a second job," Carver said.

Kirk smiled. "I suspect a lot of the models don't tell their agencies everything about their lives away from the camera. Agents can be pushy and demanding if another job gets in the way of their commissions."

"Is all of your work with Walton models?"

"Nope. Jane there"—he made a vague backhand motion toward where Jane had posed with the champagne bottle—"is with an agency over in Orlando. We deal with half a dozen agencies. It all depends on the types our clients want."

Jane came out of the room wearing jeans and a sleeveless blouse and carrying a flowered duffel bag. She seemed much shorter, and Carver realized she must have been wearing high heels in the water to make her legs look longer, even though they obviously wouldn't be visible below her ankles in the champagne photograph. All of her makeup had been removed and she looked like a teenager. She waved and said, "See you, Drew. Take care, Wilbur."

They both waved back, and all three men watched her stride from the studio, a shapely little woman who didn't at all resemble the sleek blond beauty who'd be uncorking champagne on the beach in the photograph. So much of life and love and advertising was illusion.

Carver left his card with Kirk, and Kirk assured him he'd phone and let him know if Enrico showed up at the studio.

"Let's set up for the sailboat shoot," Kirk was telling Wilbur as Carver left. "We'll need more wind to make spray."

Photography in Florida, Carver decided, could be a wet business.

As he crossed Sunburst toward the Olds, he looked around for Jane but she was nowhere in sight.

21

CARVER DROVE to his office and looked up Nightlinks in the phone directory. It was listed as an escort service and had an address on Telegraph Road on the southern edge of Del Moray. It appeared that Carl Gretch–Enrico Thomas worked as a paid escort, perhaps a male prostitute. Something Donna Winship undoubtedly didn't know.

Or did she at least suspect? Carver wondered if Gretch had used the Thomas name when working for Nightlinks. He sat back behind his desk and looked out the window at two skinny teenage girls waiting for a bus across Magellan. One was wearing amazingly tight red shorts, pretending to be annoyed when passing motorists stared or honked their horns.

Or was she pretending? Laura, his former wife, would call him a sexist for wondering that, and maybe she'd be right. Still, looking at the girl across the street, he was curious. Carver wished he understood women; it might make what he was working on easier. Might make his life easier.

Desoto, way over in Orlando, probably wouldn't know anything about Nightlinks. But Carver knew someone who almost certainly would know, a retired Del Moray police sergeant named Barney Travers who was living now in a residential hotel in Miami. Travers had worked on the vice squad for fifteen years and knew more than anyone about the dark side of sunny Del Moray.

Carver flipped though his Rolodex and came up with Travers's number, a bit surprised that it was there, then remembering he'd jotted it down and inserted it last year after Travers had sent him a Christmas card. The card had to do with elves and reindeer and was a jarring example of what fifteen years of vice squad duty could do to a cop's sense of humor.

He was about to reach for the phone and call Travers when the door opened and McGregor strutted in.

The tall man was grinning lewdly, the pink tip of his tongue oozing out between his front teeth as if struggling to emerge completely from his mouth. He was wearing the same wrinkled, ill-fitting brown suit he'd had on the last time he'd aggravated Carver, and the smell of stale perspiration mingled with cheap perfumed cologne or deodorant was still with him. He stood with his fists on his hips, staring down at Carver, his suit coat shoved back so the butt of his gun was visible in its shoulder holster.

"Why don't you ever knock?" Carver asked. "Why do you always burst in here like you expect to interrupt a Mafia conspiracy?"

"You never know," McGregor said, "I might catch you masturbating. Arrest you for indecent exposure the way they did that other comedian a few years ago."

"Since I'm not exposed or doing anything illegal," Carver said, "what do you want this time?"

McGregor jutted out his long jaw, putting on his angry expression, and glared at the lowly Carver. "Despite what I told you," he said, "the word I get is that you're still running around trying to make something out of nothing."

Carver pretended to be puzzled.

"The late happy couple," McGregor reminded him. *Flick* went the tongue. "You know, Splat and Bang."

"Ah, the Winships."

"You've been talking to people about the Winships, Carver. Trying to establish that somebody's been murdered, it looks to me."

"It is a possibility."

"You even unearthed a girlfriend of the husband, that Maggie Rourke cunt." *Flick.* "Can't say I much blame Mark Winship for going after that. But what's it got to do with anything except a guy riding a fresh pony?"

"He wasn't the type to have an affair," Carver said.

McGregor threw back his head and laughed. "Take another look at the Rourke woman, asshole. Even a jerk-off like you might leave that dark meat of yours if an operation like Maggie Rourke crooked her little finger at you and said to come hither."

Carver felt a thrust of guilt and discomfort. What McGregor said wasn't true. He told himself it wasn't true.

"Besides," McGregor said, "who knows why guys step out on the wife? The Winship marriage was private, intimate, like every marriage outside the fucking royal family."

"Even princes and princesses enjoy some privacy."

"Maybe they fought all the time."

"The Royals?"

"The Winships, dumb fuck. Maybe Donna Winship let herself get fat." He pointed out the window at the two teenagers still waiting for a bus across the street. "Look at them two skinny pieces. Probably starved themselves to get that way. Fucking bulimics upchucking in public restrooms. It's unnatural, the way women keep themselves so skinny these days. Style, sure, but it's deliberate deception. They're pretending to be what they're not. Then they get married and balloon out like the pigs they really are. Big surprise for hubby, and of course he starts looking longingly at whatever's on the other side of the fence. It's ruined the fine institution of marriage."

"Quite a theory," Carver said.

"It ain't just a theory. I seen it happen lots of times. Inside every thin woman there's a fat woman struggling to get out. Soon as they say 'I do' is when it starts to happen. The honeymoon begins and they're scarfing down milkshakes and cheeseburgers, and don't hold the onion."

"So you came here to make social commentary on the divorce rate and fast food. Now that you've done it, why don't you leave? I've got paperwork to catch up on."

"Wipe your ass with your paperwork, Carver. I'm here—"

"I know," Carver interrupted, "to warn me again not to poke around in the Winship case."

McGregor shook his head and looked at Carver as if he were hopeless. "Don't jump to conclusions like the piss-poor detective you are. Here's what's happened. Like the blind hog stumbling upon an occasional acorn, you happened to uncover a few things that change the picture."

"Like Maggie Rourke?"

"Some acorn. But what it all means is this: You got my permission to go ahead and keep nosing around."

"I thought you didn't want any unsolved murders in your jurisdiction that might mess up your chances for a promotion."

McGregor drew back as if aghast. "What kind of crap is that? I'm an officer of the law. Just because there'd be some personal gain in it for me, you think I'd sweep a homicide under the rug?"

"With a lot of other dirt," Carver said. He knew now where McGregor was going.

"If anything like murder did go down with the Winships," McGregor said, "I better be the second to know, if you're the first."

"So if you can't have a non-murder, you want a murder you can say you solved."

McGregor's tongue probed again as he smiled. "That's uncharacteristically astute of you. Now and again you show signs of not being completely brain dead."

"In a way," Carver said, "you're sort of making me an honorary member of your department."

"And under my direct command," McGregor added. "Otherwise, I'll lean on you hard. I can do that, Carver. Fact is, it'll tickle the hell out of me to straighten you out if you aren't a good soldier. I live for that kinda thing."

Carver knew it was true. McGregor wasn't above planting evidence if it was necessary to best an enemy. And anyone who stood between him and what he wanted was an enemy.

McGregor removed his fists from his hips and wiped a dirty white cuff across his nose. He pointed a long finger at Carver. "Remember, dick-face, what you know, I better know. Within seconds, if you're near a phone." He moved his lanky, basketball-center's body to the door, then turned around. "This ain't all bad for you, Carver. You don't fuck up, and the minute I become chief you get a medal. It's a promise."

Laughing, he strode from the office.

Carver watched him drive out of the lot and make a right turn on Magellan. McGregor honked the unmarked's horn as he passed the two teenage girls. One ignored him. The other, the one wearing the shorts, made an obscene gesture. Carver thought McGregor might turn the car around and make trouble for the girls, but just then a bus arrived as if to rescue them and they boarded and were gone in a haze of shimmering exhaust fumes.

Carver sat for a few minutes staring across the sun-bright street at the unoccupied bus stop, at the lonely hot metal sign and the empty bench with a liquor ad on its back, thinking about what McGregor had said.

Then he dragged the phone over to him and called Miami.

22

THE CONNECTION was bad. Barney Travers sounded as if he were a thousand miles away instead of just down the coast in Miami. Maybe that was why Travers's voice seemed old, even though he'd only been retired a few years. Carver asked him how he was doing.

"Waiting to die," Travers said.

"You sick, Barney?"

"Not as I know of. That's what retirement is, Carver, just waiting to die."

"It doesn't have to be."

"You don't know what you're talking about. But you'll find out soon enough."

Carver said, "While we're waiting, can you tell me what you know about an escort service called Nightlinks?"

"Sure. Office is over on Telegraph Road. It's a front for prostitution, like most escort services, but the women screw clients for money on their own time so it's hard to prove. Even harder to tie in with Nightlinks if any of the women do get caught taking money for sex. By the time Nightlinks gets its percentage, the deed is done and nobody's taking a fall for it."

"Ever hear of a guy named Carl Gretch, A.K.A. Enrico Thomas?"

"In connection with Nightlinks?"

"In any connection. But he works as an escort for Nightlinks."

"No, I don't think I've heard of him. That doesn't mean anything, though. Those guys change their names more often than their underwear. To get his real name, you'd probably have to go back beyond Carl Gretch."

"What about Beni Ho?"

"Hah!" Travers seemed to brighten considerably. "That one I can tell you about. He's worked as a Nightlinks escort, but he's something more than that. He does enforcement work for various people, and he loves it. The little fart doesn't have a bone in his body that isn't mean. He's a killer, though it's never been proved in court. Watch out for him, Carver. He might not be much bigger'n a midget, but he's dangerous and ornery as a wolverine."

Carver watched the traffic glisten in the sun out on Magellan. He was tired of people telling him how tough Beni Ho was. The little bastard wasn't bionic. Carver had seen him bleed. He said, "You recall if anyone ever brought charges against Nightlinks?"

"Charges, yes. Convictions, no. They've got the usual shark attorneys. I don't think they were ever in any kind of real trouble. Truth is, despite Harvey Sincliff, Nightlinks has a comparatively clean record as escort services go."

"Harvey Sincliff?"

"He owns and runs Nightlinks. A real slimeball, is Harvey. Nightlinks is set up so it looks clean on police computers, but with Harvey in charge I can tell you the girls are spreading for money and he's getting plenty himself."

"Plenty of money?" Carver asked.

"Only that. Harvey's a disciplined businessman, in his sleazy fashion. There's not much chance he's diddling any of his employees. He comes across as a lightweight who oughta be selling used cars with their speedometers turned back, but don't underestimate him. He's got brains and balls, and no scruples whatsoever. If he thinks you should be out of the game, he'll pay Beni Ho to remove you from the board." Travers paused for a moment. Violent coughing came over the line. "'S'cuse me," he said. "I been doing that more and more. One of these times I'm gonna cough up all them years I smoked cigars, then roll over and die." He cleared his throat, coughed again briefly. "You know, I kinda miss Del Moray. How's Lieutenant McGregor doing these days?"

"Up for promotion, and he's got his eye on becoming chief of police."

"That'd be a fucking tragedy."

"Any message for him, now that you're safely retired?"

"I don't waste my time these days thinking about pricks like McGregor. What life I've got left is too short for hateful reminiscing." More coughing. "On second thought, tell him I hope he eats ground glass and dies puking."

"I'll tell him verbatim. Thanks for your help, Barney. You take care of yourself."

"Speaking of taking care, be extra careful of that little weasel Beni Ho. He enjoys seeing other folks in pain, and that's the only reason he needs to start breaking small bones. There's talk about him having killed some people in imaginative ways."

Carver said, "I shot him in the leg a few days ago."

"Really? That's not very imaginative."

"Effective, though."

"Not effective enough, unless infection sets in. Shoulda been his fucking heart. But anyway, just knowing that has made my day, Carver, and it's not even time for lunch. Call me again sometime, when you feel like chatting about dentures or prostate operations. Hey, wait a minute! Don't forget to tell McGregor what I said about him. I mean that, now."

"Not to worry," Carver said, but Travers had hung up.

Lunch, Carver thought. Despite his earlier conversation with McGregor about fast food and the death of true love, he decided to grab a cheeseburger and vanilla milkshake at a drive-through McDonald's, then drop by Nightlinks and try to talk with Harvey Sincliff.

He smiled. McGregor. Harvey Sincliff. It was amazing, the people you met in this business. Not at all like, say, if you worked in a shoe store or sold nursing home insurance. Maybe.

As he started to stand up, the phone jangled. He sat back down and was going to let the answering machine handle it, but it was Beth so he lifted the receiver.

"I'm calling from the drugstore down the street from Gretch's apartment," she said. "He's back. He's in the building now."

"I'll be there soon as I can," Carver said. "If he leaves, follow him."

Beth said, "I don't think he's going to leave, Fred. He's carrying up armloads of clothes and boxes out of his car. Like he's moving back in."

23

CARVER WAS in Orlando in a little over an hour. He left Beth parked in her car outside the apartment on Belt so she could follow Gretch if for some reason he broke and ran again. Then he limped along the hot sidewalk toward the building entrance, wishing he'd had time to stop for lunch. His stomach was growling. People like Gretch caused problems large and small. The large problems kept Carver in business, but they spun off smaller ones. Such as hunger.

Gretch apparently had finished carting up boxes; his car was parked at the curb in front of the building, doors and trunk closed. A length of twine dangled from beneath the closed trunk lid, barely touching the ground.

As Carver turned to negotiate cracked concrete and enter the building, Hodgkins emerged. He was wearing overalls today over a white tee shirt, and carrying a hammer. A long screwdriver with a yellow plastic handle smeared with white paint was tucked through one of the overalls' many tool loops. He didn't look happy.

When he saw Carver, he stopped and said, "I was gonna call you. He's back."

"I know," Carver said. "How did that come to pass?"

"Billy seen his chance to collect back rent and get the apartment occupied right away, is how. That's a landlord for you when he don't live on the premises and have to cope with the trash that's there. If I was him, I wouldn't have let the little prick move back in. Not after the way he skipped out on the rent the first time. What's to prevent him from doin' it again?"

Carver didn't have an answer. "Did Billy consult you?"

"Sort of. I told him what I just told you. Told him Gretch was scum and his money was contaminated. He said money was money and didn't know nor care where it came from, so it made no difference if Gretch was scum. I don't believe that. A man with character wouldn't say it. Billy's got no character, only property."

"It happens that way a lot," Carver said. "Is Gretch up there now?"

"Yeah. He carried up some boxes and a ton of clothes on hangers, and now he's in there playin' the TV too loud."

"I'm going up and talk to him," Carver said. "I'll tell him to turn down the volume."

"You be careful of him, Carver. He's liable to do anything if you get him mad."

Carver said, "I'm liable to do anything right back."

That kind of talk seemed to excite Hodgkins. He waved the hammer in the air as if yearning for something to strike. "Know what gripes me, Carver? I cleaned up that apartment so I could show it to prospective tenants, even scrubbed and polished the kitchen and bathroom. Made everything shine. And it turns out I was only doin' that little punk's housework."

"Cheer up," Carver said. "Maybe the disinfectant will kill him."

|147|

Hodgkins shuffled away mumbling, a malcontent on a mission of repair.

Carver began sweating more heavily as he climbed the stairs to the much warmer second-floor hall. He wasn't in a good mood when he knocked on Gretch's door.

He stood for what seemed a long time, listening to what sounded like people having sex on the other side of the door. "Oh, yes, yes, yes!" a woman shouted, as music reached a crescendo. The woman yelled something unintelligible. Then the door opened. "Oh, yes!" the woman said again.

Gretch looked out at Carver and said, "Oh, no! I figured you'd show up here again."

Behind him on the TV screen a man and woman were lying nude on a round bed and lighting cigarettes, smiling dreamily at each other. Gretch started to close the door, but Carver placed the tip of his cane against his chest and shoved him back, then pushed inside. The apartment wasn't any cooler than out in the hall.

"Okay, okay," Gretch said, "so you're insistent." He glanced at the TV, then walked over and turned off the adult video he had playing. "I saw this scene before."

"I'll bet."

"Next they take a shower together, get all excited with the shampoo and soap and all, then go at it again."

"No kidding?" Carver said.

Gretch was still dirty from moving in the boxes that were stacked against a wall in the living room. His blue shirt and khaki pants were smudged and his hands and arms were streaked with perspiration and dirt. A half-empty bottle of Corona beer sat on the floor near the sofa that faced the television.

Gretch sat down on the sofa, leaned forward, and picked up the beer. He took a sip, grinning at Carver. "I figure maybe we owe each other an apology. I mean, you followed me around when you had no right, and I guess I shouldn't have pulled a knife on you." He said it as if apologizing for taking Carver's parking space. He drank some more beer, dribbling some down his chin, and said, "I guess you want whatever it was you wanted before."

Carver moved closer to Gretch, watching his hands, prepared to lash out with the cane if Gretch tried to pull the knife again. He stood silently for a moment, letting Gretch get nervous. Watching him make a show of taking another sip of beer. But the bottle was empty now. Gretch pretended it wasn't, licking his lips as he put it back down on the floor.

"So whaddya want?" he finally blurted out.

Carver said, "Talk to me about Donna Winship."

"Sure. Donna." He took a deep breath, then said, "Whew!," as if emotion had almost derailed him before he'd gotten it under control. "Donna's the reason I had to get away for a while. Try'n make some sense outa what happened. I loved her." He bowed his head. "Whether or not you believe it, I loved her. When I heard about it, the accident, I got a little crazy. I just had to go off by myself, spend some time alone and get used to the idea of Donna being gone. I still ain't sure I've gotten used to it. I mean, I feel like if I picked up the phone and called, she'd still answer and we could meet someplace."

"Where have you been?"

"Staying with a friend in Miami. But it wasn't working out. I mean, his wife started bitching about me being there. Then she went the other way when her husband was right in the next room, and I had to fight her off to keep her from unzipping my pants. She held it against me. You know the way some women do. I knew it was time to come back here anyway, try to pick up my life again." He looked up at Carver, started to take another drink of beer, then remembered the bottle was empty. Looked up at Carver again, hope in his eyes. "That what you wanted to hear?"

"It's what you wanted me to hear."

|149|

Gretch shook his head, slowly at first, then violently, in a display of agonizing dismay. When he stopped, he said, "You don't believe a guy like me could love somebody like Donna, but it's true. I loved her with all my heart." He touched the side of his neck gingerly; he might have hurt himself, shaking his head that way.

"How'd you two meet?" Carver asked. He hadn't expected this soap opera story line from Gretch, didn't know quite how to take it.

"I was with another woman at a convention, a female insurance executive from out of town, when I met Donna and fell for her right there. She was with some other people from the insurance company where she worked. I saw right away there was something between us, so I phoned her the next day at work, kept phoning her until she agreed to meet me someplace for coffee. That's how it started." He sniffed and wiped away tears with dirty knuckles, making it look as if he had two black eyes. "You know how it ended."

"Did you know she was married?"

"Not at first. She told me the second time we went out. We were both too far gone on each other for it to make any difference then. She said for me not to think I was breaking up her marriage, she was unhappy anyway."

"The female insurance executive. How'd you meet her?"

Gretch clenched his hands in his lap and stared at them. "This some kinda test?"

Carver said, "Yes."

"I'm a model, but I work sometimes as a paid escort. She called and I went with her to the convention. There's nothing wrong with that. Men and women, they come into town for those kinda things, they sometimes like to be seen with somebody at important functions, you know? They got their own reasons. Like, the insurance woman prefers girls but knew that wouldn't go well with the company brass. She wanted me to help establish the impression she liked men."

"You do anything other than escort these women?"

"I don't see as that's any of your business. What it's got to do with anything, anyway?"

Gretch was starting to build up some indignation, the mood that helped carry a guy like him through life. Carver said, "What about Donna Winship's husband?"

"What about him?" Gretch shrugged. "He ain't the first guy whose wife stepped out on him. From what Donna said, the marriage going sour was his fault. He'll survive."

"He didn't," Carver said. "He's dead."

Gretch stood up, wearing an astounded expression. He sat back down immediately, as if too affected by the news to remain upright. Carver couldn't tell if the display of surprise was genuine or if modeling skills extended to acting.

"Mark Winship shot himself when he learned about Donna's death," Carver said.

For a long time Gretch said nothing, staring at the opposite wall, or maybe the blank TV screen where the man and woman had recently enjoyed sex and cigarettes.

Then he said, "You can't lay any guilt on me for that one. I didn't plan for things to work out this way." He slumped forward, elbows on knees, and stared at the floor. Carver was surprised to find himself feeling slightly sorry for Gretch.

He said, "The police are calling his death a suicide. Right now, anyway."

Gretch glanced sharply over at him. "What's that supposed to mean?"

"Means some people think Mark Winship might have been murdered."

Gretch rubbed both hands over his thighs with a lot of pressure, as if trying to scrape something unpleasant off his palms.

"I wouldn't know anything about that, and I don't wanna know."

"No idea who'd want to kill Mark?"

"No. And I figure if the cops say it's suicide, it probably is. They know about those kinda things."

Carver said, "What about Maggie Rourke?"

Looking at the floor again, Gretch shook his head. The back of his neck was dirty where he'd rubbed his hand over it while lugging stuff up the hot stairs. "I don't know any Maggie Rourke."

"The Walton Agency."

Gretch raised his head and stared at Carver. "Yeah, yeah. Now I know who you mean. Real pretty brunette. I don't really know her, though. She's another Walton model, and we worked on the same shoot last year. It was a lung shot."

"Lung shot?"

"Group photo for a cigarette ad. You know, the tobacco companies like to show good-looking people having fun on a picnic or skiing or whatever. Healthy people with healthy lungs. We were all smoking and playing volleyball on the beach."

"You ever meet any of Donna's friends?"

"Are you kidding? She wasn't the type to share that kinda secret. She wanted to keep our affair quiet. So did I. Nobody wanted anybody else to get hurt. Then it all turned to shit, like a lotta other things have happened to me in my life."

"You know a man named Beni Ho? Little Oriental guy."

"No, I don't think so. Should I know him?"

"Nobody should."

Gretch stared at him earnestly. "I gotta say I'm not completely sorry to hear about Mark Winship, not after some of the stuff Donna told me about him. It's just a goddamn shame"— his voice broke and his eyes misted over again—"just a goddamn shame she was married at all, that any of this ever happened. Especially to somebody as good as her. I never woulda gone near her if I knew how it'd turn out. Life's fucking funny sometimes, isn't it? I don't mean like 'ha-ha' funny, but, you know . . ."

"I know," Carver said. He planted his cane and moved back a few steps, toward the door. "You plan on being at this address for a while?"

Gretch looked surprised. "Of course. I gotta be. I'm on a lease."

Carver left the apartment, closing the door behind him.

He stood in the stifling hall for a few minutes, listening. There was only silence.

Then faint music and voices from the TV.

The sound of a shower running.

24

BETH FOLLOWED Carver back to Del Moray, then to the taco stand on Magellan, where they sat in the shade of an umbrella over one of the tiny round tables and ate a late lunch–early supper. A warm salt breeze was wafting in, carrying the scent of the ocean. The sun was still bearing down hard, and Carver's knee and forearm that were outside the circle of the umbrella's shade were hot.

Beth bit into her brittle taco, chewed, swallowed with apparent difficulty, and said, "I don't understand why you like this place, Fred. Stuff tastes like a cardboard meat-pie."

"Try more sauce."

She tore the corner off one of the little plastic containers of hot sauce and squeezed some onto her taco. She took another cautious bite, chewed, said nothing, and sipped Pepsi-Cola through a straw.

As they ate, Carver told her about his conversation with Carl Gretch. As *he* ate, actually. Beth only sipped soda and watched the sunlit pleasure boats bobbing in unison at their moorings as he talked.

When he was finished talking, she continued staring at the boats. "Not much of what Gretch told you rings true, Fred."

"Of course not. Not even his story about how he met Donna Winship. Question is, why would he tell me how much he loved her? Why would he care what I thought?"

"I think we should find out. I keep trying to imagine Donna and Mark both dying as suicides, and I can't. The more we learn, the more questions present themselves."

"Starting again tomorrow," Carver said, "you keep a loose watch on Gretch's apartment and see where he goes if he leaves. Or who visits him if he stays put. When we're finished here, I'll drive over and try to talk to Harvey Sincliff at Nightlinks."

She discovered taco sauce on her index finger and licked it off. "Gonna phone first?"

"No. I'd rather catch him unprepared."

"I've gotta do some work on an article for *Burrow*," Beth said, "then I'll drive back to Orlando tonight and stay in a motel so I can be outside Gretch's apartment early in the morning."

"He strikes me as the type who'd sleep late."

Beth winked. "You'd just rather have me with you than in a motel."

"Can't deny it."

She glanced at her watch. "I'd better get going now and warm up my computer." She slid the uneaten half of her taco over to Carver. "You consume this instrument of culinary masochism."

"I don't think Gretch will suspect he's being watched now, but be careful anyway," he said, as she stood up to leave.

Tall, tall woman, she leaned far down to peer beneath the edge of the umbrella at him. "You figure Gretch thinks you actually believed his story?"

"No, but he knows I can't do anything about it one way or the other."

She straightened up and he could no longer see her face. "I might stop for a hamburger on the way home, Fred. *Viva la* Mexico, but screw their food."

He watched her walk away. Then he slid his chair over so he was completely out of the sun and ate the rest of her taco.

THE NIGHTLINKS office address was on the end of a strip shopping center in an otherwise desolate stretch of Telegraph Road. The office's glass door and show window were tinted midnight blue and had gold scrollwork on them but no lettering.

The shopping center was one long, continuous building with a brick facade and a flat roof with air-conditioning units mounted on it. The units were partly shielded from view by low, wooden privacy fences that looked more as if they belonged in someone's backyard than on a roof. Power and phone lines ran from a pole with a large transformer on it to a corner of the building. A row of birds sat on the top cable, looking out over the parking lot. The shop next to Nightlinks was closed and its windows were soaped solid. Next to it was a dry cleaner, then a used-book store, a pharmacy, an Everything-Is-A-Dollar store, then a tavern called the Aero Lounge that had a sign with a three-bladed yellow propeller that slowly rotated. On the other side of Nightlinks was a driveway that led around the cinder block wall to the rear of the building for deliveries, then a vacant lot high with weeds.

Carver parked in the nearest space, about halfway down the row of shops, and was about to climb from the car when he saw an attractive redheaded woman come out of Nightlinks. He watched her lower herself with a great show of legs into a black sports car and drive away.

She hadn't been gone more than a few seconds when a well-dressed man of about thirty entered Nightlinks.

Carver thought he'd sit where he was and watch for a while.

Ten minutes later, the man came out accompanied by a blond woman in a red dress and very high heels. Just behind them walked a small, lean man dressed as a cowboy. The cowboy drove away alone in a battered pickup truck with a gun rack in the rear window. The other man and the blond woman left together in a yellow Lincoln Town Car.

Except for a Federal Express delivery, there was no activity during the next twenty minutes. The Olds was heating up and some men in work clothes who'd entered the Aero Lounge had given him a curious glance. Suspicious character in an old convertible, he knew he couldn't stay where he was much longer without answering some questions. He decided it was time to see if Harvey Sincliff was in.

It felt good to get out of the hot car and straighten up. As he got closer to the building, he noticed small gold lettering near the bottom of the blue-tinted window, spelling out the name of the company. Very discreet. When he opened the door, a bell chimed and a thin woman of about forty seated behind a low gray reception desk smiled at him. The office was surprisingly plush, done in grays and blues. The reception area was small, though. There was a door behind the woman's desk that no doubt led to bigger and better things.

The woman, who was attractive despite protruding teeth, asked if she could help Carver.

He said that maybe she could.

Her eyes took him in, assessing and categorizing. Part of her job. "We have several escorts available," she told him, "though not for tonight."

"I only want to talk with someone," Carver said.

"That's fine. Our people are all very good listeners." She reached into a desk drawer and got out a pink and white form.

"We take all major credit cards but no personal checks. We'll need to know a few things about you.".

"My name is Fred Carver," he said. "It's Mr. Sincliff I need to see."

Her smile stuck but her teeth retracted half an inch. "Are you in sales?"

"No. It concerns one of his employees. Carl Gretch."

Now she stopped smiling altogether. It made her look years older, emaciated rather than fashionably thin. It was as if the smile, the thinness, were all an act, as McGregor had said. McGregor would assess her as single and on the hunt, searching for a man and a cake.

"Are you with the police?" she asked.

"No."

She looked uncertain for a moment, then said, "It's almost five o'clock; I'm not sure Mr. Sincliff is still here."

"Could you please check?"

He thought she might refuse, but her smile returned. She asked Carver to excuse her and went through the door behind the desk. She was much taller than she'd appeared sitting down, and had long legs with remarkably slender ankles.

A minute later she came back and sat down, leaving the door open. A medium-sized man with a stomach paunch appeared there. He wore a harried expression, a neat white shirt, and plaid suspenders, and looked like an accountant with books that refused to balance. His dark hair was thinning and combed sideways from a clean part, and there was an expression of abstract concern on his face that appeared permanent. His head was too small for his body, and his tiny dark eyes were set so close together that at a glance he appeared cross-eyed. It was the eyes that gave him the concerned expression.

He smiled, somehow still looking troubled, and said, "Please come in, Mr. Carver."

Carver followed him through a hall to a door near the far end of the building. Then he stepped aside and let Carver pass ahead of him into a spacious, musty-smelling office with a blue area rug over a gray tile floor. There was a large desk in the office, a table with a computer, printer, and copy machine on it. There was a window with closed blinds to the left of Carver, a wooden bookshelf and a line of dark gray file cabinets to his right. A cigar-store Indian that looked genuine stood stoically in a corner. Collector plates were arranged in a diamond pattern on the wall near the desk. John Kennedy was there. Elvis was there. So was John Wayne.

So was Beni Ho.

But not on a plate.

He was standing as still as the wooden Indian, leaning against the wall near the plates and smiling.

Carver heard the door close behind him, and Harvey Sincliff moved out in front of him and sat down behind the desk. Beni Ho stepped out a few feet from the wall and lifted the cane he was using for support to show it to Carver.

"You and I are alike now, Carver."

Carver said, "I'm taller."

"I don't think that's what you came here to talk about," Sincliff said. "My receptionist said you mentioned Carl Gretch."

"Why is Mr. Ho here?" Carver asked.

"He's my employee."

"Does that mean bodyguard?"

"If you like. Mr. Ho is still a capable man, even with his cane. Something you should understand, Mr. Carver." Beni Ho continued smiling, but he lifted his arm slightly, elbow out, so Carver could see the holstered handgun tucked tight against his ribs beneath his jacket.

"Why would you think you need protection to talk to me, Mr. Sincliff?"

"I'm not a violent man," Sincliff said, "and you have a formidable reputation, Mr. Carver."

Mr. Ho, Mr. Carver, Mr. Sincliff. We sound like the *New York Times*, Carver thought. "While Mr. Ho is here," he said, "we might as well talk about him. I understand he works for you as an escort as well as a bodyguard?"

"On occasion. He's versatile."

"What about Mr. Carl Gretch?"

"Not as versatile, I'm sure. And he doesn't work for me, whoever he is. I've never heard of him."

"Then why did you agree to see me?"

"Politeness. And curiosity. As I said, you have a reputation."

"So you don't know Carl Gretch, even by reputation. Do you know Enrico Thomas?"

"Of course. He's one of our escorts, but on a part-time basis. I believe he has another job."

"Thomas and Gretch are the same man."

"You don't say."

"How did he get involved with Donna Winship?"

"The woman who was struck and killed by a truck? If Enrico was dating her, it had nothing to do with Nightlinks. Though we have plenty of repeat business, usually it's with out-of-town clients who come to Florida infrequently. Executives who need an escort for the evening to attend some official function. Whatever you might think, ours is a respectable enterprise."

"Then why him?" Carver nodded toward Beni Ho.

"He works for me," Sincliff said. "His life outside this business is no concern of mine. A lot of folks have the wrong idea about what we do here, and some of them make threats. I knew of Mr. Ho's expertise in the martial arts, so I added protection to his duties. Other aspects of his reputation are immaterial."

"Is Enrico Thomas good at his work?"

"All our escorts are ladies and gentlemen who know how to behave in public."

"And in private?"

"That's their business. That's why it's called private." Sincliff leaned forward and picked up a paper clip from the desk. He began bending it back and forth. "I have to be honest, Mr. Carver, I don't like it when someone assumes the worst of my business, then comes in here talking as if I'm guilty of some sort of crime. People sometimes need escorts, and I supply them and make a profit. It's that simple and there's nothing more to it. If you can't see it as an exercise in capitalism, think of it as the grown-up equivalent of a date for the prom."

"I don't dance anymore," Carver said.

"You will at least one more time with me," Beni Ho hissed softly through his smile.

Ignoring him, Carver said to Sincliff, "A city the size of Del Moray wouldn't seem to have enough conventions or trade shows to support a business like Nightlinks."

"We don't just do business in Del Moray. We're linked by computer to branches in Orlando, Miami, and the Tampa area. That's why I didn't realize Carl Whazzisname and Enrico Thomas were the same man. I hardly know Enrico. Most of our communication is done by phone or fax."

Sincliff dropped the mangled paperclip into a glass ashtray and stood up. Explanation time was over. "Did you learn anything useful here, Mr. Carver?"

"Probably. In time, I'll know for sure."

"Time's something I'm short of today, I'm afraid. Mr. Ho will walk you out."

Carver headed for the door, aware of Ho trailing him off to the side, like a shadow of a man with a cane.

Carver passed through the reception area, careful to keep Ho at a distance on his right, a blurred figure in his peripheral vision. If Ho moved closer, Carver was ready to act with the cane.

The toothy woman at the desk was silent as he went outside. The door opened and closed again seconds after he'd stepped out into the heat. Ho was still following him.

They played the same shadow game as Carver made his way to where the Olds was parked. As he reached the car door, he heard Ho stop walking behind him on the gravel.

He turned and faced Ho, not surprised to see that he was smiling. Leaning on his cane about five feet away and smiling.

Ho said, "We've become mirror images."

Carver said, "I hope not."

"I have a gun just as you do, Mr. Carver. Is it my turn to shoot you in the leg?"

Carver didn't answer. He was close enough to strike Ho's arm with the cane if the little man went for the gun inside his jacket.

"I come from a very hard place, Mr. Carver. Fear lived in me like an animal that devoured me from the inside. First my youth, then my trust, then my love and compassion, and finally my ability to feel even fear. But I have other feelings. I can and will do anything necessary to achieve my desires."

"You sound hardly human," Carver said.

"You should know."

Carver didn't ask what he meant.

"I will choose when and where, Mr. Carver, and I will make you regret you shot me. It's a point of honor."

"You've been seeing the wrong kind of movies."

"No. You understand me, I know. Because I understand you. Though unfortunately, that understanding came too late to prevent my being shot. As I said, we are mirror images. We both know the code and live by it."

"Then you know I'll shoot you again," Carver said. "And not in the leg."

"Yes, I'm sure now that you will if you can."

Sincliff appeared in the office entrance and waved for Ho to come back inside.

"We have our understanding," Ho said, shifting his weight

over his cane and beginning to back away. "I don't like being hindered, having to wait to heal."

Carver said, "Nothing in life is easy, least of all me."

Ho nodded ever so slightly, then turned completely away from Carver and hobbled back inside with his cane.

Carver stood in the sun and watched him, for more than one reason not liking what he saw.

25

BETH HAD decided not to drive into Orlando that evening and instead worked late in the cottage, bent over her Toshiba laptop computer with an elegant intensity. Carver left her alone and sat out on the porch, smoking Swisher Sweet cigars and looking out at the sea, trying to put everything together in his mind and failing.

She was still working at eleven o'clock when he went inside and said goodnight. He was unable to fall completely asleep. It was almost one when he felt her crawl into bed beside him. The springs groaned and the mattress shifted in her direction as she settled in. Still only half-asleep, he heard a steady, persistent pattering sound and realized it was raining. A semi over on the highway gave two long, lonely blasts of its airhorn as it ran through bad weather. The room was illuminated as if by a flashbulb, and a moment later thunder roared and rumbled. Glassware in the kitchen vibrated shrilly on shelves. Within seconds, more lightning washed the cottage with light.

"You asleep?" Beth whispered.

"No," Carver said, "I was just lying here hoping for high winds."

"I finished my *Burrow* article. It's gonna make some people in the mail-order business mighty uncomfortable."

"Good."

Lightning glare danced over the walls and ceiling. "You get to talk with Sincliff?"

Carver waited until a sharp peal of thunder faded into a silence occupied only by the rain. Then he told Beth about his visit to Nightlinks.

She lay quietly for a while, then said, "Beni Ho's more dangerous now than before he lost some use of a leg."

"He's that sort of guy," Carver agreed.

"You need to be more careful, Fred. Since he's temporarily crippled, Ho's liable to use something long-distance, a gun or throwing weapon."

"I don't think so. He likes to see the eyes of the people he kills." Another roll of thunder, this time without lightning. The storm was moving away. "I wonder if the women he escorts for Nightlinks suspect what he's capable of doing."

"On a certain level, probably. But they still might request him next time. You know how it is, Fred. Some women like dangerous men."

He moved his hand over and felt the smooth warm surface of her bare thigh. "Is that why you and I are here together?"

She rolled onto her side and kissed him on the lips, then drew her head back and smiled seductively at him in the faint illumination of a distant lightning strike. "Maybe. On the other hand, some men like dangerous women."

CARVER AWOKE alone to bright sunlight.

Beth had left quietly before dawn to resume her watch on Gretch's apartment before Gretch got out of bed.

Carver remembered last night and passed his hand lightly over the cool sheet where she'd lain beside him. He looked out the window, and another hot and glaring Florida day looked back at him. The only indication it had rained heavily last night was that the air felt more humid than usual. It was only a little past nine, and already the cottage was uncomfortably warm. He wished Beth had switched on the air conditioner before leaving.

He lay for a while gazing out the window at blue sky and darker ocean rippling with a diamond glint of sunlight, listening to the wavering snarl of a speedboat playing out of his line of sight. Then he located his cane where it had fallen on the floor during sex last night, knocked by one of Beth's long legs from where it had leaned against the wall.

He struggled out of bed and hobbled into the bathroom, relieved himself, and splashed cold tap water over his face. Then he got down his swimming trunks from where they were draped over the shower rod, worked them on, and left the cottage for his morning therapeutic swim.

The speedboat had gone somewhere else and the sea was quiet except for the sighing, slapping sound of the swells rolling in from the eastern light and hunkering down in white foam beyond Carver as they encountered the shallows and ran for the beach. He rode the swells easily, rising and falling in the timeless rhythm that had worn away continents. He floated and thought again of last night and realized anew how much Beth meant to him. And how much a woman like Maggie Rourke must have meant to Mark Winship, even in the agony of guilt he'd apparently suffered knowing what he'd done to his wife. Mark and Maggie must have experienced nights like last night, yet Mark had taken his own life rather than face the dilemma of Donna's death. Of course he'd felt grief and remorse, and perhaps he'd turned on himself, but still there was Maggie, waiting for him. Maggie, possible now for the rest of his life without complication. Mark's Maggie, like Carver's Beth. It wasn't getting any easier for Carver to believe Mark Winship had committed suicide.

The sigh of the swells had become a low roar, and he saw that he'd drifted too far from shore. He rolled onto his stomach and swam with the hot sun on his back.

He'd returned from his swim and showered and shaved, and was eating a late breakfast of eggs, sausage, toast, and coffee, when the phone rang.

The abruptness of the first ring made him start and almost knock his cup over. He hurriedly chewed the bite of toast he'd just taken and reached for the phone where it sat on the breakfast counter. Swallowed and said hello.

"Me, Fred."

He knew by the flat tone of Beth's voice that something had happened.

26

IT WAS eleven-thirty when Carver parked the Olds behind Beth's LeBaron and crossed Belt Street toward Gretch's apartment.

Hodgkins was standing outside in the hot sun, smoking a cigarette and waiting for him, watching him cross the street. The old man drew hard on the cigarette, as if it might be his last and life-prolonging inhalation, then flicked the butt off to the side in a wide arc that left a trail like a tracer bullet.

He must have been holding his breath. When Carver got near him, he exhaled loudly and the morning breeze shredded the smoke that had been in his lungs.

"We did like you said," he told Carver, "which was exactly nothin' and don't let nobody else do otherwise."

Carver sorted that out and concluded that Hodgkins and Beth had followed his instructions.

They went inside and Hodgkins led the way up the creaking wooden steps. Though he appeared composed, excitement urged him on; Carver had to hustle with the cane to keep up with him. Their footsteps and the clatter of the cane echoed in the bare, enameled stairwell, but no one opened a door to peer out at them.

"I was the one that found him," Hodgkins said over his shoulder. "But I knew enough not to touch anything and mess up the scene. Mizz Jackson had told me she'd be watchin' the place, so I knew she was parked across the street. I went and told her about what I found, then she phoned you."

The door to Gretch's apartment was slightly ajar. Hodgkins, breathing heavily from taking the stairs so fast, stood to the side and let Carver enter first.

Beth was standing and staring out a living room window whose venetian blinds were raised crookedly. When she heard them enter, she turned. She looked older, but she was calm. The dead weren't strangers to her.

She said, "In the bedroom, Fred."

She led the way into Gretch's bedroom. The first thing Carver noticed was the old blue carpet that had been on the floor, wadded now against the far wall. Sprawled on his back on the bare wood floor was Carl Gretch, his limbs in close to his body but at odd attitudes. His face was so swollen that his eyes were dark slits that looked like folds of pinched flesh. No matter. He wouldn't need eyes where he was now.

"I seen earlier this mornin' that his door was open," Hodgkins said, "so I stuck my head in and called. Didn't get no answer." He looked apprehensive and scratched his scalp beneath his gray hair. Dandruff flakes settled on the shoulder of his blue shirt. "I know I shouldn't have, but I figured maybe somethin' was wrong, maybe a prowler'd been there, so I went on inside and seen nobody was home and the carpet had been rolled up in here. I knew right away somethin' was inside it, so I lifted one end and unrolled it, and that's what fell out." He nodded toward Gretch's body.

"What then?" Carver asked.

Hodgkins looked at Beth.

"I saw Mr. Hodgkins staring at my car earlier," she said, "when he'd come out to empty some trash. So I let him know why I was there. When he found Gretch, he came and got me. That's when I phoned you."

Carver supported himself with his cane and leaned down to look more closely at the corpse. Gretch was wearing only white Jockey shorts. He'd fouled them in death. Carver held his breath. There were several ugly dark blotches on Gretch's thighs and torso, as well as his face, but the skin was unbroken.

"Whaddya figure happened to him?" Hodgkins asked. He was whispering now, as if he feared waking Gretch.

"I think he was rolled up in the carpet and then beaten to death," Carver said. "It might have taken a long time."

Hodgkins said, "Jesus H. Christ!"

Beth said, "More likely Beni Ho."

"Probably," Carver said. "He could have held a gun on Gretch, or knocked him unconscious, to get him in the carpet. One turn of the carpet and Gretch would have been helpless, like being wrapped in his shroud before he was dead. Then Ho could have his sport."

"Sick, sick bastard," Hodgkins said.

"Could anyone have entered the building last night and sneaked into Gretch's apartment?"

"No reason why not," Hodgkins said. "In fact, I mighta heard someone on the stairs about two in the mornin', but I didn't think nothin' of it and went back to sleep."

"The beating itself wouldn't make much noise, considering Gretch was rolled in the carpet, even if he screamed. But somebody might have heard. Who lives directly beneath this apartment?"

"Old Mrs. Carpenter. She's deaf as a stone. She sleeps with her hearing aid turned off and wouldn't have heard cannon shots right next to her bed."

Beth said, "This building needs better security."

Hodgkins said, "Hah!" and made a face as if about to spit. But he didn't. He said, "Tell it to Billy. I have, often enough!"

"Who's Billy?" she asked.

"The landlord," Carver said. "He keeps losing Gretch as a tenant, then getting him back."

"Well," Hodgkins said, "he ain't gonna get him back this time. And if he got a security deposit, it'll be the first time he came out ahead dealing with Gretch."

"Where from here?" Beth asked Carver, glancing down at Gretch and wrinkling her nose at the odor.

"We phone Desoto and report this to the police."

"I gonna get in any trouble?" Hodgkins asked. "I mean, for comin' in here like I did when I found him?"

"You're the manager and the door was open," Carver said. "You thought something might be wrong so you investigated. If you'd come in and saved Gretch's life, you'd be a hero."

"Or dead," Beth said.

"Fella can be both," Hodgkins told her. "I'll tell the cops that, Carver, case they give me any shit." He stared down at Gretch, looking nauseated and furious. "Gretch was no good," he said, "but I hate to see anybody die like he did." He stared at Carver as if angrily seeking answers. "Who'd do somethin' like this to a man? What kinda person'd be so cold?"

"The kind who might show up as your escort for the evening," Carver said.

He went to the phone and called Desoto.

THE POLICE were at the scene within five minutes. First two polite and efficient uniforms who asked Beth, Carver, and Hodgkins the basic crime scene questions, then requested they stay in the apartment. Then Desoto and two plainclothes detectives. The plainclothes cops took Beth and Hodgkins to Hodgkins's apartment to take their statements separately. Desoto took Carver's statement, then said they'd all have to go down to headquarters and repeat them all again for the recorder so they could be transcribed and signed.

Also so any discrepancies in the three statements would be noted, but Desoto didn't mention that to Carver. They both knew there was no need. Carver understood how the game was played.

"Beni Ho did this," Carver said, when Desoto had closed his notebook and they were off-the-record.

"Seems that way," Desoto agreed. The police photographer and assistant medical examiner had finished, and the paramedics passed through the living room carrying Gretch zipped tight in a body bag. Each paramedic had hold of an end of the bag with one clenched fist. Neither man was straining. Gretch had been a small man and wasn't much of a burden. Not in death, anyway. Carver and Desoto stood silently watching.

"Let's go outside," Desoto said. The technicans were still vacuuming the area where the body had been found and dusting the entire apartment for prints, like a somber and efficient maid service. "We should get outa these people's way."

They went downstairs and stood outside the building, where Hodgkins had been standing and smoking when Carver arrived. Two unmarkeds and a cruiser were lined at the curb. The ambulance, lights flashing in the sunlight but siren silent, was pulling away with Gretch's body. Carver and Desoto watched it turn the corner off of Belt and disappear.

"You gonna talk to Beni Ho?" Carver asked.

"Sure, but if he did Gretch, we both know he'll have his alibi ready." Desoto buttoned his caramel-colored suit coat. His tie was tightly knotted and gold cufflinks winked on his white French cuffs. He wasn't sweating and looked entirely comfortable and at ease, a darkly handsome guy who might have been one of Walton's catalog models. He said, "Why would Beni Ho kill Gretch?"

"Because Gretch knew something about Mark Winship's death and he wasn't a stable character. In fact, he was a flake and a hothead. He might have talked, so killing him was the lesser risk."

"What about Donna Winship? You think she was murdered too?"

"No," Carver said. "Hers looks like a genuine suicide."

"That's what doesn't feel right," Desoto said. "Donna kills herself, then somebody thinks Mark has to die."

"That's how it was."

"Give me a reason."

"I can't yet, but I think there is one. After what happened to Gretch, I'm convinced Mark was murdered."

"The police won't be convinced, though. Not officially."

"And you?" Carver asked.

"I'm with the police, remember?"

"I mean, how do you feel personally?"

"Personally, I more or less agree with you that Mark was murdered."

"McGregor won't."

"Well, Gretch didn't roll himself up in a rug and beat himself to death," Desoto said, "so this one's definitely a homicide. And it's in my jurisdiction even if the Winship deaths aren't. I can keep you informed of any possible connection between Gretch and Mark Winship that might come up during the investigation."

"Donna was the connection."

"Sure. But we don't know what that means. It doesn't seem to be the stuff that murders are made of unless they're crimes of passion. Donna killed herself and Mark died and that's how it went, passion and grief. I mean, that's how it could have gone if Mark actually committed suicide. But Gretch's murder wouldn't fit into the picture unless Mark was also a murder victim. This thing with Gretch muddies the waters considerably." He smiled sadly and shook his head. "Life is a mystery, hey, *amigo*?"

Carver said, "It doesn't hold a candle to death."

27

CARVER KNEW what they wanted to hear, so they were finished with him first.

He left police headquarters on Hughey before Beth and Hodgkins, knowing they might be there considerably longer. The polite, insistent questions would come faster when they were tired, when they'd be more likely to contradict themselves or each other if they were lying. The interrogators were aware he'd been one of them and knew their tricks, so the game had been cut short. He'd given his statement again to Desoto and two other officers while a recorder was running, then verified and signed the transcript.

As he lowered himself into the Olds, he glanced at his watch. Three-twenty. He'd had a doughnut and several cups of acidic coffee in the interrogation room. He looked over at the beige brick and graystone building with its pinched, fortresslike windows and wondered when Beth would finally walk out. There was no way to guess. Homicide cases had top priority and created their own timetables. And it wasn't every day someone was found who'd been beaten to death while rolled in a carpet. Desoto had told him the M.E.'s preliminary report had stated that almost every bone in Gretch's body had been broken and there had been massive internal bleeding. The victim had died slowly and in great agony. Carver felt a rush of anger that anyone, even Gretch, had to die that way.

He started the engine and got the car's air conditioner huffing and gurgling, then drove to a McDonald's and had a Big Mac, large order of fries, and a diet Coke. He'd swum this morning, so he figured he could afford the calories, and the Coke assuaged his dietary conscience. And it wasn't as if he did this every other day; there was no reason to think of himself as weak.

It was almost four when he called Burnair and Crosley from a public phone and asked to speak with Maggie Rourke. He was told Miz Rourke had left for the day. He stuffed more change into the phone and called Maggie's cottage. No one picked up. He let her phone ring ten times before replacing the receiver.

He got back in his car and pulled out into traffic, aiming the Olds's long, prowlike hood toward Del Moray. When he got there, he'd call Maggie's cottage again. If she still wasn't there, he knew where he might find her.

MAGGIE'S BLACK Stanza was parked on Gull Avenue half a block from Shellie's.

Carver didn't bother trying to conceal himself this time. He entered the bar, leaned over his cane, and looked around.

The place was cool after outside, and more crowded now. Half the stools at the long bar were occupied by men in work clothes, a few in suits, and women mostly in casual clothes. Almost all the tables were taken. The TV above the bar was soundlessly showing the local news, two flawlessly coiffed talking heads miming half-sentences at each other, maybe about

Carl Gretch. A karaoke setup was on a small raised platform at the rear of the bar, but it was too early for anyone to be at the mike pretending to be a celebrity. Soft rock with a deep bass beat was pounding at low volume from large box speakers that were angled out from the walls in each corner so they were aimed down at the customers.

Maggie was at the far end of the bar, perched on the same stool Carver had seen her on the last time he'd been there. She was easily the best-dressed woman in the place, with her gray business suit and white blouse with a ruffled collar, her black high heels hitched over the barstool brace. She had a drink in front of her and was staring into it, her hands folded in her lap. There was a white napkin next to her glass with three red swizzle sticks laid out on it in no particular pattern. She'd been there a while. Carver figured she'd found the dismembered doll on her bed and maybe that was why she looked so disconsolate. Or maybe she'd heard about Gretch's death and it meant something to her. He couldn't ask her about the doll without her knowing he'd been in her cottage, but he could ask her about Gretch and try to catch her reaction. She had to have a lot of alcohol in her; it might be the best time to talk to her.

She didn't notice him until he'd taken the stool next to her. Then their eyes met in the mirror behind the bar. She didn't seem surprised to see him, only nodded, then stared back down into her drink.

"That looks diluted," he said, nodding toward her glass. "Buy you another?"

She didn't answer.

When the bartender, a short, stocky woman with black hair and no makeup, walked over, Carver ordered a Budweiser and another of whatever Maggie was drinking.

It turned out to be scotch and seltzer. When the drinks were in front of them on the bar, Maggie stirred hers, then laid the plastic swizzle stick on the napkin with the others. She sipped her fresh drink as if testing it, seemed satisfied, and placed it carefully on its coaster. "You followed me."

"Sort of."

"I don't like that."

"I don't, either," Carver said. "It's an unpleasant part of my job, following people."

"I'd certainly appreciate it," she said—and he realized her words were coming slow and slurred—"if you wouldn't mention to anyone at Burnair and Crosley I was here. You understand. Bad for the corporate image."

"You come here a lot?"

She turned her head and studied him with blurry but still beautiful eyes. "It's not the first time."

"Or the second?"

Her despondent little laugh was more like a cry. Her right hand began to move on the bar in time to the music, the tips of her fingers barely brushing the polished wood surface, almost a nervous twitch. She was making an effort to seem sober. "So I gotta admit I have this problem. I'm a recovering alcoholic. It was okay until Mark died. I mean, I could cope with it. Stay away from it. Then, when I learned about his death, I fell off the wagon. Hit the ground hard." No slurring that time. Good.

"Anybody at Burnair and Crosley know about your problem?"

"I don't think so. I lost my previous job in the recession. Or the reshtru—restructuring, as it was called." She smiled hopelessly. "No, that's not true. I lost it because I drank. Anyway, I couldn't find work, so I did some modeling, then I got involved in a bad—no, a disastrous—love affair. He had influence, and he used it to place me at Burnair and Crosley just before we broke up, gave me the highest recommendation that didn't mention alcoholism. He helped me to stop drinking, too, and I stayed stopped until Mark died. So now I'm drinking again and trying to stop again."

"Are you trying your best?"

"Not at the moment." She sipped. Replaced her drink squarely on its coaster. "And now you know I'm a drunk who handles other people's money. So what are you gonna do, have me executed?"

"Not me."

"I'm cold clean sober at work, Carver. Always." Her hand began to move again in time with the music.

"I believe you." He worked on his beer for a minute. "Speaking of people dying, have you heard about Carl Gretch?"

No visible reaction. "Who?"

"Enrico Thomas. Donna's lover."

Now she blinked. Her hand stopped moving. "That guy? He's dead?"

"Died sometime last night," Carver said. "Died hard." Pushing it, watching her.

"What? How?"

"He was rolled up tight in a carpet and beaten to death."

She swallowed, then lifted her glass and took a huge gulp of her drink so she'd have something for her throat to work on. Delicately, she dabbed at her lips with the backs of her knuckles, making it seem like a gesture taught at finishing schools. "I never met him, so why should I care?"

"He knew you. You were fellow clients at the Walton Agency."

She swiveled slightly on her stool and stared at Carver, looking genuinely confused.

"He said he met you at a lung shoot," Carver explained.

"What the hell is that?"

"It was a photographer's shoot for a cigarette advertisement. You and Gretch were playing volleyball on the beach with some other models."

She chewed on the inside of her cheek, probably shredding it without feeling what she was doing to herself. "Yeah," she said finally, "I remember that job. Gretch. Little guy? Latin?"

"He's the one."

"*He* was Enrico Thomas? Donna's lover?"

"They were the same man."

"I'll be damned." She swiveled back to face the bar and her drink. "And you say somebody beat him to death?" Trying to get it all straight in her mind.

"I think Beni Ho did it."

"Isn't that a Japanese restaurant?"

"He's the man I shot in front of your cottage."

"Really? Police gonna arrest him?"

"No. There's isn't proof, and there won't be. Ho's very much a professional who takes everything into account." He leaned closer to her. "Is everything all right with you?"

" 'Course not. That's why I'm here doing what I'm doing, because of Mark. Trying to get over how goddamn unfair it all is."

"I mean, has anyone threatened you in any way?"

She shook her head no firmly. "Why should anyone threaten me? Donna's dead, now Mark is."

"And Gretch."

"I didn't—I hardly knew him."

"Think about it," Carver said softly. "Try to focus. First Donna, then Mark, and now Gretch."

After a moment she said, "I see what you mean. All three sides of a love triangle." She slowly stirred her drink with the tip of her finger, red nail swirling amber liquid in the soft light from behind the bar. "But I don't get it. Why? Why did any of it happen?"

"I was hoping you could give me some insight."

"Uh-uh, I can't. You know more'n I do about it, that's for sure. Maybe . . . maybe it's just fate. You believe in fate, don't you?"

"Sometimes. I believe in geometry, too."

She cocked her head as if listening to music coming from her glass and looked puzzled. "Meaning?"

"It's why I asked you if you'd been threatened. It wasn't a love triangle, it was a square. And there's one side left."

She bowed her head, then moved a hand to caress her stomach. Swallowed several times noisily. "S'cuse me!" she said, and almost fell off her stool, using it for support while she stood and got her balance. "Might be a little sick . . ."

He watched her stumble on numbed legs toward the restrooms at the rear of the bar. They were only about ten feet away or she might not have made it. The door marked GULLS slammed shut behind her. The other door was marked BUOYS. Carver had seen that a few times in Florida.

She'd left her purse, so he was reasonably certain she wouldn't try to leave through a back exit or window. He wasn't sure if it mattered much anyway. Where could she go?

When she came out of the restroom ten minutes later she was still walking unsteadily and was very pale. The stocky bartender gave her a look. Gave Carver a look.

Carver picked up Maggie's purse from the bar.

"What're you doing?" she asked, leaning with one hand on the bar's padded edge.

He planted his cane and got down off his stool. "I'm gonna drive you home."

"I don't need anyone to do that."

"You do if you want to stay alive."

The bartender leaned over the bar so her black hair hung down over one side of her face. With her sturdy build and lack of makeup, it somehow made her seem ominous. "I can't let you walk outa here and drive, ma'am. It could mean my job, and maybe a lot worse for you."

Maggie looked as if she might argue some more. But she sighed and licked her lips with a disgusted expression, then grabbed her purse from Carver and wove toward the door. Every man at the bar turned to stare. A few of them smiled. Carver followed her.

He thought she might make for her own car and continue to object, but she was waiting for him outside the door, holding her purse clutched to her stomach with both hands. She was swaying slightly and had a look on her face as if she might be nauseated.

"Which?" she said.

Carver pointed to the Olds parked across the street, then gripped her elbow and helped her steer a straight course to the car. She smelled of alcohol and vomit, yet beneath that was an oddly appealing and persistent scent of perfume. Lilacs, Carver thought. He'd had his rough time with alcohol after Laura had left him and he'd been shot, and again after his son had died. He wondered how long Maggie would remain a beautiful woman if she stayed wed to the bottle.

On the highway she fell asleep with her head propped on his shoulder. By the time they'd reached her cottage, she was impossible to rouse.

He climbed out of the car, walked around to the passenger side, and opened the door. He shook Maggie's shoulder, shouted at her.

She blinked at him and smiled, then closed her eyes again.

There was no other way to carry her, walking with a cane. After fishing her keys from her purse, he wrestled her out of the car, slung her over his shoulder, and limped with her to the cottage door. She didn't weigh much, and it was little effort once he'd gotten her up and balanced.

When he'd unlocked the door and opened it he found a light switch and flicked it upward. A lamp on one of the tables came on. He carried Maggie to her bed and laid her down where the dismembered doll had been, then worked her remaining shoe off her nylon-clad foot. The other shoe must have dropped off somewhere between the car and the bed. She moaned in her sleep and rolled onto her side, drawing her knees up as if her stomach ached.

Carver lifted one side of the bedspread and covered her up to the shoulders with it, then returned to the living room.

The missing shoe was on the floor just inside the door. He picked it up and closed the door, then walked back and dropped it beside its mate next to the bed. Maggie hadn't moved and was breathing evenly with her mouth open, making soft little snoring sounds. Her face was unlined, her expression blank. The alcohol had brought her some peace; the price would be paid later.

After walking around the cottage and making sure the sliding glass door and the windows were locked, he placed her purse on the table with the lamp and left, locking the door behind him.

When he reached the highway, he cranked down the Olds's windows and let the wind chase the mingled scent of her from the car's interior.

28

BEVERLY DENTON was eating lunch in the park across from Burnair and Crosley the next afternoon. Carver passed through dozens of foraging pigeons waddling about on the grass and pecking for morsels among the coarse green strands. They took to the air all at once with a great whirring and flapping, causing Beverly to look up from the book she was reading and see him. She smiled, but it was an uncertain smile.

"I thought I might find you here," Carver said, as she glanced at his cane and scooted over on the bench to make room for him. He didn't like that and remained standing.

She put down the sandwich she was eating and closed her paperback book, a Sue Grafton novel. So she was a fan of fictional detectives. "I haven't gotten anyone in trouble, have I?" she asked.

"No. In a roundabout way, you're helping people."

She lifted the sandwich again, then hastily put it back down, as if deciding it would be bad manners to eat in front of him. She was wearing slacks and a matching green blazer, and the same oversized gold hoop earrings she'd had on the last time Carver had seen her. "I guess that means you've learned something about Donna and Mark."

"Nothing conclusive," he said. "But you were right when you told me their deaths should be investigated."

"Do you think they really did commit suicide?"

"I think Donna did. I think Mark was murdered."

She seemed to mull that over, staring out at the traffic on Atlantic Drive, squinting as if the sun hurt her eyes. "What do the police think?" she asked.

"They think it would be more convenient if he committed suicide."

"Just like in books," she said, tapping a fingernail on the glossy cover of the Grafton novel that was almost luminous in the sunlight.

"More like in books than most people think," Carver said.

She smiled at him, with certainty this time. "You're here because you want something from me," she said.

"Yes, just like in books. How long has Maggie Rourke been with Burnair and Crosley?"

"I'm not sure exactly. Less than a year, though."

"She was recommended for her position by a lover she later broke away from. I need to know his name."

"I can't help you there. I never heard of the guy."

"You can help," he said. "You can find out his name."

"Maggie would never tell me, even if I asked."

"No, she wouldn't. But I'm reasonably sure he wrote a letter of reference for her."

Understanding, Beverly tilted back her head and ran her fingers through her short brown hair, causing sun to spark off an earring. "You want me to sneak a look at her personnel file."

"Can you manage it?"

"I think so."

"Will you?"

|185|

"I don't know," she said slowly. "It's risky."

"You're the one who told me the Winships' deaths needed to be investigated. That's what I'm trying to do. It's important that I learn this man's name."

"You've got to understand, I'd lose my job if someone discovered me raiding Personnel's files. They're not locked, but they're supposed to be private."

He wondered for a moment if she was actually fearful or if she might be trying to work some money out of him.

Then she said, "But I'll do it. At least I'll try."

"Thanks. You still got my number?"

"I think so. I'll phone you when I know. *If* I know. You want half a ham sandwich? I'm only going to feed it to those squirrels otherwise."

He accepted the sandwich and sat down for a while beside her on the hard concrete bench, eating and watching the two squirrels she'd referred to edge ever closer to them, moving then posing and giving them sideways glances, seeming to feign disinterest. Finally she laughed and began breaking off pieces of bread and tossing them to the squirrels, who pounced on them voraciously. The pigeons returned but kept their distance. The hierarchy of nature.

Carver finished most of his sandwich, tossed the rest to the pigeons beyond the squirrels, then said good-bye to Beverly. She assured him again that she'd phone him if she found out what he needed to know. She picked up her detective novel and seemed already engrossed in it as he turned away.

After leaving Beverly Denton, Carver drove to Telegraph Road and found a spot to park adjacent to the strip shopping center that contained Nightlinks' offices. He was some distance away, up the road and beyond the vacant and overgrown lot alongside the center. Still, he had a clear enough view of Nightlinks through the foliage.

He got out his Minolta and affixed its 200-millimeter lens, then focused on the area of Nightlinks' entrance.

He spent the next several hours photographing the attractive people who came and went. Nightlinks might have done a lot of business by phone and fax, but someone entered or left the office every twenty minutes or so. Once Harvey Sincliff emerged and walked with a tall, well-dressed man to the Aero Lounge at the other end of the shopping strip. An hour later, the tall man drove away and Sincliff returned alone to Nightlinks while Carver sat in the hot car and watched.

Carver's back began to ache but he continued to keep the camera trained and steady. The Minolta's long lens would provide some good close-up shots. It might be interesting to see if Desoto, Beverly, Maggie, or Ellen Pfitzer would recognize any of the subjects.

Long shots in every sense of the word, Carver thought, rotating the lens to draw a beautiful Latin woman closer and tripping the shutter.

HE'D DROPPED off the film for development and was in his office doing paperwork a few minutes before five o'clock when Beverly Denton phoned.

"Got it, Mr. Carver," she said as soon as he'd picked up the receiver and identified himself. She sounded breathless and proud of herself. Clandestine operations could be addictive. "Maggie was recommended by a man named Charles F. Post. He was a wealthy yacht broker in Palm Beach when he and Maggie were an item. He's not so wealthy now."

"How do you know that?"

"Remember I told you my fiancé Warren refurbishes yachts? Well, when I saw Post was in the boat business I called Warren, and sure enough Warren had heard of him. Post was something of a character, a real charmer and ladies' man even though he was married. And a shrewd businessman. A yankee trader, Warren called him. Post Yacht Sales did millions of dollars in business a year."

"Why past tense?" Carver asked.

"Two reasons. Gambling and divorce. Charlie Post—Warren said everybody called him Charlie—liked to gamble and dropped a lot of money at the dog track and in Atlantic City. Also, last year he and his wife were divorced, and she got most of what he owned."

Carver wondered if the divorce was because of Maggie. Probably, he decided. He could think of worse reasons.

"Did Warren tell you where Post is now?" he asked.

"He didn't know. After the divorce, Post moved out of North Palm Beach. It takes money to keep up with the Joneses there, and he no longer had it."

"What about the wife? She still in Palm Beach?"

"Warren said she was."

"Did he know her name?"

"No, but she should be easy to find. She owns and manages Post Yacht Sales."

"You gave me more than I asked for," Carver said. "Thanks."

"I hope it helps."

"Thank Warren, too," Carver told her.

AFTER HANGING up on Beverly, Carver phoned Post Yacht Sales in Palm Beach and asked to talk with Mrs. Post. He was told she wasn't in, but he did manage to wrangle her first name from the woman on the phone. May. Then he pretended to be an old business associate of Charlie Post and tried to get Post's address. No luck there.

He called Palm Beach information and asked for the number of May Post and was told it was unlisted. So he called Beverly

Denton back and asked if she'd see if Warren could call Post Yacht Sales and get Charlie Post's address, citing unfinished business in the refurbishing of a yacht.

Half an hour later, she called and told him Warren had been successful. Then she gave him an address on Collins Avenue in Miami Beach and the name of a residential hotel.

Carver recognized the hotel as one of the South Beach remnants of the Art Deco era that hadn't yet been gentrified and reopened for tourists. Not exactly a flophouse. Not exactly.

Charlie Post had fallen a long way from North Palm Beach.

29

THE HOTEL MIRANDA on Collins was two buildings south of a gleamingly rehabilitated luxury hotel that was a forerunner of what the "Florida Riviera" was beginning to provide.

Each time Carver came to the area, he marveled at the changes taking place. The crumbling Art Deco buildings were one by one being restored to their former ornate and stylish selves. Entire blocks of forlorn residential hotels that housed the poor and the desperate were becoming high-toned resorts. The poor were moving out. Money was moving in, and gaining momentum the way money did when it became concentrated.

The Hotel Miranda hadn't yet succumbed to the process. It was a faded and mottled green stucco structure five stories high and topped with an ornate neon sign that probably hadn't glowed since the forties. Its wooden window frames, once white and now a muddied cream color, were chipped and peeling. Wide glass double doors, webbed with finely turned wooden framework, formed the entrance. Above them a fan-shaped window bore the name of the hotel in fragmented gold letters. The doors had been painted recently, though not scraped or sanded, and the wood was in slightly better condition than the window frames. The oversized brass hardware was ornate and polished, even if irretrievably tarnished. Carver eased his shoulder into the flat brass push-plate and entered the lobby.

It was dim in the lobby and smelled musty, and the past was almost palpable. He was standing on a black-and-white tiled floor darkened by years and ground-out cigarette butts. Faded green carpet stretched in front of the scarred old registration desk, then up a wide flight of stairs. Beyond the desk were elevators with clocklike brass floor indicators above the doors, fancy arrows that rotated along Roman numerals. One of the elevators had an Out of Order sign taped to its door. It looked as if it had been there since 1967.

Two old women sat in oversized brown vinyl chairs and talked around a dusty artificial fern as if it were the ghost of a husband being snubbed. They glanced at Carver as he made his way to the desk, then resumed their conversation.

The desk clerk was a man of about sixty with a lean, lined face and thinning hair so black it had to be dyed. His unshaven left cheek was concave, as if all the molars on that side were missing. He had on a threadbare blue suit, white shirt, and red tie, a stab at respectability in a hopeless situation.

"Charles Post's room number, please," Carver said. The two old women looked over at him at the mention of Post's name.

"We don't give out our guests' room numbers," the clerk said with a whiff of morning gin. "I can give you Mr. Post's extension and you can phone upstairs to him."

Carver said that was good enough, and the clerk directed him to the house phones that squatted on a gray marble shelf, two yellowed plastic units without dials or punch pads.

Charlie Post answered on the second ring and didn't even bother to ask why Carver wanted to talk to him. He seemed eager for company and invited him up to his fifth-floor room.

He was standing with the door open when Carver stepped off the elevator. Though he was at least in his midseventies, he was still a handsome man, with erect posture, broad shoulders, silver hair, and a waistline that had spread but was under control. He was wearing pleated brown pants, a blue-striped white shirt open at the collar, and a navy blue ascot.

"Charlie Post," he said with a creased and handsome smile as Carver moved within handshaking range.

Carver introduced himself and shook Post's cool, dry hand, wondering if after a certain age people stopped perspiring.

Post stepped back and waved an arm in a reserved yet gracious motion for Carver to enter. He didn't smell of age, like a lot of old people; there was about him the scent of soap and shampoo. Not perfumed, though; some brand of masculine cologne Carver couldn't place. Carver saw that Post's thick gray hair was still damp in back from his morning bath or shower.

"I can offer you coffee," he said in his firm, amiable voice.

The room was large, well worn but comfortable, with a double bed with a white spread, dark mahogany dresser and wardrobe, and the same green carpet that was in the lobby and hall. A window was open about six inches and white sheer curtains undulated softly in the slight breeze that pushed its way in. The room was clean and filled with the scent of fresh-perked coffee sitting on a hotplate on a small table near the bed. A clear glass cup of black coffee on a chipped saucer sat on a low table in front of a brown sofa with ball-and-claw legs.

Carver declined coffee, and Post waved him into a well-padded if threadbare wing chair, then sat down on the sofa. He looked smilingly and inquisitively at Carver, waiting for whatever it was Carver wanted to say. It occurred to Carver that anyone selling anything could have gained entrance as easily as he had, and he wondered how naive Post had become in his not-so-golden years.

He said, "I'm here to ask you about Maggie Rourke."

Post's smile faded and for an instant was replaced by an expression of hope. Carver recognized the look, the dreamer dreaming the dream. "Maggie, huh?" Post said. He seemed lost in memory for a few seconds. The sound of traffic down on Collins drifted into the room with the breeze. "That Maggie . . . You know where she is?"

"Don't you?"

"No, she left my life the way she entered it—like a visiting angel."

Surprised, Carver said, "That's poetic."

"Maggie's the kind of woman that inspires poetry."

Carver didn't argue. "Your former wife May told me I might find you here," he said, bending the truth a little.

Charlie Post sipped coffee, then placed the cup back in its saucer, clinking glass against china. His hand was trembling. "May inspires things other than poetry." Carver wondered if the trembling hand was the result of his mentioning Maggie, or May. Or maybe it was simply due to advancing age. Seemingly in complete control of his emotions again, Post pretended to examine his fingernails, as if to demonstrate to himself and to Carver that his hand was now steady, and said, "May took everything I owned. My business, my home, my old life."

"Was the divorce because of Maggie?"

"Oh, yes and no. May knew I was seeing someone else, even had us followed and obtained . . . er, indelicate photographs of us. But the truth was, Maggie wasn't the first of my indiscretions, and May knew it. I won't say May drove me to infidelity; it's never that simple. I'm a man who should never have married. I love beautiful women the way I love beauty in nature and in the line of a fine ship. So I suppose it wasn't entirely May's fault. I've always liked the opposite sex, and they've always appreciated my appreciating them."

"Was Maggie named as corespondent in the divorce?"

"No. Maggie dropped out of sight the day after we were

photographed in the stateroom of a yacht. She couldn't stand what she knew was coming, the embarrassment and shame. I wasn't about to give out her name, and May never learned it. Actually that worked in May's favor, that I seemed not even to know the name of the woman in the photographs, like I was a real lowlife who went to bed with anyone on short notice. One-night-stand Charlie. That's how she painted me, anyway. It tilted things even more in her direction in court. So Maggie had nothing to do with the actual divorce proceedings, but she would have if I'd fought May. I was glad when Maggie disappeared. I mean, the thought of those photographs being made public. I couldn't have that, so I was hobbled in the divorce negotiations despite the slickest attorneys I could buy. May cleaned me out."

"And you've never seen Maggie since?"

"Nope. We had an arrangement we both understood. I know she wasn't heart-throbbing in love with me, but I thought eventually she might be. We talked about my leaving May, but I think Maggie figured that's all it really was, just talk and wishful thinking. So she broke it off the quickest, cleanest way possible." He smiled, his blue eyes clouding. "Still, I'd like to see her once more, tell her everything's all right between us."

"*Is* it all right?" Carver asked. "I mean, your former wife has everything you owned."

"Sure. But on a certain level—the important level—I don't regret what happened. I know what you're thinking: For love of a woman a kingdom was lost. I'll tell you, Carver, Maggie was worth it. And at that point in my marriage, May really didn't care that I was being unfaithful. Hell, she probably only married me for my money in the first place. After a while, we didn't love each other at all and didn't mind saying so when we argued. Which was often, until we got tired even of that. Then along came Maggie." He sipped more coffee and looked wistful. His hand was still steady. "Sometimes, Carver, you have to grab life

| 194 |

by the balls and live it and damn the consequences. Maggie wasn't like the others. I knew right away she was a one-time thing for me, maybe a last chance at the grand prize. I admit I became obsessed. She was the whole unimagined world and I wanted her, and for a short time she was mine. Whatever I've lost because of it, I say it was worth it and I'd do it again."

Carver thought about that, then said, "I see what you mean."

"Do you really?"

"I'm afraid so."

"Liberating, ain't it," Post said, grinning hugely.

Carver laughed.

"Not so long ago I was one of the most successful businessmen on the Gold Coast, now here I am and I'm not complaining. Know why?"

"You just told me," Carver reminded him. "Maggie."

"Maggie, all right, but also the fact that this pisshole isn't my last stop. Nothing can whip me but time, and it hasn't yet. I've been getting in touch with some of my old contacts, raising capital. I've lost more than one fortune, Carver, and made them back. And I'll bounce back from this loss, too. Bet on it."

"If I could afford it," Carver said, "I would bet on you." He shifted his weight and leaned his cane against his chair arm, thinking age hadn't robbed Post of his deviousness and charm. "Did you ever come in contact with anyone named Enrico Thomas or Carl Gretch?"

Post didn't even have to think about it. "Nope."

"Beni Ho?"

"Sounds like a restaurant. Oriental fella, I assume. Nope, never heard of him, either."

"Your ex-wife May," Carver said, "does she know how to manage Post Yacht Sales?"

"Oh, sure. May's wicked smart. That's how she nicked me for damn near everything I had."

Carver thought, Some nick. He said, "Maggie told me you wrote her a letter of reference, got her a position at Burnair and Crosley in Del Moray."

Charlie Post glanced sideways at Carver and grinned like a kid caught in a schoolyard lie. "Did she now?"

"I thought you told me you didn't know what happened to her after she left you," Carver said.

"I said such a thing?"

"Sure did. Not five minutes ago."

"Well, let's just say I was protecting her privacy. It is true I've never seen her since the night of those photographs. She phoned about two weeks later though, asking for help after she lost her job in the brokerage firm where she was an account executive. She was desperate, even doing part-time work modeling. That didn't sound like her at all, though she sure had the looks. Well, I'd done plenty of business with Burnair and Crosley, and Ken Crosley was an old friend of mine. So I wrote a letter of reference for Maggie and they made an opening for her. I tried phoning her there a few times, but I was always told she wasn't in."

"So you did know where to find her, but you never tried to see her."

"That's true. Because I know when something's ended, Carver. Much as I don't like it, I can swallow it. That's one of the best things to know in life, when something's over. Even better'n recognizing opportunity when it knocks. Keeps you outa lots of trouble."

Carver didn't know what to believe. Post was a disarming conniver and equally persuasive about both sides of a story. It was easy to understand how he had his way with women.

"I figured Del Moray was small and out of the way enough that she wouldn't be bothered. She still there, Carver?"

"Sure. Even if she won't accept your calls."

Charlie Post shrugged and smiled, a high roller accepting his losses gracefully. "I guess she knows when things are ended, too. I've got no hard feeling or second thoughts. I had my time in heaven and I'm just passing through on my way to nothingness, like you and everybody else."

Carver leaned his weight on his cane and stood up out of the overstuffed chair. His back ached from sitting in the thing, even though it had seemed comfortable. "Thanks for your time," he told Post.

The handsome old man pursed his lips and studied him. "You going to talk with May?"

"If I can."

"Don't believe anything she tells you, Carver. May's a liar." He said that with a face that could bluff at poker.

"If she contradicts anything you told me," Carver said, "I'll know she's fibbing."

As he moved toward the door, Post said, "Don't let her sell you a boat."

|30|

CARVER PARKED beside Beth's car outside his cottage.

As he walked toward the plank front porch, he wiped perspiration from his face with the tail of his pullover shirt and was glad to hear the air conditioner droning away. Beth wasn't bothered much by heat and often only opened the windows on some of the hottest, most humid days of summer.

It was cool inside. She was sitting at the breakfast counter, eating a sandwich and using her laptop Toshiba. A Budweiser can and a glass half full of beer sat beside the computer.

Carver peeled off his perspiration-soaked shirt and went into the bathroom.

"Hot, lover?" she asked, not looking up from her computer.

He didn't answer. Instead he splashed cold water over his face. He felt water drip and run down his forearms and bare chest. Some of it made it down his ridged stomach and felt cool beneath his waistband. He ran more cold water over his wrists, holding them beneath the tap for several minutes. Then he toweled his face and chest dry and returned to the cottage's main area. Though the air conditioner was on, a window was open and the sound of the surf dashing itself on the beach infiltrated the cottage.

"I figured you'd turn up soon," Beth said, "so I switched on the air conditioner just for you."

"Thoughtful," he said, and got another Budweiser out from behind some very old barbecued chicken in the refrigerator. He carried the beer to the sofa, sat down and rolled the cold curvature of the can back and forth on his forehead, then gazed out at the ocean. A few white triangles of sails were banked at identical angles. Beyond them, far in the sun-hazed distance, was what appeared to be a cruise ship. Nothing out there seemed to be moving; maybe it was too hot. Behind him, Carver could hear Beth's fingers clicking and clacking the computer's keyboard with amazing speed. It sounded like a maniac abusing a typewriter inside a padded room.

He said, "I thought you were finished with your mail-order-scam story."

"I am. This is a telephone boiler room piece," she said, continuing to play the computer's keys. "It'll expose some of those jerks who are talking the old folks out of their ready cash. Some of the people involved in the phony mail-order business are mixed up in this. That's how I got onto it. It's like a web full of spiders."

"Gonna send any of them to jail?"

"Hope so."

"That'll just leave more helpless flies for the televangelists," he told her.

"You're too cynical, Fred."

"I've been told."

After she relayed her story via modem to the *Burrow* offices, she sat down next to Carver on the sofa, leaned back, and extended her legs, as if her muscles were stiff from sitting a long time at her computer. She was wearing black shorts and a red halter that didn't do much of a job restraining her breasts. Carver didn't mind. Her feet were bare. The black leather sandals she'd been wearing were lying upside down on the floor next to her crossed ankles. They were the kind with soles made from tire treads and were probably good for another thirty thousand miles.

"I still haven't heard anything on Dredge Industries," she said. "I've got Jeff Mehling working on it."

Mehling was *Burrow's* resident computer genius. He'd helped Carver before, but they'd never met. Beth had told him Mehling mainly communicated with friends via electronic mail. Carver hadn't wanted to hear any more about that.

"Jeff told me he'd have something soon," Beth went on. "He's still experimenting, finding his way into various data banks."

Carver wondered if the government knew about Mehling.

Beth laced her fingers behind her head, inhaled deeply as she stretched her long body, and gave him a sloe-eyed glance. "You talk to Post?"

Not looking at her breasts, he told her about the conversation with Charlie Post at the Hotel Miranda in Miami Beach.

"Pussy broke," Beth said. "That's how some people I know used to describe Post's condition. And some men'll go out and find the wrong woman and do it all again. It's a masochistic thing with them, giving up their money for love."

"Post didn't strike me as masochistic."

"Nobody's how they strike people, Fred. You oughta know that."

Then he told her about stopping briefly in Palm Beach on the drive up the coast. May Post hadn't been in her office at Post Yacht Sales, and she hadn't answered her home phone.

"Why didn't you hang around until she showed up?" Beth asked.

"Because the office workers were frantically finalizing arrangements for a party that night on a yacht they had listed to sell, the *Stedda Work*. Woman in the office who was calling to check on the caterer explained to me that was how they showed some of their yachts to prospective clients. Like a floating open house with booze and hors d'oeuvres."

"And May Post is sure to be on board," Beth said, her head resting back so she was staring now at the ceiling. "It's a pretty smart tactic, getting the rich sales prospects liquored up and maybe bidding against each other."

"Charlie Post told me May was smart."

They both were quiet for a while, listening to the low hum of the air conditioner and the soft rush of the surf. Not far away outside a gull cried. Beth idly moved a bare foot over and rested painted toes on Carver's moccasin. He could feel the pressure of each individual toe through the supple leather.

She said, "I'm assuming you're going to drive back to Palm Beach tonight and crash the party."

"No. I'll be there as a guest. I managed to pick up a few unused invitations when no one was looking."

"A few?" She sounded interested.

Carver said, "We'll have to look as if we belong with the Palm Beach set and could afford a yacht or two. Got something suitable to wear?"

"Don't worry," she told him, "I'll be the richiest and the bitchiest. But you I'll have to supervise, Fred. When you get dressed up you look like a gangster."

31

THE *STEDDA WORK* was, according to a color brochure available at the foot of the gangplank, a 94-foot Broward Motoryacht built in 1985. It was a beautiful white vessel with red trim, three luxury staterooms, two salons, an on-deck galley, a 170-bottle wine cooler, a teak swimstep with stairs and transom door, and a range of 3,000 miles so you could get far away from land and enjoy it all without being disturbed.

All of this could be had for only 2.3 million dollars, described in the brochure as a bargain reduced price. Since it was a reduced price offer, Carver considered it for a few seconds before pushing it out of his mind.

Ushering Beth before him, he handed his two invitations to an attractive and smiling blond woman in a blue yachting outfit, then limped up the canopy-covered gangplank to where a dozen or so people were wandering about the deck holding drinks and helping themselves to hors d'oeuvres offered by white-coated waiters balancing silver trays. It was, as Carver had suspected, a well-turned-out crowd devoid of polyester. Most of the men and not a few women turned to appraise Beth as she and Carver boarded. She was wearing a simple black dress with laced sleeves, a jade necklace and pin, black high heels. She looked like a princess. Carver looked like a gangster in his black slacks, pearl shirt with black and gray tie, and gray silk double-breasted sport coat, but he figured that was okay; it was something these people understood.

A waiter with a tray of champagne in tall continental glasses approached them. The glasses looked like expensive crystal, Carver noted, as he and Beth helped themselves. The champagne had the taste of fizzy old bank notes. Carver liked it.

He and Beth nodded to a few people who glanced at them as if they might know them, then they made their way toward the stern where more guests were lounging about and chatting. Carver noticed one of the women he'd seen that morning in the Post Yacht Sales office, but she was busy smiling and talking to a fat man in a gray suit and didn't have eyes for anyone else. Carver didn't try to avoid her. Even if she did recognize him, she'd probably figure he'd made contact with May Post and been invited.

Beth nodded and smiled at an elderly man who nodded and smiled at her. There was a lot of nodding and smiling all around. A lot of quiet calculation.

Beth sipped champagne and said, "This is a great vessel, Fred. You think we should make an offer?"

"What we should do," he said, "is find May Post."

"What does she look like?"

"I don't know. I've never seen her."

"No matter," Beth said. "She's the hostess and should be easy to spot. She'll be smiling too much and moving too fast." She swirled her remaining champagne around in her glass. "Isn't that a certain U.S. Senator?" she said, nodding toward a handsome gray-haired man talking to a man and woman near the rail.

"Probably."

Beth said, "Excuse me, Fred," and started toward the man.

"Where are you going?" Carver asked, knowing where and not liking it. She acted as if she hadn't heard.

The party had been going for a while. Music suddenly came over the yacht's sound system. Laughter and conversation became louder. Carver watched Beth talking earnestly to the Senator, who seemed to be listening just as earnestly. Over near the opposite rail, he saw an elderly woman standing with her arm around a handsome young man in his twenties, not in a motherly way. Carver thought he'd seen the man at Nightlinks the day he'd photographed people entering and leaving. It would be interesting to look at the prints when they came back from the lab. Conversation continued buzzing around him. Two men waving drinks at each other were talking about bow thrusters. Carver didn't know what a bow thruster was, but this boat probably had one. Or was it a ship? Someone had once told him that a ship was any vessel large enough to carry a boat. The *Stedda Work* qualified. "Talk to May," a woman's voice said somewhere near him. "She's in the Blue Salon."

Carver decided to follow that advice, even though it had been meant for someone else.

With a final glance at Beth and the Senator, who were both laughing now like old chums discussing schoolday pranks, Carver made his way below deck.

Outside sounds were nonexistent there, but the music and conversation were louder. Shuffling along a narrow companionway, he squeezed past a heavyset woman in a sequined blue dress, traded his empty champagne glass for a full one as a white-coated waiter with a tray squeezed past him, and found the salon. It was crowded with people watching a card game, and it was red.

A man with a dead cigar in his mouth looked over at Carver and grinned. "You a gambler, sport?"

"No, just looking for the Blue Salon," Carver explained.

"Above deck," the man said around the cigar, then returned to watching the game, which was seven-card stud. "I raise you back," a woman said firmly, as Carver edged away.

The Blue Salon was above deck and lined with windows that looked out over the party on deck and the lights of the marina. It wasn't as crowded as the Red Salon. Most of the guests there were clustered around a small bar where the woman who'd collected invitations was now dispensing drinks. The sound system had been turned off and the music seeped in softly from the rest of the yacht, heavy with violins, pleasant at lower volume.

Moving closer to the bar, Carver braced himself with his cane and stood pretending to gaze out the window, actually studying the reflections of the guests in the salon and eavesdropping on their conversation. Within a few minutes he heard a woman seated on a plush window seat referred to as May.

He turned around and looked closely at her. Beneath a tight sequined red dress her body was thin enough to hint at anorexia. Her short hair had been dyed blond too often and was stiffly arranged so it angled sharply over one of her penciled eyebrows. She had a long, bony face that held a kind of angular attractiveness. As she crossed her legs, she noticed Carver staring at her. Quickly she drew on the cigarette she was holding and turned her attention back to the sincere-looking middle-aged man seated beside her. He puffed on a pipe and listened. Carver noticed for the first time that most of the people around him held cigarettes. Apparently Blue was the smoking salon, which accounted for the dead cigar in the mouth of the cardplayer below deck.

When the man with the pipe stood up and walked away, Carver approached May Post.

She smiled up at him with the kind of almost genuine, high-voltage smile seen on virtually everyone who sold expensive merchandise. For all she knew, Carver was a potential buyer. She couldn't know everyone she'd invited.

"Make the deal?" he asked.

The smile didn't quite disappear. "Hardly. That was Jason Orondo, my sales manager." She drew on her cigarette, exhaled slowly, and studied him through the haze with a smoker's narrowed eyes. He could tell he didn't set quite right with her, though for the moment she couldn't figure him out. Her eyes said she knew he wasn't Palm Beach, though; that was for sure.

He gave her his own warmest smile. "Care to talk about something other than yachts?"

Melting but still wary, she met his eyes and said, "Okay. Unless you're from the Internal Revenue Service."

He laughed and sipped his champagne. Debonair Carver. "Nothing like that, I assure you."

"They can be sneaky."

"It's a sneaky world," he said sadly, "full of misdirection."

"Then do be direct."

"I'm a private investigator and I'd like to talk to you about Charlie Post."

She looked thoughtful. "Charlie? Is he being investigated?"

"Not really. He's on the periphery. I'm looking into a couple of deaths up in Del Moray."

"Homicides?"

"Maybe."

She grinned, liking that. "Charlie's capacity to get into trouble knows no limits."

"He told me you divorced him because he was unfaithful."

"He was wrong. I divorced him because I was tired of him. He happened to be going out with some bimbo at the time, and that was convenient. I hired somebody like you to follow him. Charlie and the bimbo were photographed in a compromising position, not to mention an uncomfortable one."

"Who was she?"

"Just the latest in a long line of women with big boobs and round heels. She ran out on Charlie the next day. It was a one-night stand that didn't work out well. Even he didn't know her name, and I'd never seen her before. Charlie wasn't particular when his worm was wriggling. Probably she was some waitress he picked up. It didn't matter that she probably couldn't have been found even if we'd searched; we had the photographs. Most of the divorce agreement took place out of court." She caught something in the corner of her vision, smiled and waved across the room at someone, then looked back up at Carver. "Charlie knew I didn't love him, Mr. . . . ?"

"Carver."

"He knew I didn't love him and was going to leave him sooner or later. He didn't love me, either. He did everything but ask me to leave. Finally I got sick of him and I obliged." She smiled again, but not in the way she had at her guest across the room. "Is that direct enough?"

"Sure is. So you don't think Charlie took the other woman seriously."

"Of course he didn't. Charlie never took any woman seriously except for an hour at a time. Plenty of them, though. He's got more energy than any man his age I've ever met; I'll give him that much."

"Was it a fair divorce?"

"I think so. Doesn't Charlie?"

"He didn't mention."

She sucked hard on her cigarette, using it for a prop, then turned her head to the side and exhaled a long trail of smoke as she stood up. He was surprised by how tall she was. She seemed even thinner than she'd appeared sitting down. "I think we just stopped being candid with each other," she said, looking down at him.

He shrugged. "Sorry. It always happens."

"It's been a pleasure talking to you, Mr. Carver. Explore the yacht. Enjoy the rest of the evening." She turned and began walking from the salon.

He said, "Would you consider a million and a half?"

She didn't look back.

"WHAT DID you say to the Senator?" Carver asked Beth as they sped north on the Florida Turnpike toward Del Moray. He was driving but they were in her car. It put in a better appearance than the Olds.

"I thanked him. He gets little enough of that. What did May Post say to you?"

"Pretty much the same thing Charlie Post told me."

"So now you know Post isn't a complete liar."

"The best liars are never complete. That's why what they say smacks of the truth."

"True enough."

They drove for a while in silence, listening to the tires tick over seams in the pavement. Then Carver glanced over at Beth and said, "You were the most stunningly attractive woman on the boat."

She moved close to him, kissed his ear, and said, "What were you doing looking at every other woman on board?"

"Part of my work."

"That's a lie."

"Not completely."

"You don't have to sweet-talk me, Fred."

That was true.

Partly.

|32|

WHILE CARVER swam the next morning, Beth drove into Del Moray to pick up the photographs of Nightlinks clientele. She'd left before he'd gone into the sea, and she'd already returned by the time he'd showered away salt water along with oil from the offshore freighters and dressed.

She was seated on a stool at the breakfast bar. Before her were two coffee cups, a box of doughnuts, and the fat white envelope containing the photographs.

Carver saw that her cup was full. He went to the Braun brewer and poured coffee into the cup she'd set out for him. Then he sat down on the stool diagonally across the counter from her.

"Bought glazed," she said.

"Good." He opened the box and withdrew one of half a dozen glazed doughnuts. Took a generous bite out of it, then set it down on a piece of the opaque paper that doughnut shops used because for some reason iced and sugar-coated doughnuts didn't stick to the stuff. The doughnut was fresh and still warm.

Beth took a bite out of another doughnut, brushed sugar and icing from her hands, then very deftly opened the envelope in a way that wouldn't get it sticky. Carver sipped coffee and watched her thumb through the stack of photographs with equal dexterity. When she was halfway through, she gave him the ones she had seen.

The camera and lens had worked well. Though blurred foliage in the foreground spoiled some of the shots, in most of them the unknowing subjects were framed as tightly as if the camera had been only a few feet from them.

"Nice-looking folks," Beth said, still studying the photos. "I guess you gotta be a looker to work as a paid escort."

"It can't hurt," Carver said.

Beth examined some more photos, then said, "Hey! This guy."

Carver looked up at her.

"This guy right here." She laid a photograph on the counter.

It was a shot of Harvey Sincliff and another man walking toward the Aero Lounge.

"I saw him enter and leave Gretch's apartment building more than once," Beth said. Her long red fingernail tapped the image of Sincliff rather than his companion. A flake of glazed icing dropped from her finger onto the photo.

"You sure?"

"He was there at least twice," Beth said. "I didn't actually see him with Gretch, but Gretch was home each time he was in the building. I made a note of that, but didn't think it was important. For all I knew he was there to see somebody else. Maybe even lived there." She leaned forward and blew the flake of icing from the photo. "Who is he?"

"Harvey Sincliff. He owns Nightlinks."

"Oh. Well, Gretch worked for him as an escort. Maybe that's why he was there to see him."

"Sincliff told me he knew Gretch as Enrico Thomas, and

then only slightly. Didn't even recall who he was until I prodded his memory. He also told me he hadn't seen Gretch in months."

"I guess he lied, then," Beth said around a bite of doughnut. "No surprise. Question is why."

Carver finished his doughnut, then ate another one, pondering that question.

"Maybe there's more to Nightlinks than just an escort service," Beth said.

"There is. Sincliff is into prostitution, but it's difficult to prove."

"I took that for granted. Most escort services are fronts for prostitution. I mean, maybe there's even more to it than that."

"Any ideas?"

"No. But people have died, Fred. It might be worth finding out Sincliff's real connection with Gretch, and what, if anything, Nightlinks has to do with it."

He'd been thinking about the best way to do that. "Busy tonight?" he asked.

"Last night was fun," Beth said. "What have you got planned for tonight?"

"We follow some of the escorts, see who they meet, where they go, what they do."

She washed down a final bite of doughnut with coffee. "The 'what they do' part shouldn't be difficult."

Carver said, "I'm more interested in the who and where. And the why."

"There might be something in this for a *Burrow* piece," Beth said. "Following Nightlinks escorts could serve more than one purpose."

Carver said, "Too much in life serves more than one purpose, has more than one face."

Beth swiveled off her stool, stood at the sink, and poured the rest of her cooling coffee down the drain. "Maybe Donna learned that too late," she said.

. . .

AFTER BREAKFAST, Carver left Beth to her *Burrow* work and drove into Del Moray. He managed to see Ellen Pfitzer at the country club. Between sets of tennis she looked carefully at the Nightlinks photographs. She told Carver she recognized no one. If she was lying, nothing about her gave her away.

He watched her bounce and struggle through a few games of the next set. Her opponent was a lanky woman in her fifties who went to the net too soon and too often, possibly because the sun was obviously making her suffer.

Ellen was winning one of life's battles and having a good time as Carver waved goodbye and went back to the Olds.

After phoning Beverly Denton and setting up another meeting in the park across from Burnair and Crosley for that afternoon, he drove to his office and checked his messages.

A woman whose missing daughter he'd located last year called to thank him again and assure him her check for final payment was in the mail. The realty company that managed the building where his office was located called to ask him why the rent check he'd assured them was in the mail hadn't yet reached them.

McGregor had left the same message twice, instructions for Carver to call him back without delay. At least Carver assumed he was "Dick-head," since the message was on his machine.

McGregor had nothing if not timing. Carver was reaching for the phone when the towering lieutenant strode into the office. The way he acted, it was possible he'd just bought the building.

"I left a message to call me back, dick-head," McGregor said. "Where you been?"

"Swimming, eating doughnuts. You should knock. You're liable to charge through a door someday into new construction, step on a nail."

"Knock you on your ass is what I'm liable to do. I thought I better drive over here and see you personally. You don't possess the etiquette gene. It's possible you might not have returned my call."

"I was about to do just that," Carver said honestly. It felt strange, being honest with McGregor.

"Sure, sure," McGregor said with his lewd grin. "Probably you been fucking your jungle bunny all morning and you was about to call her and tell her you loved her."

"It's good you're in police work, with all your sensitivity."

"You're such a politically correct fuck-head yourself." McGregor hitched up his wrinkled pants and glowered down at Carver. The usual funk that emanated from him hung in the air from when his suitcoat had flapped open with the extension of his elbows. "It's actually last night I'm interested in," he said. "I had no idea you were such a party animal, knew so many rich and important people."

"Old friends, most of them."

"Don't bullshit me. You and your dark meat were trespassing there. You crashed the party for a reason. And don't tell me you were thinking about buying that yacht."

"There was no way to crash that party," Carver said. "It was by invitation only, and they checked all the guests at the gangplank. You know that, otherwise you would have been on board scarfing down free food and liquor. The truth is, an old friend of Beth's knew somebody who used to crew on the yacht, and he gave her a couple of invitations to repay a favor."

"Yeah?" McGregor didn't sound convinced. "What's this old friend's name?"

"I'm not sure. His friends call him Ishmael."

McGregor wrote that down in his leather-covered notebook. "Last name?"

"I don't know. He tells everyone just to call him Ishmael."

"Black guy, I'll bet."

"No. Why?"

"Sounds like one of those black basketball players that change their names. Something about religion."

"He's tall enough. He might be."

"What? A basketball player?"

"Religious."

McGregor slapped his notepad shut and shoved it into his pocket. "I heard enough of your smart-ass chatter, Carver. You remembering to call me whenever you learn something?"

"You bet."

McGregor waited for Carver to say more. Carver didn't.

After several seconds, McGregor took a few long paces, then stood squarely facing Carver, closer to the desk than before. "Know what worries me, piss-for-gray-matter?"

"Yeah. Connections. You probably noticed Beth talking with the Senator."

"Senator?" McGregor faded back a step.

"What worries you is the fact that I might know somebody well who was at that party, and that the muscle that goes with money might be dangerous to you if you fuck up so close to promotion time."

McGregor probed between his front teeth with his tongue, then smiled. "Well, you're smarter than you look, but stupid at that." Gone was the smile. "Sure, I get nervous automatically when there's that kinda money involved. I been corrupted for so much less. But if you do me wrong, Carver, money and influence won't bring you back to life."

Carver got the Nightlinks photographs from a desk drawer and laid them on the desk. "Know any of these people?"

McGregor picked up the photos and looked through them. "The ugly one's Harvey Sincliff. Owns Nightlinks escort service." He dropped the photos back on the desk so they landed in a jumble. "Sincliff involved with the Winship suicides?"

"Maybe. Donna Winship was going out with a guy who used to do escort work for Sincliff."

"What guy?" McGregor asked. "Give me a name."

"Enrico Thomas."

"So Donna and Mark were going out on each other. He was porking the Rourke woman and wifey was hiring an escort. Ain't a woman alive won't fuck around on her husband if the timing's right."

"She didn't hire Thomas as an escort," Carver said. "She didn't even know he worked for Nightlinks. His main profession was working as a photographer's model. He's in catalogs, cigarette ads, that kind of thing."

"So she got tired of hubby and went for some guy with looks and a bigger dick."

"Could be," Carver said, letting McGregor's imagination roam.

"That it?" McGregor asked. "That's all you know?"

"So far."

McGregor cleared his throat noisily. Carver thought he was going to spit on the floor, but he swallowed instead. "I don't believe that for a second, Carver. Even a dim bulb like you has had enough time to figure out more than what you just told me."

"Well, it's your job to be skeptical."

McGregor ran his tongue around the inside of his cheek for a while, as if seeking morsels from his last meal. Carver had seen him do that before when he was thinking hard. "Carver, you get something on Harvey Sincliff and maybe you and I can be friends for about two seconds. Everybody knows he's into prostitution, but it's tough to nail him, what with the setup he's got and the dumb-ass Constitution always getting in the way. Running an escort service isn't against the law."

"If he shows up dirty and it can be proved despite the Constitution," Carver said, "I'll let you know."

"Let me know what you were really doing at that swank party sometime, too," McGregor said.

"I'll do better than that. Next time I'll make sure you get invited."

McGregor wasn't sure if Carver was kidding, so he played it safe and didn't reply. He placed his palms flat on the desk and leaned close enough for Carver to smell his fetid breath. "This has been a productive little visit, despite your lies. We'll talk more often, and you better have more to say."

He straightened up in sections, the way extremely tall men do, then turned around and walked out of the office.

Carver sat for a few minutes, then decided he'd leave, too. Any room was unpleasant for a while after McGregor had been in it. He seemed to taint the air wherever he went.

Grabbing his cane from where it leaned against the wall, Carver stood up. After erasing his messages, he left the office. Possibly he'd be lucky and not see McGregor for a few days, he thought, locking the door behind him.

But he knew it wouldn't be much longer than that. He'd only tossed McGregor so much meat to chew on.

|33|

BEVERLY DENTON had only a few minutes to spare that afternoon. Burnair and Crosley were in the middle of a market upturn prompted by a drop in interest rates, and employees were taking abbreviated lunch hours. Standing in the shade of the palms in the pocket-sized park on Atlantic Drive, she examined the photographs Carver had handed her, going through them slowly, but she recognized none of the men or women who'd frequented Nightlinks.

"Was this important?" she asked, giving the photos back to him. Her tone of voice suggested she thought she had let him down by not knowing any of the subjects.

"It could be a help that you *didn't* recognize any of these faces," he told her, no doubt easing her regret but adding to her confusion. Not a bad trade, Carver thought. Unless you were in the business of clearing up confusion.

She glanced over at two young boys climbing on the jungle gym under the supervision of a woman dressed as a nurse, then smiled at him.

"Thanks to you and your fiancé," he said, "I found Charlie Post and was able to talk with him."

"Warren tells me Post is a real womanizer, a kind of charming swashbuckler entrepreneur."

"That's how he came across, all right."

"You have an interesting line of work," she said, "meet interesting people."

"Yes, I'm here talking to you."

She laughed, then looked across the street at the gleaming vertical planes of Burnair and Crosley with something like trepidation. "I better get back. The place is a zoo today. The market's in a rally and nobody wants to be left behind."

"Does that happen often?"

"About as often as when the market's falling and nobody wants to fall with it."

"Aren't you going to have lunch?"

"I already ate a sandwich at my desk." She turned to cross the street, then said, "I hope you find whoever killed Mark Winship."

"Probably it's the same person who killed Carl Gretch."

"Carl Gretch?"

"Enrico Thomas."

She looked at him blankly. They'd never talked much about Donna Winship, mostly Mark. "Thomas was Donna's extramarital friend."

Beverly's eyes widened. "And he was murdered?"

"Beaten to death by an interesting person."

"Jesus!" It was the first time he'd heard her use profanity. It surprised him. "That's proof somebody's trying to conceal the reasons for Mark and Donna's deaths."

"Maybe not proof," Carver said, "but strong indication." He wanted to keep her there a few more minutes, though he wasn't quite sure why. It was as if some part of him sensed she knew something he must learn. He used to think disdainfully of people who acted on instinct, but now he knew it could be as useful as logic. "How has Maggie Rourke been acting?"

"Maggie? Normally enough, though she seems to be under a lot of stress. There was some kind of minor fuss at work this morning, I think."

"Fuss?"

"I heard somebody came in and wanted to talk to Maggie but she refused to see him. He raised a bit of a ruckus, then went away quietly. At first I thought it might have been you, but nobody mentioned the man walked with a cane, and it didn't seem like your style anyway."

"It wasn't me. Do you know anything else about him?"

"No, this was just something I heard mentioned in the rest-room. That's the kind of thing that happens to women who look like Maggie; they have their admirers, men who become obsessed."

"It upsets lives," Carver said. "At least she's working today."

Beverly grinned. "Everybody's working today." She tapped her wristwatch with a fingernail. "Which reminds me."

"Okay," Carver said, "thanks again."

"Anytime, Mr. Carver. I read the papers, catch the news on TV or the car radio. I'd like to see some justice for a change."

He watched her wait for a break in traffic, shifting her weight from one leg to another like a marathon runner eager for the gun. Then she hurried on her high heels across Atlantic Drive to be reflected and distorted and absorbed by the glimmering mirror-angled building that loomed like a tribute to the sun.

Some justice for a change, he thought, driving back to his office.

Maybe this time.

A DUSTY blue Ford with rental plates was in the shady space where Carver usually parked. Annoying. Shaded parking slots were at a premium in Florida. He pulled into a slot several cars down and climbed out of the Olds.

He was plodding through the sun, feeling heat working through the thin soles of his moccasins, when he noticed someone sitting behind the Ford's steering wheel.

Nearing the car, he saw the head of thick silver hair and recognized Charlie Post.

Post was slumped with his head bowed, as if trying to figure out the car's controls. He must have caught a glimpse of Carver in the corner of his vision, because he raised his head suddenly. For an instant there was fear in his eyes, then he grinned in relief. There was something wrong with him. When Carver got within a few feet of the car, he saw that one of Post's eyes was swollen almost shut and a thin trickle of blood had wormed from his nose to meet his upper lip.

As Carver opened the Ford's door, Post said, "Had a minor altercation." His clothes—gray slacks, white shirt, same blue ascot as in Miami—looked whole and unwrinkled, suggesting no injuries beneath.

"Can you walk okay, Charlie?"

"Sure. Just been sitting here waiting for you."

"Come on into the office where it's cool."

Carver tried to help him out of the car, but Post refused his proffered hand and stood up by himself.

He was shaky for only a moment, leaning with his hand on the car roof until he gained his balance. "Damned heat," he said. "Good for you only if you're an orange."

Walking near each other, but refusing to lean on each other for help, the old man who'd been beaten and the man with the cane walked through the sweltering tropical heat into Carver's office.

It was plenty cool in there. "Sit down, Charlie." Carver rolled his vinyl-padded swivel chair out from behind the desk for Post. Then he sat on the edge of the desk and waited until the injured man was situated.

Post seemed to realize for the first time that his nose was bleeding. He drew a white handkerchief from a pocket and dabbed at it, examined the blood on it and shook his head. "I don't think it's broken," he said.

"Doesn't look like it."

Post dabbed again, wincing this time. "Violent people," he said reflectively. "There are more of them than there used to be in Florida. More crazies with guns. The drugs, maybe."

"Maybe," Carver said. "Can I get you some water?"

"No, I'm fine. I'm not as frail as I look."

"What happened, Charlie?"

"I'm not sure."

"Why are you in Del Moray?" But Carver had a good idea why.

"Maggie," Post said. "After talking to you, I kept thinking about her. I decided I wanted to see her one more time, get everything clear between us so the memories were unsullied. It's not as if I'm an old man trying to set everything in order toward life's end," he added defensively, "it's just this seemed like personal business that needed wrapping up."

"Sure," Carver said.

"So I rented a car in Miami, drove up here, and tried to see her where she worked."

So this was the man who'd tried without success that morning to talk with Maggie at Burnair and Crosley.

"She was there but she wouldn't see me," Post said. He sounded more mystified than disappointed.

"One of the stockbrokers get rough with you?" Carver asked.

Post broke out his creased and charming grin. "I'm more lover than fighter, Carver. Not that I haven't been beaten up in the stock market before. Not this time, though. I was outside the building, walking back to my car, when a fella approached and asked me to get into a car with him if I wanted to talk about Maggie Rourke. I asked why we couldn't talk out on the sidewalk, and he said it was too hot. So we got into a big car, a Chrysler, I think. It was black and the windows were tinted. Right away he started beating on me. Not as hard as he could, just as hard as he had to so I couldn't fight back. He was good. He was experienced. Nobody could hear me or see in through those tinted windows, and it all happened fast."

"What did he look like?" Carver asked.

"Big, dressed casual but nice. Dark eyes, I think. Brown hair. About forty. I asked him who he was, and all he'd say was that he was Maggie's special friend and I was to leave her alone, not try to see her again."

"You agreed, I hope."

"Sure did. He had all the cards and all the chips. When I was bent over trying to get my breath after a punch in the stomach, he started the engine and drove away. I got plenty scared then, but we only went a few blocks and he pulled to the curb again. He asked if I got the message about staying away from Maggie. When I said yes, he reached over, opened the door, and told me to get out. I did, made it back to my car, and drove to the address on your business card. You weren't here, so I went to a motel and checked in, rested a while, got cleaned up and came back. I thought I felt okay, but the engine started to overheat sitting there at idle with the air conditioner on, so I had to turn it off for a while and the heat caught up with me. A little while later, you came along."

"Would you recognize the man if you saw him again?"

"Definitely. But I think he was somebody's hired goon. I've been around in my life; I've known people like that, and he had all the earmarks."

"You think Maggie would hire that kind of guy?"

"Maggie? No, not her. But somebody looking out for her, maybe that person would hire professional muscle."

"Did you ever notice Maggie having a problem with alcohol?"

"You mean drinking too much? Not a chance. Never seen a sign of that in Maggie."

"Uh-huh," Carver said, thinking even the recollection of love could be blind.

He asked Post to excuse him, then went out to the parking lot and got the envelope with the photographs from the Olds's glove compartment. When he returned, he removed the photos and handed them to Post. "Is the man who beat you in any of these?"

Post looked through them, then shook his head. "Don't recognize a soul here." He handed the photographs back to Carver.

Carver laid them next to the phone, then leaned back with his buttocks against the desk, holding the cane loosely and horizontally with both hands. "I think you oughta do what the man said, Charlie. About leaving Maggie alone."

"I intend to. But what about Maggie? I've got some concern there. She fall in with some rough friends?"

"At least one," Carver said.

"You don't think that muscle was really her boyfriend?"

"I don't know," Carver said honestly. "Maggie's a mystery."

"Isn't she, though?" Post said, grinning.

"You want me to take you to a doctor?" Carver asked.

"No. Nothing's broken. Anyway, I'm between medical insurance policies right now. I'll just go back to my motel and soak in a warm bath." He stood up, looking strong and steady. "I thought you'd want to know about this, thought maybe you had some idea what it was all about."

"I wish I knew."

"All I wanted was to tie loose ends, but apparently Maggie's not of the same mind. Like I said before, I know when something's over and done with. I'm going back to Miami in the morning."

"Feel well enough to drive?"

"Sure. There won't be any problem. It's good highway the whole trip."

"I mean back to your motel."

"Of course. I got here, didn't I?"

Carver considered that one of the few questions he could answer just then with certainty.

WITH POST'S permission, Carver drove behind him to the Sea Horse Motel on the coast highway to make sure he got there okay. It wasn't easy. Post drove the way he'd lived, fast and with risk and a sense of immortality. The car rental agency in Miami had no idea what it had loosed onto the highways.

They had a few drinks in the cool and dim motel bar, sitting in a booth and talking about women and yachts and the way Disney World was going to grow and grow and devour Florida.

"You make sure Maggie doesn't get hurt in whatever's going on," Post implored several times.

Carver assured him he'd do what he could.

Post began to talk about making his next fortune when Cuba was open for travel again and would be a boat and tourist mecca. It all sounded good. All it needed was for Castro to move out of the way of dreams.

When Post was finally settled in his room, Carver drank two cups of black coffee to shake the effects of the liquor. Then he left the motel and drove to meet Beth so they could follow some of the Nightlinks escorts into the dark and humid unknown.

|34|

THEY KILLED time, then had an early supper before arriving in separate cars to park at the far end of the lot where Nightlinks was located.

Beth drove from the lot first, following the man Carver had photographed walking to the Aero Lounge with Harvey Sincliff. Twenty minutes later, Carver left the parking space he'd used before to take his photographs. When he reached Telegraph Road he turned left and fell in behind a sleek black Miata convertible driven by the beautiful redhead he'd seen on his first visit to Nightlinks.

Despite the flamboyant package of car and woman, she was a cautious driver and easy to follow. She left the Del Moray city limits and took A1A north along the coast for a few miles. The Miata's convertible top was lowered and her red hair whipped and waved like a proud flag as the little car cut through the ocean breeze.

After passing a row of motels along the shoreline, she slowed and made a right turn into the parking lot of the Red Dolphin Inn, an upscale motel overlooking the sea.

Carver followed and parked at the other end of the lot. The Red Dolphin Inn was built of heavy red and brown stone and exposed rough-hewn beams. The office sported particularly bulky and graceless architecture and was built in an A-frame that was fronted with darkly tinted triangular glass and had a slate-shingled roof and heavy wooden doors fitted with iron rings for handles. Jutting from each side of the office was a long, two-story wing where the rooms were located. The wings looked like cheaply built blockhouses that had been added as afterthoughts and didn't fit in with the heavy rustic quality of the rest of the motel.

The redhead had parked near the office, but she didn't enter it. Instead she climbed from the Miata and went through a door to the right of the main entrance.

Carver waited a few minutes. A silver minivan containing a man and woman and two kids drove into the lot and parked in front of the office. The man, a skinny guy still in his twenties, got out of the van, stretched as if he'd just awakened from a ten-year nap, then walked stiffly inside to register. The woman sat still, but the kids were bouncing around inside the van as if they were on fire.

A dark blue Mercury pulled in and looked as if it were going to stop behind the minivan. Then it drove around the boxy little vehicle and parked halfway down the wing nearest Carver.

The driver, a middle-aged man wearing sunglasses and a gray suit, climbed out and walked directly to one of the lower-level rooms. He unlocked the door but didn't enter. After poking his head into the room and glancing around, he shut the door again and walked back toward the office. He moved into the stark shadow of the peaked roof and entered the office just as the minivan driver was coming out clutching a key with a big green plastic tag as if it were a prize.

Wondering if the redhead had simply used another entrance to the office and registered, or if she'd gone directly to a room out of his vision, Carver worked his way out of the Olds and headed toward the door she'd used. The sun was low but still hot; its energy seemed to resist him like warm liquid until he reached the cool shade of the building.

He opened the door slowly, feeling a rush of cool air, and found that it led to the motel lounge. When he stepped all the way inside he saw the redhead seated in a dim booth near the back. The guy who'd gotten out of the Mercury was with her. He must have come through the door between office and lounge. He'd removed his dark glasses and he and the woman were staring at each other over drinks and a generous flower arrangement in the center of the table. Neither of them noticed Carver. There were only four other customers in the lounge: two men seated at the bar, and two women in business clothes in another booth, studying and conferring about something on a notebook computer.

Carver slid into a secluded booth away from the door and ordered a Budweiser from the tired but smiling woman who plodded over from behind the bar.

He sat sipping his beer from its frosted mug, waiting for the redhead and the Mercury driver, knowing he could see them if they left by the outside door or passed through the doorway into the office.

When they'd finished their drinks twenty minutes later, they went directly outside. They were holding hands. The man glanced at Carver without interest while the redhead, even more beautiful up close, stared straight ahead with a slight smile on her very red lips. It was the kind of smile even a monk might read a lot into.

Carver followed just in time to see them enter the room whose door the man had opened earlier.

He went back to the Olds, jotted down the Mercury's license

number, then waited in the heat. Quickly he settled into the patient, seemingly half-asleep mode of a cop on a stakeout or a sniper surveying terrain from cover. He was actually super-alert to everything around him. He saw the young mother from the minivan plod down the fancy iron stairs and get four cans of soda from a machine. Watched her go back upstairs, a pair of cans clutched close to her body in each hand as if she were applying cold compresses to wounds. In the darkening sky beyond the horizontal line of the motel's roof, a gull was soaring in abrupt, measured patterns, as if trying to spell out something in the air. A riddle for Carver that he might solve too late.

It was dark when the redhead opened the room's door and stepped out, smoothed her skirt over her hips, and strode to the Miata. With practiced ease, she raised the little car's canvas top before driving away. There still was no sign of the man as Carver started the Olds and followed her out to the highway, then back toward Del Moray.

She didn't drive far. After a few miles, she parked in the lot of another motel and followed much the same procedure. This time she drank alone in the lounge for about fifteen minutes before a tall man with raven black hair and wearing a black suit showed up.

He didn't even sit down. Didn't say hello or so much as nod to her. The woman rose, wearing her siren's smile, and they walked together from the lounge and up a flight of inside stairs to the upper rooms. Carver followed halfway up the stairs and then paused, watching them enter one of the rooms and noting its number: 203.

He had a second beer before returning to wait in the Olds. It was easy to find the outside entrance to 203 from the catwalk that fronted the building. If the woman and the dark-haired man left by either door, he'd be able to see them.

He was surprised when a crack of dim light appeared as the room's door onto the catwalk opened. More surprised when he caught a glimpse of a dark figure entering the room. He sat up straighter, staring through the windshield.

The room's drapes were closed but glowed several times in quick succession in brilliant flashes of light. The door opened again, a shadowy figure ran out, and Carver saw a short man in dark clothing hurl himself down the stairs, then run across the parking lot. He heard but didn't see a car roar away, glimpsing twin red taillights and nothing more as it reached the highway.

The whole thing had taken less than a minute.

The room's door was still open. A light came on, and for an instant a nude man appeared in the doorway, body hunched and long black hair wildly mussed. Even from this distance Carver could see the look of horror on his face as he slammed the door.

Less than fifteen minutes later the black-haired man, fully dressed now but carrying his suit coat, emerged from the room with the woman. She was dressed as before but had her hair pinned in a pile on top her head. They stood for a few minutes at the base of the stairs, talking earnestly in the faint glow of the vending machines. The man was waving his long arms, obviously upset. The woman touched his cheek gently from time to time, calming him. He slipped into his suit coat and stood still, listening to her. Then they kissed briefly and parted. Carver had a chance to get the license number of the man's black or midnight blue Cadillac before following the Miata.

This time the redhead drove all the way back into Del Moray. She parked in the dark lot of a small, seedy motel three blocks from the ocean and went directly into one of the detached cabins, using a key she'd fished from her purse. Lights winked on inside the cabin, providing a view of a wall with an arrangement of framed prints on it, some of them hanging crookedly. Then the woman appeared at the front window and closed the drapes.

Half an hour passed. A paunchy but muscular man with tattooed arms came out of another of the run-down cabins and gave Carver a curious and hostile look as he swaggered to a dented gray pickup truck. Rap music blared from the cab as the truck kicked back gravel and roared away. Carver figured it would be wise not to be there when the man returned.

The shade was raised on the cabin window that held the air conditioner. Carver climbed from the Olds and walked along the line of cabins as if he had a firm destination. Yet he was moving slowly; a man with a cane could do that without attracting suspicion even if he were seen.

He moved even slower as he veered at an angle to where he could see inside the window, getting so close to the cabin that he could feel the hot breath of the wheezing old air conditioner.

He glanced quickly around. Took a chance.

Edging to the window, he tried not to breathe in the air conditioner's fumes and peered inside.

The woman was wearing only black panties and bra, half reclining on a small sofa and talking on the phone. Her free hand held what looked like an ice pack on the side of one of her thighs. As Carver watched, she hung up the phone, then stood and walked into a small kitchenette, where she tossed the ice pack into the sink. The cabin was small; she was alone. She sat on the edge of the bed and unpinned her hair, let it fall and shook it out, her head hanging low. Something about the long red hair, swinging side to side and almost brushing the floor, held Carver spellbound.

A truck whined past out on the street, shifting through gears noisily and breaking the mood.

Feeling like a Peeping Tom, Carver backed away. He glanced guiltily around the shadowed parking lot. No one was on the lot or at any of the cabin windows. In fact, only two cabins' lights were glowing other than the one near the street that served as the office.

Relieved, he went back to the Olds, got in, and started the engine. There was no more reason to be a voyeur. The redheaded woman was home—in her own motel room, anyway. He could leave and they could both go to bed and get some rest.

As he eased the big Olds as soundlessly as possible from the gravel lot and turned right onto the street, he thought of the gull he'd watched tracing patterns in the sky earlier that evening, and of the hypnotic spray and graceful arc of the woman's long red hair swinging and almost touching the floor.

He tapped the brake and glanced back for a moment, not knowing quite what he was feeling, then drove away.

35

BETH WAS waiting for Carver on the beach the next morning when he came in from his swim. As he crawled up from the surf to where his cane protruded from the damp sand, he felt like some creature of early evolution, more at home in water but compelled by destiny to walk on land.

He grabbed the cane and levered himself to his feet, suddenly cool even in the morning sun, and joined Beth as she sat cross-legged on a large towel. She was wearing her red swimsuit but he doubted she would go into the water. She seldom swam or sought the sun. It amused her at times that some of the people who scorned her because she was black worked so hard to become one tenth as dark.

Beside her lay a white beach towel with a scene of a glorious setting sun and soaring gulls on it. Carver lowered himself onto the towel and leaned back toward the terrycloth sunset, supporting himself on his elbows and feeling the genuine sun and the soft sea breeze evaporating the salt water from his tanned flesh. Beth had been asleep when he'd returned last night, and still sleeping when he'd crept from the cottage half an hour ago to swim.

"How did you do last night?" he asked.

She remained sitting Indian fashion with her legs crossed, watching the sea. The sun was sparkling on the water like strewn diamonds. "I followed that good-looking dude to a hotel outside town where he met a woman about three times his age. They went to an expensive restaurant, then shopping. She tried on clothes for him and he made over her like she was young Liz Taylor, then they had a few drinks at a seaside lounge and he drove her back to the hotel."

"He go upstairs with her?"

"Nope. He went home, to an apartment over on West Tenth. He did what an escort's supposed to do, it seemed to me." Squinting against the morning sun, she looked over and down at Carver. "What about that redhead you followed?"

Carver told her about the two men the woman had met, and the apparent photographing in the motel room of the woman and the second man having sex.

"Sounds like prostitution," Beth said, "not to mention blackmail shaping up."

"It might be a variation of the badger game," Carver said, watching a pelican splash into the sea in an awkard dive for a fish, then come up empty. "The woman lures the man to a motel room, her confederate breaks in and photographs them, then says the woman's husband hired him. The guy in the photos with the woman buys prints and negatives from the photographer and bribes him not to tell the woman's husband. He can feel good about that. Not only won't his wife find out he's been a bad boy, he's also nobly protecting his lover."

"Why not simply the badger game?" Beth asked. "The man with the camera pretends to *be* the husband, and after threatening and arguing with the john, he calms down and generously agrees to accept a bribe not to tell the john's wife."

"The photographer wasn't in the room long enough," Carver said. "He got in and took his shots within seconds, then ran from the scene. There was no time for conversation."

Beth brushed sand from her ankles, then flicked it off her towel. "That guy in Miami, Charlie Post, told you his wife had photographs of him and Maggie Rourke together."

"I haven't forgotten."

"Seems too much of a coincidence."

"Maybe. People have extramarital sex, other people photograph them to nail them with proof of infidelity. Happens all the time."

"I figure there's probably a common thread there," she said.

"Maggie isn't connected to Nightlinks."

"You sure?"

"She says no."

"Nixon said no about Watergate. Bush said no about Irangate."

Carver grinned. "Maggie might not even be a Republican."

Beth looked at him with disgust. "Woman probably don't even vote. That's not the point. She says no, and you believe her because she speaks through kissable lips. Jesus, Fred!"

He sat up straight so he was at eye level with her. "There isn't anything suggesting Maggie even knows Nightlinks exists."

Her expression of disdain lingered on her dark features, per-spiring now in the glare of the sun. "That might be an acorn you haven't stumbled across yet. But it might exist. Might even grow into an oak, you give it half a chance, a little of that fertilizer you spread around so well."

"McGregor said something about me being blind and stum-bling onto acorns."

"Man must know a few things."

"He calls you my dark meat."

"Fuck McGregor!"

He laughed.

"You like getting me pissed, Fred?" She punched him on the upper arm. Hard. "You like it, do you?"

He laughed harder, but his arm was aching.

She punched him again, in precisely the same way in precisely the same spot, adding injury to injury. "You think it's funny, do you?"

"No, no!" he said, still laughing.

She waited, not smiling.

He stopped laughing.

"You could be right," he said.

"So what you gonna do about it, Fred?" She jokingly drew back her fist as if about to punch his arm again where it was still throbbing, only much harder this time.

He guessed she was joking, anyway.

"I'm going to talk to Maggie Rourke," he told her.

It wasn't exactly the answer she'd wanted, but she didn't argue. She stood up gracefully and shook sand from her towel, snapping it like a whip. The breeze caught some of the sand and blew it on Carver. "You're gonna have breakfast first," she said.

He found his cane and gained his feet, dragging his towel up with him. "We going out to eat?"

"I got some biscuits ready to go in the oven," she told him. "We can eat in this morning."

She'd surprised him again. She wasn't one to use the kitchen for much other than rinsing her hands.

"Biscuits?"

"Biscuits. Like your Aunt Jemima used to bake."

"Why the spurt of domesticity?" he asked.

"'Cause I felt like some biscuits," she said, straight-faced.

He followed her up the beach toward the cottage. She was walking slower than usual so he could keep pace, her heels kicking up small rooster tails of sand. He loved walking behind her, watching the beautiful undulating flow of her lean body as she strode with confidence and elegance. It was difficult to imagine her in a kitchen wearing an apron, busying about and tending to biscuits.

"Did you make those biscuits from scratch?" he asked.

She didn't answer.

He thought for a moment of twisting up his towel and flicking her in the buttocks.

Then he decided that would be a bad idea.

She was domestic only up to a point.

WHEN CARVER phoned Burnair and Crosley he was told that Maggie wasn't expected in that day. He asked to talk to Beverly Denton, who said that Maggie had called in sick that morning.

His stomach still churning from Beth's biscuits, he drove A1A toward Maggie's cottage.

He didn't really believe there had to be a connection between the man photographing the redhead and her john, and Maggie's being photographed with Charlie Post. Adultery, photographs, and divorce had been close partners since the invention of the camera. But he wanted to talk with Maggie about Post's being roughed up when he'd attempted to see her.

Or maybe he simply wanted to talk with Maggie.

She opened the door right away when he knocked. She must have just returned from the beach; she was wearing a black one-piece swimsuit cut high on the thighs, and there was a sheen of perspiration on her tan face and the swell of her breasts. She smiled when she saw it was Carver, knocking him slightly off balance. He'd imagined she might reward his persistence by throwing something at him.

"You *are* determined about that conversation we're supposed to have," she said. Her eyes were a deep and nondescript color in the dim light of the cottage, pulling at him so that he had to look away for a second.

"Obsessed, even," he said. "Apparently you bring that out in people."

"Some people. The ones who need to be obsessed."

She stepped aside and made room for him to enter.

The cottage was cool, not so dim now that he was inside. She didn't ask him to sit down, but she still wore her slight smile as she stood facing him. She was obviously aware that she fascinated him; it was a familiar phenomenon for her.

"It's a new swimming suit," she said, backing away a few steps and turning, modeling so he could see her from every angle. She was one of those women whose compactness lent the impression of full perfection. Her smile was wider as she stopped turning and faced him. "Well, how do I look?"

"Like a flavor."

The smile burst into a short, musical laugh.

"I called you at Burnair and Crosley," he said. "They told me you'd called in sick."

"It passed," she said. She ran a hand absently along a well-turned forearm, then was perfectly still for a second in an exquisitely graceful pose, like something Michelangelo might have created if he'd worked with warm flesh instead of stone. "The sun heals everything if only you give it time."

"Maybe it's the time that heals."

"No, it takes the heat of the sun to purge body and soul."

Carver found himself staring at her cleavage above the bra of her black suit. He quickly looked into her eyes and saw amusement there, and a kind of cruel pleasure. She was a woman who understood the power of her sex, what she possessed that she might give or withhold.

"I saw Charlie Post yesterday," he said, trying to get to business. "He looked a bit rough after his beating."

"Beating?" Parallel frown lines of concern appeared above the bridge of her nose, then disappeared. "Charlie was beaten?"

"Not long after trying to see you."

Maggie hitched up the top of her swimming suit as if it might be about to fall from her breasts, but she didn't move to tie the string designed to loop around her neck for support. "It isn't a good idea for Charlie and me to see each other again. I think even Charlie would tell you that."

"He's more convinced of it now," Carver said.

"Is he all right?"

"He'll heal. Time and the sun and all that."

"Who did it to him?"

"A large man driving a big black luxury car."

She made a show of trying to think, actually looking up and off to the left, as if her memory were suspended there like a balloon. "I don't know anybody like that. At least anybody who beats up people. Poor Charlie. He's a prince of a guy, and he doesn't deserve all the trouble he's had. I mean, that wife of his. Ex-wife. My God, what a curse she turned out to be."

"Charlie would agree. He doesn't feel the same way about you, though."

"But I was a curse nonetheless. I mean, it was his affair with me that really sent May off the deep end so she divorced him."

"It would have happened sooner or later."

"Sure. But it doesn't feel good to be the one who made it happen sooner."

"What do you know about Nightlinks?" Carver asked.

Her expression remained one of concern for Charlie, but she glanced off and up to the left again at her hovering memory. "You asked me that before and I said I knew nothing. What *is* Nightlinks, anyway?"

"An escort service."

"Well, I never heard—Wait a minute, you don't think Charlie and I met through an escort service, do you?"

"I don't know. How *did* you meet?"

"In a more conventional and respectable manner." She

walked to a small credenza, moving slowly and deliberately, knowing he was watching. That he couldn't not watch. The confidence of beautiful women within the context of their familiar worlds always amazed him. They moved through the waters of attraction and seduction with the ease of bright tropical fish.

Striking a too-casual pose with one hip jutting out, she poured herself a glass of white wine. Then she looked over at Carver as if just remembering he was there. "Would you like a drink?"

"No. Too early."

"Well," she said a little sadly, "it's too late for me. Would you like anything else?" She made it sound innocent, but there was a glitter in her eyes that reflected something deep within. Eve in the apple orchard.

"Maybe it's too late for that, too," he said.

"But only maybe." She placed her stemmed glass on the credenza and walked boldly over to him. She kissed him on the lips, leaning into him with her breasts. She smelled fresh and damp and eager. Stepping back, but with a hand on his arm where Beth had playfully punched him this morning, she said, "Am I a flavor you like?"

"Can't deny it," he said, and ran the backs of his knuckles gently, weightlessly, down the line of her cheek.

"Then don't deny yourself anything," she said, smiling dreamily.

"I can't mix pleasure with business."

"That's one of those old saws that're hardly ever true."

"True this time, though."

"Then forget about business."

"Is that what you're trying to get me to do?"

She moved away from him, not bothering to conceal her annoyance. "You've got me wrong, Fred. It is Fred, isn't it?"

"Sometimes it's Fred. Sometimes it's Fool. And I don't have you at all," he said, hearing the lament in his voice.

She heard it too and smiled. "It's not really going to be Fool this time, is it?"

"I don't know. I'll have to sort it out later."

"Well, that 'maybe' is still hanging in the air, so it's still Fred for the time being." She strode back to the credenza and picked up her glass. "Sure you won't have something to drink?"

"Maybe later," he said.

She rolled the roundness of the cool glass across her cheek where he'd touched it, then briefly across the tan swell of her breasts. A trickle of moisture ran beneath the black material of her suit. "Maybe's good enough for now," she said.

He nodded, shifted his weight over his cane, and limped to the door. He hated to leave. Hated it! He felt as if he were walking on the bottom of the sea.

"Is Charlie still in town?" Maggie asked behind him.

He turned around. "No, he went back to Miami."

"Good. I'm still fond of Charlie. That old man really is one of the best. I want to see him happy."

Carver couldn't help smiling. "You saw him happy for a while."

"Didn't I, though?" she said, and raised her glass and sipped.

He went out into the heat and got in the Olds. Seated behind the steering wheel, he noticed his hand was trembling.

Beth. He knew it was Beth who'd kept him from Maggie inside the cottage.

Beth had become almost a physical part of him, had burned her way deep into his life so that he couldn't be unfaithful to her without being unfaithful to himself. He despised that kind of oneness and dependency. He knew it for a weakness. He'd guarded against it, hadn't wanted it to happen.

But it had.

When the trembling stopped he drove away, but he couldn't help glancing back.

36

THAT NIGHT they switched.

Beth followed the redhead and Carver the man who'd escorted the elderly woman the night before. That way neither escort would notice the same person in the background, a tall black woman or a bald man who walked with a cane. And this evening they picked up on them outside their homes instead of at Nightlinks.

The man, a darkly handsome guy who looked like an Arab terrorist who'd shaved off his beard, didn't strike Carver as being as young as Beth had described. And he didn't go to Nightlinks tonight. He was working, though, all dressed up and with someplace to go: black slacks, gray shirt open at the throat to show off a gold chain, unconstructed darker gray sport jacket. He got into his late-model maroon Buick, and Carver followed him to the Sea Lord Hotel.

He was in the lobby about twenty minutes before emerging with a roundish, pretty brunette on his arm. She had on a silky black skirt and a sleeveless white blouse with a glittering gold design down the front. She looked about forty and was staring up at her escort as if he'd been manufactured only for her delight.

Carver thought, Some way to make a living, as he slipped the Olds into drive and followed the maroon Buick back out onto A1A.

Nightlinks and the woman turned left and dropped south all the way to Lauderdale-by-the-Sea. It was dark when they pulled into the parking lot of the Holiday Inn on El Mar Drive. El Mar ran east of A1A at that point, the last street before the beach and ocean.

Carver parked nearby and watched.

The woman waited in the Buick while the man went into the hotel lobby. He returned five minutes later, climbed back into the Buick, and the woman climbed all over him. They kissed as if interested in the Guinness record, then the man got back out of the car and walked around to the passenger side. Out of sight of the woman, he ran the back of his hand across his mouth, then worked his cheeks between thumb and forefinger. Maybe she'd loosened a tooth. It had to be an occupational hazard.

Gallant and smiling, he opened the door for the woman. She took his offered hand and climbed out, tugging down her skirt with unnecessary modesty. She was grinning as if she'd just happened upon the potential of the opposite sex. Possibly she had.

Holding hands, the two of them strolled along El Mar to a restaurant a few blocks away. The sign outside said the name of the place was Aruba. It was crowded, but somehow they got a table after only a short wait. Maybe love working its wonders.

Aruba was a good restaurant from Carver's point of view. It was located on the beach near a wooden pier that jutted far out and was softly lighted. Tourists were out enjoying the night, some of them wandering around holding ice cream cones from a shop across the street.

He went over and bought a frozen custard cone, then found a spot where he could sit as if watching the ocean, which was kind of feisty this evening, with a strong landward breeze. Actually he was watching the Nightlinks escort and his client eating at a table by the window. From where he sat, he could also see the corner doorway where the man and woman would emerge from Aruba after their meal. He wished the people he followed would always be so cooperative.

An hour later they left their table and stepped out onto the sidewalk. The man was carrying his sport jacket. He draped it over the woman's shoulders like a cape to protect her from the sea breeze. Carver made a mental note to remember that move.

They wandered around the area for about half an hour, not going far as they ducked in and out of souvenir shops. Carver found it easy to stay relatively out of sight and keep an eye on them. When they came out of the third shop, the woman was wearing a wide-brimmed straw hat with a colorful bow on it. She removed it as the man drew her close and kissed her with conviction. Carver wasn't surprised when they finally ended the kiss and walked hand in hand toward the hotel where the Buick was parked.

Not surprised either when they walked past the Buick. The man had already registered. He unlocked the outside door to one of the rooms and ushered the woman inside, his hand resting gently against the small of her back.

Carver went to the Olds and sat watching, listening to a Braves game on the radio.

The lights in the room were turned off in the seventh inning. Didn't come back on until the postgame interview.

Went out again an hour later. Love and money, Carver thought, could be effective aphrodisiacs.

It was almost 2:00 A.M. when the lovers came out of the room. The woman waited in the car again while the man checked out. This time she sat with her head tilted back against the headrest, as if she might be napping.

She sat up straight when the man came outside and got into the car. They talked for a few minutes, then the Buick's lights came on and it backed out onto El Mar.

Carver followed as it cut west on Commercial, then drove all the way to I-95 and turned north. Love and money having been spent, they were taking the fast way back to Del Moray, rather than the scenic and romantic route along the ocean.

The woman was dropped off back at the Sea Lord, where the man had picked her up. There was a goodnight kiss, but it was perfunctory, almost businesslike. Then the man drove to his apartment on Tenth Street and presumably went to bed, this time to sleep.

Everybody seemed happy but Carver, who was tired and irritated, though he'd actually expended little energy.

Beth was in bed asleep when he got back to the cottage.

He left a note instructing her not to wake him in the morning, then lay down beside her and felt his weariness make his body seem heavy enough to sink all the way through the mattress.

Staring into darkness, he thought about the man and woman he'd followed, and the artificial happiness and passion that had seemed so real, and maybe been as real as many of life's sustaining illusions. The ocean rushed noisily onto the beach, and the wind off the sea was moaning softly in the cottage eaves. Beth's long thigh was resting lightly and warmly along his own. She moaned the same soft song as the wind and stirred, moving her leg closer, then away, leaving him detached and alone in the night.

He was thinking about waking her, holding her, when he fell asleep.

· · ·

SHE HAD coffee ready for him when he struggled out of bed the next morning.

"Figured you'd need this, Fred." She handed him his cup with the leaping marlin on it.

He needed it, all right. His mind was still webbed with sleep and his body seemed to respond to each of his brain's commands a few seconds after they were given. He sipped. The coffee was too hot but his tongue was thickly coated and didn't get scalded. That was how it felt, anyway; maybe he simply hadn't yet picked up the sensation of pain. "Time's it?" he asked.

"Nine-thirty. Late for you to be getting up."

"Got in late last night. I'm getting too old for that kind of thing, stolen wild sex in hotel rooms."

"Is that why you look so used up this morning?"

"Probably. I feel foggy and deprived."

"Deprived, huh? We can fix that."

"Not now," he said, "or someone would have to fix me."

"Poor Fred. Voyeurism can be so wearing." She got the glass pot and topped off his coffee. Maybe she wanted it hot enough to sear his entire intestinal tract. "Gonna have your swim?" she asked, returning the pot to its burner.

"Not this morning."

"Say, you *must* have had some workout last night!"

He was getting tired of being punctured by verbal darts. He sipped some more coffee, feeling it burn the roof of his mouth this time, then found his cane and stood up. He made his way into the bathroom and showered and shaved. As he got dressed in the screened-off bedroom area, he smelled bacon frying.

When he returned to the cottage's main room, he found that Beth had a plate of bacon and eggs on the breakfast counter for him along with a fresh cup of coffee.

"You act very much like a wife sometimes," he said, sitting on a stool.

She didn't answer. Instead she carried her coffee outside onto the porch.

By the time he'd finished eating he felt human again. Up to the Bronze Age, anyway. He joined Beth on the porch.

She was sitting in one of the webbed aluminum lounge chairs. She had on some kind of wispy white dress that the wind parted to reveal her calves and a good stretch of thigh. . . . *Some workout you didn't have last night.*

Carver sat down in the chair next to hers and propped his good leg up on the porch rail. He stared out at the ocean rolling beyond his moccasin. Clouds were stacked high on the horizon but didn't seem to be moving.

"What about your night?" he said.

"Same old same old," Beth told him. "Our redheaded friend spent time with a man in a motel room, then returned to Nightlinks. She was inside the office for about fifteen minutes, probably looking at profiles, then she came out and drove to meet another man at another motel. She was back home by ten o'clock."

"Looking at profiles?"

"Escort services usually ask a prospective client certain questions, develop a kind of profile of the man—or woman—so they can provide the right escort. But the service and the escorts also use the profiles to screen clients. The redhead is hooking, Fred. My guess is she takes on the late callers, goes into the office sometimes to see what's acceptable, the least risky. Otherwise she'd do business from home. She probably wants to talk to whoever's handling the phone at Nightlinks and get their personal impression of the men she might go to meet."

"Did you get the johns' license plate numbers last night?" Carver asked.

"They're in my notebook on the table with my computer."

She adjusted her dress so it covered her legs, reminding him for an instant of the plump woman working herself out of the Buick last night. "What about your guy?"

"He's hooking, too," Carver said.

"Sometimes it seems like the whole world's hooking, one way or another," she said.

"Sometimes." He let his foot drop from the rail to thunk on the plank porch. Reached for his cane. "Gotta make a phone call."

"Man's gotta do what he's gotta do," Beth said, not moving.

Carver couldn't quite make out what kind of mood she was in. But he knew that was part of why he loved her, not knowing exactly where he stood or what to expect next. She was a package of surprises, some of them harrowing. Hadn't she said some men were drawn to dangerous women?

He phoned Desoto and asked him to run the license plate numbers he and Beth had collected during the last two nights. He also told Desoto why he wanted them.

"You give this information to McGregor yet?" Desoto asked.

Carver knew what he was thinking. "Not yet. But don't worry, I'm not withholding information in a homicide investigation, since McGregor insists the Winships' deaths were suicide."

"What about Carl Gretch?"

"That's murder, but it's your case, not McGregor's. That's why I just gave you this information."

"And asked for information from me."

"Sure. But I wouldn't take for granted there's any connection between Nightlinks and Carl Gretch's death."

"Everything's connected in some way or other with everything else. Haven't you noticed?"

"I've noticed you're the second person I've met this morning in a philosophical frame of mind."

"Murder does that to people. To the people who weren't

murdered, anyway. Speaking of murder, what's going on with the little Oriental destruction machine?"

"Beni Ho? He's walking with a cane now. Also with revenge in his heart."

"He's all the more dangerous crippled."

"That's what Beth said."

"Hm. Listen to Beth on this one. I'll get back to you soon as I can on the license numbers."

Carver hung up the phone, then he returned to the porch and sat down again next to Beth. She was still staring straight ahead at the ocean. The sea wind hadn't budged the clouds stacked on the horizon, but it had parted her dress again, revealing her legs.

"What now?" she asked, not looking at him.

"We wait for Desoto to call back."

"You ask him to run those plates?"

"Uh-huh."

"Might be a little while before he calls."

"Might."

She finally looked over at him and smiled. It was a smile he knew. "Know how we might pass that time?"

"Not charades?"

"Not charades," she said.

|37|

DESOTO DIDN'T phone until noon.

He gave Carver the names and addresses of the Nightlinks clients and escorts who'd apparently engaged in prostitution. Two of the clients were from out of state, driving rental cars.

Desoto had taken so much time to get back to Carver because he had had to check the rental car agencies for names and addresses. Also a woman's mutilated body had been found in Lake Eola Park, floating out by the fountain near the center of the lake. Some tourists in one of the boats built to resemble swans had discovered it. The experience was nothing like Disney World. Much of Desoto's morning had been spent taking the sobered tourists' statements.

After telling Carver what he needed to know, Desoto had to terminate the conversation rapidly. The medical examiner's preliminary findings on the woman in the lake had arrived. Someone in the background was yelling something about a saw.

Carver hung up the phone and sat staring at the paper on which he'd scrawled the Nightlinks information with a black felt-tip pen. Beth had showered and was dressed in tight slacks and a gray tee shirt lettered SAVE THE MANATEE across the chest. The propagation of the sea beast was a cause with many Floridians, and the sluglike animal appeared on license plates, bumper stickers, and souvenirs up and down the state. Carver wondered why there wasn't as much enthusiasm to save the human victims of crime in Dade County.

Beth kissed the back of his neck and peered over his shoulder. "That's our list of bad boys, huh?"

"And girls. The redhead's name is Mandy Jamison." He traced his finger down the list. "This is the one that interests me. The driver of the blue '93 Cadillac."

"The one that got himself photographed?"

"Reverend Harold Devine," Carver said. "He's pastor of a church in Miami and does a weekly TV spot."

"He's more than that," Beth said. She was still looking over his shoulder, and her breath was warm in his ear. He didn't mind.

"Desoto mentioned he was director of something called Operation Revert."

"That's right, Fred. They oughta be called Operation Regress. *Burrow* did a piece on them last year when some of their members chained themselves to the doors of a television network affiliate in Miami. They believe all of society's ills can be traced to the disintegration of the family, and they think the media are the primary cause of that decline. They want to turn back the clock to 'Ozzie and Harriet' time, reestablish the dominance of the American family. The problem is, they don't care how they accomplish it."

"And you don't care for them," Carver said.

"More'n a few of those true-blue model families had colored maids at minimum wage."

"And 'Ozzie and Harriet' time was also separate drinking fountains time."

"Not to mention separate lynchings." Beth walked to the other side of the breakfast counter and perched on a stool facing Carver. "Also not to mention Barney Fife time. Funny little guy, sure. But how'd you like to be hassled by that jerk for real if he had the power to get you convicted?"

Carver knew she had a thing about Barney Fife, believing the Mayberry TV character had made a generation of abusive cops seem sympathetic, so he said nothing. He didn't want to get into an argument over reruns.

"Devine's the one got himself photographed," she said, "so that makes the blackmail scenario most likely."

"The Cadillac has dual registration. He has a wife, according to Desoto. Cindy Sue, believe it or not."

"I believe," Beth said.

"Maybe Cindy Sue hired a detective to follow her pious husband and get the goods on him. Or maybe his political enemies wanted something heavy to hold over his head. Plenty of folks might want to take advantage of the fact that the good reverend has a weakness for prostitutes."

"What about the others on the list?"

"Nothing about them jumps out," Carver said. "One's a furniture dealer from Wisconsin, another sells cars up in Jacksonville. Guys with money to spend and looking for a good time, most of them probably married. It'd be a shame to shake up their lives by making it public record they were Nightlinks customers."

"Oh, really?" Beth drew back and glared at him. "I always regarded prostitution as a crime it took two people to commit. And sometimes there's a crime within a crime, and no legal recourse for the victim. I know what I'm talking about, Fred."

He didn't ask what she meant by that. He knew part of the price she'd had to pay to escape her upbringing. Some parts he didn't want to know. Most men and women should keep some things secret from each other, and shouldn't pry. One of the reasons for the disintegration of the American family, he thought, was that there was too much communication within marriage.

"I guess I agree with you," he said. "But I'm not so sure it should be a crime at all. Society ought to grow up and decriminalize it, leave both parties undisturbed."

"Very progressive of you, Fred. A lot of men think the same way, some of them in the legislature. But the women doing for men are the ones still getting dragged into court, while the guys who pay them for their services walk and don't even get their names in the paper."

"It's not a fair world," Carver said.

"That your explanation? Well, the wives of those guys who are going out and diddling with strange pussy would agree with you. Think of that hypocrite bastard Devine preaching family unity and urging the government to withhold welfare payments to single mothers, then going out and lying down with some poor woman who probably loathes him but needs his money to feed her kids."

"I doubt if Mandy Jamison has any kids," Carver said. He could see Beth getting more annoyed by the second, yet he kept saying things that made things worse. He wondered if, on a certain level, he might be doing it deliberately.

"You really think that redhead's the only strange wiggle he's paid for?"

She was slipping into street slang, getting angry deep down. Carver knew that was a sign he should back off. "For all we know she does have kids," he admitted.

"Fuck Reverend Harold Devine and his whole army of hypocrites. They're the assholes would have been wearing white sheets not too many years ago. Might even wear them now. If the two-faced bastard is getting blackmailed, good. If you need to make his name public to get the answers on the Winship deaths, you do it. And if you don't, I will!"

|252|

She stood up and he saw that her fists were clenched into tight brown knots. The bright red of her painted nails made it appear that each hand was squeezing something that was bleeding. She strode to where her portable computer sat and snatched it up, then made for the door.

"Where you going?" Carver asked.

"Going to *Burrow*. You damn well better remember what I said, Fred!"

"About what?"

She slammed the door hard on her way out.

He didn't get a chance to tell her he agreed with her.

HE HAD a ham sandwich and a Budweiser for lunch, then drove into Del Moray and parked at his vantage point where he could watch the Nightlinks office. He'd developed a sense for where the energy in a case emanated from, where the epicenter lay. More and more, what had happened to Donna and Mark Winship seemed to be connected to Nightlinks. He wasn't sure what he might learn from a daylight stakeout of the escort service, but maybe things went on here by the light of the sun. Maybe Mandy Jamison arranged for child care and worked days. Carver the cynic.

But Mandy didn't appear. Only three people came and went at Nightlinks in the two hours he sat sweltering in the Olds, a man and two women. Early afternoon was obviously a slow time for escort services.

Carver sat up straighter when he saw Beni Ho emerge from the office, slip a pair of dark glasses onto the bridge of his nose, and get into a black Porsche that looked like the Batmobile. Ho was moving better but still limping along with a cane, like Carver, and he was carrying a briefcase. The last time Carver had seen him leave Nightlinks he was carrying a briefcase.

The Porsche either needed a muffler or its exhaust system was set up to roar mightily in a projection of power. It rolled smoothly and noisily from the parking lot.

Things were slow here anyway, and stifling, so Carver wiped sweat from the corners of his eyes, started the Olds, and drove down to Telegraph Road.

Ho knew his car, so Carver had to be especially careful. He stayed far back, sometimes losing sight of the black Porsche in the bright traffic and sun glare, but he was able to stay with it.

Ho drove to an apartment building on Seventh Street, a four-story blue and white structure with a wooden railing around the perimeter of its flat roof. Carver parked beneath a bent and shaggy palm tree a block down and watched, listening to the drooping fronds rattle in the breeze.

Ho entered the building carrying the briefcase, then returned to his car about five minutes later, still with the case.

He drove over to Egret Avenue and made a similar visit to a small, vine-covered house. Then it was all the way to the other side of town for another brief stop at an apartment building. He headed east then, toward the ocean.

Carver followed, but he was getting worried. Ho was driving at the speed limit, not behaving in any way unusual, but he wasn't the sort anyone could follow indefinitely without being seen. Carver hoped the little assassin's dark glasses obstructed his vision enough to take the edge off his awareness.

It wasn't until Ho had parked and climbed up out of the Porsche again that Carver realized where they were. At the motel where he'd last seen Mandy Jamison after her date with Reverend Devine. The place she seemed to call home.

He took a chance and let the Olds's idling engine ease it down the street so he could see where Ho was going.

The little man limped directly to Mandy's cabin. He rapped on the door with the crook of his cane, as Carver might have done. Mandy opened the door. Carver caught a glimpse of her, wearing jeans and an oversized blouse and looking ghostly pale without makeup, as she moved back to let Beni Ho enter.

Ten minutes later, Ho hobbled outside and back to his car. He drove over to Ocean Drive, then south. Turned right on Wellington. There wasn't much traffic now, so Carver had to stay even farther behind the Porsche. At one point he even cut over to run parallel to Ho in the next block for a while, sneaking looks at the black Porsche at intersections, guided at times by only the throaty roar of its powerful engine.

The neighborhood began to decline. Run-down office buildings, some of them boarded up, lined the streets. Here and there stood a desolate house or apartment building with despondent-looking old men or women on the porches or stoops. More of the businesses on the street seemed to be permanently closed than open.

When Carver cut back to the next block to fall in behind the black Porsche again, he was surprised to find that the neighborhood looked familiar. He was on Gull Avenue.

Then the Porsche's brakelights flared. Carver slowed the Olds and pulled to the curb.

Ho parked across the street from Shellie's Lounge and limped inside.

Carver drove past, then parked around the corner. He walked back to Gull and found a spot near a bus stop where he could stand back in the doorway of a boarded-up shoe store and not attract too much attention. Passersby would take him for a man waiting for a bus, or for a wino or junkie seeking shade.

He settled back, sweated, and waited.

Ho was inside Shellie's for almost half an hour. When he returned to the Porsche and drove away, he didn't have his briefcase.

Carver stood watching the Porsche travel north on Gull Avenue, gliding fast and shiny like some huge beetlelike insect working up nerve to test its wings.

He watched it until, as it flashed past a line of parked cars, he noticed a red plastic rose taped to an antenna.

Maggie Rourke's car was parked at the curb.

|38|

CARVER PAUSED just inside the door. It was dim and cool as a cave inside Shellie's, and the low-volume sound system was playing something forlorn and slow by Eric Clapton. There were about a dozen customers scattered around, four or five of them at the bar. The TV above the bar was tuned soundlessly to a cable channel showing jai alai from Miami, but nobody was paying attention except for the bartender, not the stocky woman today but a fat man with sandy hair and a white shirt.

Maggie was seated on a stool at the end of the bar, a drink in front of her and the briefcase lying at her feet like a weary pet she'd been walking. Her clothes were casual—baggy red tee shirt and skin-tight black shorts that came down almost to her knees. She was wearing black sandals, letting the left one dangle so loosely from her toes that it seemed an instant away from dropping to the floor and subtly changing everything in her world.

When Carver approached, she looked over at him with a flash of surprise and then careful disinterest.

"Still sick?" he asked, sliding onto the stool next to her, not glancing down at the briefcase.

"Why should you care?"

"Is this the woman-scorned act?"

"Don't overestimate yourself."

She was working hard to get him to leave. He didn't blame her. The bartender sauntered over to them, never taking his eyes off the TV. Carver asked for a Budweiser. It was set before him, half of it poured into a glass, all without a word from the bartender. Carver wondered if he had a bet down on the jai alai match.

"Listen," Maggie said, turning toward him, "excuse my bad manners. I'm a little drunk, early as it is." Since he wasn't leaving, she'd apparently changed her tactics.

"Going into work when you leave here?"

"Huh?" She smiled. "Not a chance. Why would you ask that?"

"Your briefcase. I thought maybe you stopped here on your way to work."

"Actually I was in early this morning and picked up some papers to take home and study."

"What kind of papers?"

"Information on an initial public offering. Savings and loan going public. You interested?"

He smiled. "Nothing to invest."

"Damn, damn, damn!" the bartender said, reacting to something on television. Clapton began crooning achingly about love lost forever.

Maggie took a sip of her drink, then rested her hand on the back of Carver's. Her fingers were cool from being curled around her glass. "Last time we were here you offered to drive me home."

"I thought you were drunk then. You're not drunk now."

"Nice of you to think not. You're a gentleman, Ferd."

"That's Fred. I'll be glad to carry your briefcase out to your car for you, gentleman that I am."

Her eyes picked up the light from the TV and glowed with alarm and lucidity. "No, thanks. I'm not leaving yet. Not for a while."

"Me either, I guess."

She was quiet for a moment, staring into her drink. Then she said, "You still think Mark's death was murder?"

"Yes."

"Any proof?"

"Not yet."

"If it was murder, Fred, I'd like to see you catch the bastard who did it."

"You're not convinced anymore it was suicide?"

"I've found it hard to stay convinced of anything since Mark died. The world keeps shifting on me, meaning one thing then another. I turn around and everything's changed." Her sandal dropped to the floor, and she absently lowered her foot and snagged it with her toes without looking. "It scares the shit out of me."

She didn't sound scared, even though she should have been. Carver remembered the mutilated doll in her bed. He thought maybe she really was feeling the effects of the liquor.

"Everybody's scared from time to time," he said.

"Even big bad Fred?"

He said, "You scare me, Maggie."

"I scare a lot of men. Then they try to prove to themselves they're not scared. It's a pattern."

"Life's full of patterns, only sometimes they're hard to see. Like those optical illusions that are one thing then another, depending on how you look at them."

"That's your job, I guess. Seeing the patterns, the real shapes of things in the fog." She sounded sad.

Maybe she sensed what he was thinking, what had emerged

from the fog. Maggie, Beni Ho, Carl Gretch—they formed a tighter and tighter pattern. He knew now they were all connected in some meaningful way with Nightlinks. Mark's lover, Donna's lover, and a killer. And Donna and Mark and Gretch were dead. Maggie should be more frightened than she was. She should be scared sick.

He could think of only one reason why she wasn't. He swiveled on his stool and stood up. Laid some ones on the bar to pay for the beer he'd only sampled.

"Thought you were gonna hang around," she said.

"Changed my mind. Work to do."

"Don't mention to anyone at Burnair and Crosley you saw me here, okay?"

"Sure. There's not much chance I'd run into someone from there anyway."

"Well, you never know."

"I'm trying to change that."

"Fred!" she called, as he was leaving. When he turned around she was smiling at him.

"You scare me, too," she said.

HE RETURNED to the shoe store doorway across Gull and waited less then five minutes before Maggie came out of Shellie's, blinked at the sunshine, then strode to her car.

She was walking a straight line and didn't seem the least bit drunk. Maybe she'd been scared sober.

She was carrying the briefcase.

He hurried to the Olds and climbed in and followed her, first to the Florida Federal Bank of Del Moray on Blue Heron Drive, then to Burnair and Crosley.

39

CARVER DROVE to his office and fielded phone calls and correspondence until almost four o'clock. It was cool and quiet and peaceful there. The view out the window was of the wind off the sea ruffling the tall palm trees beyond the buildings on the other side of Magellan so they looked like towering, absurdly thin women shaking their heads so their hair flew. The only sound was the soft, monotonous hum of the air conditioner doing full battle with the relentless heat and winning for the moment. He almost would have resented a prospective client walking in.

He sat staring at the glaring view beyond the window, thinking about how he seemed to be learning more about the circumstances surrounding the deaths of Donna and Mark Winship, and about how little of what he'd learned was sufficient proof for an indictment. A sharp attorney would call most of it circumstantial, hearsay, and assumption. The sharp attorney would be right.

But that same attorney would have difficulty explaining the relationships of the people involved, the dead and the survivors.

Somewhere in those relationships lay the impetus for suicide and the motive for murder, if only it could all be reasoned out.

Explaining it wasn't a job for an attorney, Carver had to concede. It was his job. And he was sure that if he didn't do it well, there would be at least one more murder.

He hated all violent death, but especially homicide. Hated the arrogant presumption, the loosing of chaos, and then the ruins that inevitably spawned more tragedy, that were always pieces of the puzzle of murder. He hated the sudden transformation of someone alive into something no more animate than a piece of furniture. He hated the death of beauty and the return to dust.

Another thing he didn't like was the workable parts of his lower body falling asleep. His pelvis and the base of his spine were numb from sitting too long in his chair. He stood up, leaning first on the desk and then on his cane, and waited for the tingling of returning circulation to stop and full feeling to return to his lower extremities.

He was standing that way, staring across Magellan at two potbellied elderly men in white slacks and pastel golf shirts talking animatedly with each other, maybe arguing, when the phone rang.

He didn't move, letting the answering machine pick up the call after the fourth ring.

Beep!

"Beth here, Fred. When you get a chance call me at the cottage. Or if you happen to be in the office—"

He lifted the receiver and sat back down in his chair simultaneously, cutting in on the machine to speak direct: "I'm here, Beth."

"Seen the evening edition of the *Gazette-Dispatch*?" she asked. The *Dispatch* was the newspaper of choice in Del Moray, after the *Miami Herald*, which covered much more than the *Dispatch*'s regional news.

Dreading what she might tell him, he said he hadn't read a paper since this morning. Across Magellan, one of the elderly men was emphasizing a point by rhythmically poking the other in the chest with a forefinger. The other man stood calmly with his hands at his sides, like a fixed object in a flooded wild stream, waiting patiently for the water to recede.

"You were right about who hired that photographer, Fred. Looks like it was Cindy Sue, and she didn't waste any time. She filed for divorce from Reverend Devine this morning. She must have been waiting to move as soon as the film was developed."

"Were the photographs mentioned?"

"No. Cindy Sue claimed incompatibility. No details. It's a small item on page six of the front section, a sidebar to a story about Reverend Devine and his flock obstructing entry into a high school that was scheduled to show a sex-education film titled *Sex in and out of Marriage.*" Beth paused, then chuckled with satisfaction. "Don't you just love irony?"

"Unless I'm the one getting ironed."

"Well, even a hypocrite's private life should remain private, unless he or she makes a hypocritical public issue of it. Then the rules change. Reverend Devine is getting what he deserves, and I hope his wife makes those photos public."

"You're an uncompromising woman."

"Way I feel about it, Fred."

"I think I'll always be honest with you."

"Wisest choice."

After hanging up, he went outside to buy a newspaper from the vending machine on the corner. He inserted a quarter, wrestled a *Gazette-Dispatch* out of its blue steel enclosure, then carried the newspaper back to the office to read.

The news item was as Beth had described. And there was a photo of Devine that had been shot at some sort of protest demonstration. A man and two women behind him were leaning angrily toward the camera with their mouths open, snarling something at the photographer. The man and one of the women had what looked like stick handles of signs resting on their shoulders. In the photograph's background was a parked car and a blurred flurry of activity involving several people moving fast in the same direction. Devine looked younger than he had the night Carver had glimpsed him at the motel, a sternly smiling man with a slightly bulbous nose and the gaze of a crusader. There was also a photo of Cindy Sue, a round-faced brunette who was attractive despite a hairdo that resembled a Buckingham Palace guardsman's tall headgear.

Carver folded the newspaper in half and laid it on the desk.

He understood now what Nightlinks was really all about. Something so simple, even if devious, that it was a miracle it wasn't done more often. Or maybe it was, and only some of those involved were aware of it.

Carver now understood why Donna and Mark had died, and why Gretch had been made to follow them in death.

And he knew what his next move should be and didn't like it. Not completely.

After using his cane to slide the phone across the desk to him, he called McGregor at Del Moray police headquarters.

He felt like a man reaching into a hole for a snake.

40

"ODD," McGregor said, "you phoning me. Usually I've gotta run you to ground and yank conversation outa you like it was back molars."

Outside the office window a huge motor home lumbered past on Magellan. There were suitcases and bicycles strapped to its roof and it was towing a small car whose windows displayed clothes and boxes stuffed inside. Florida attracted people who found it impossible to travel light.

"We had a deal," Carver said, turning away from the window. "I'm honoring it."

"I don't understand that."

"No surprise there."

"I mean about the honor part. That's the kinda word politicians toss around like Frisbees. I do understand why you're making good on what I forced you to agree to; it's because you know for sure I'll skin you slow and hang your hide out to dry if you don't. You might be stupid, but you are yellow."

"You're not making this easy," Carver said.

"Life's never easy. It only seems like it sometimes, just before the bottom falls out. What have you got to tell me, dick-head? Go ahead and unburden yourself."

"Harvey Sincliff."

"The human cesspool that owns Nightlinks?"

"The very cesspool."

"If you've got something that'll stick to Harvey Sincliff, we definitely can talk a while. We've been after him and his escort service for years, but he knows the ropes and always wraps them around our necks. Yeah, we can sure have a chat about Sincliff. Him and his fucking high-price lawyers are a disease."

"You can be the doctor who finds the cure," Carver said. "I can give him to you."

He knew how McGregor must be salivating. Not so much over collaring Sincliff and shutting down Nightlinks as over the inevitable news coverage and celebrity status for the police officer who got credit for the investigation and arrest. He'd be a hero. Heroes got kisses and prizes. Heroes got promoted.

"Sincliff's into prostitution and everybody knows it," McGregor said. "He's been turning out his escorts for years. Thing is, he's set up so it's impossible to prove."

"You can arrest him and make it stick like Superglue. I can give you the names of employees and clients who engaged in prostitution, along with the names and addresses of the johns. Beth and I will back it up with our testimony, and some of the johns are sure to break and cooperate with the prosecution."

"Goin' after the johns too, huh?" A note of caution now. Here was something that wasn't usually done. The sound of McGregor's brain working might have been audible over the line.

"Why not the johns? Prostitution's a crime that takes two to commit."

"Still, some of 'em might have toes too important to step on."

"There are no toes like that connected to the names I'll give you. Except maybe for Reverend Harold Devine's."

"Devine? The family-values turd that's always yammering on TV and picketing?" There was unmistakable delight in McGregor's voice. "So that's the reason his wife filed for divorce; the good reverend was getting a little pussy donation on the side. I never seen it to fail with them praise-the-Lord-and-pass-the-collection-plate assholes. They all got sexual problems, or they wouldn't be so high on telling everybody else not to have fun."

"You have a philosophy that covers every situation," Carver said.

"Because I got the balls and brains to live with the truth," McGregor told him, obviously feeling complimented by Carver's observation. "I see the world the way it is and you see nothing but your idiot pipe dreams that make you feel better. Now spit out what you got, and there better not be anything floating in it that doesn't belong."

Carver told him about the Nightlinks stakeouts and following the escorts and their clients. He gave him names, addresses, and license plate numbers. He didn't mention that Reverend Devine had been photographed with Mandy Jamison at the motel.

"The bagman is an Oriental named Beni Ho," Carver said. "He collects the previous night's proceeds and turns them over to a woman named Maggie Rourke. My guess is she invests the money for Sincliff under a dummy account at Burnair and Crosley Brokerage. She's an account manager there."

"And she's the one that ties the prostitution to Nightlinks and proves the escorts aren't acting on their own. That oughta make a nice package for the prosecutor. But will she break easy and cooperate with us?"

"She won't have any choice, once you follow the money."

"All this sounds good," McGregor said, "but what's it got to do with the Winships crossing the divide?"

"Probably nothing. It's information I came across while working on the Winship case, and I thought you could use it."

Carver wasn't about to tell McGregor what he thought Nightlinks was really involved in. He wasn't sure that what he suspected was true. But true or not, McGregor would love it and plant evidence if necessary to make it seem like fact. That it was a path to promotion and power was more important to him than the truth. And the path would be clear and shining to him, beckoning with the realization that the media would close in like sharks on the story and bleed and shake it for circulation and ratings for weeks. It would make Sincliff's arrest for running a prostitution ring barely noticeable in the news.

"So I'm to believe you're telling me this out of generosity?" McGregor asked.

"Why not?"

"I don't believe in generosity, Carver, any more'n I believe in Santa Claus. They both have the last laugh and they shake like a bowl fulla puke, and they're both phony."

"I'll bet you're a joy around Christmas."

"I don't like what Christmas has become," McGregor said, catching Carver off guard.

"You mean the commercialism?"

"Not that. The other. They oughta forget all that religious stuff entirely and concentrate on jacking up prices and selling crap to the suckers to give each other. Better for the economy that way. Get people out shopping instead of sitting on their fat asses praying and sipping eggnog."

Carver thought he might have something there, but he didn't say so.

"Only thing still bothers me about this," McGregor said, "is that to make it really stick like Superglue we'll have to bring in all the johns as well as the whores. I don't like that. Some poor guy knocking off stray for pay, next thing he knows he's standing limp-dicked in front of a judge. And despite what you say, he might be important."

"That's a double standard."

"Sure it is. I might not believe in Christmas, but I do believe in double standards. Fucking the people under you is what life is all about. It's God's plan, otherwise why would they be under you if not to get fucked? That's why you're there on the bottom, Carver."

"When are you going to move on Nightlinks?"

"I don't know yet. But you can be sure of one thing. We won't even think about making a move without checking with you first for approval and authorization." He hung up the phone. Laughing, Carver thought.

Even before replacing the receiver, Carver had made up his mind to be at Nightlinks when McGregor and the Del Moray police made the arrests and confiscated the files. It should be easy enough to find out when that would be. Carver and Beth had connections in the news media, which were sure to be notified ahead of time. If he knew McGregor, there would be journalists and cameras there, probably even before the law.

McGregor had a politician's understanding of the power of imagery, as well as a politician's lust for influence and authority. He'd played the press more than once. They were willing participants in his game.

Carver sat wondering if he'd done the right thing. If it turned out he was mistaken about Nightlinks, lives would be damaged, some of them permanently, because of a victimless crime he didn't really believe should be criminal.

The escorts would be able to cope. They'd probably had dealings with the police and the courts, and when they found their way out of this storm in their lives they'd continue much as they had before, even if they served brief sentences. But the clients and their spouses and children might find their worlds suddenly changed from daylight to darkness. Faith would be lost and marriages might end. All because of Carver's suspicion. His compulsion to reach conclusions. His need to discern the shapes in the fog and understand.

|41|

McGREGOR MOVED fast, before word could get out; papers could be shredded and opportunity might elude him. His boldness was perhaps the only thing about him that Carver sometimes in weaker moments admired. A contact of Beth's at Channel 6 News, alerted to coming developments, called her and said the police had leaked to the news department that there would be a raid on Nightlinks that evening at six o'clock, when the escort service would still be open and taking calls for that night's clientele.

Carver parked the Olds in front of the Aero Lounge and sat looking toward the other end of the strip shopping center where Nightlinks was located. Heat moved into the parked car, masquerading as a breeze through the cranked-down windows. A mosquito came with it and sampled blood from the back of Carver's hand. He slapped at it and missed, hearing a faint drone as it navigated past his ear. He hadn't averted his gaze from the length of the sun-punished strip of shops.

McGregor was on top of things. It was 5:45 and there was

no sign of anything unusual. People were walking in and out of the dry cleaners and the Aero Lounge. A few entered or left Nightlinks, though no one Carver recognized. He figured McGregor would hit at least ten minutes before he'd told the news media he'd be there, so no one at Nightlinks would be tipped to what was going on by looking outside and seeing some overeager news channel van festooned with call letters and satellite dishes.

But ten minutes passed, counted in gradually building heat and trickles of perspiration down the back of Carver's neck, and he began to wonder if McGregor was actually going to arrive. Carver and the news media might have been set up, for some reason not yet clear. McGregor might be engaged in another of his Machiavellian games.

The mosquito returned, or one just like it, and droned around Carver's face, tickling as it tried to flit up a nostril. He swatted air viciously with his cupped hand, hoping the turbulence would drive the pesky insect away.

Then he noticed a blue work van parked near Nightlinks, unlettered and with two people sitting in the front seats, motionless as mannequins behind the wide tinted windshield. The pedestrian traffic in the shopping strip seemed to pick up. Several cars arrived, and people in business clothes got out. Another van. A gray Pontiac of the sort used for unmarked police cars by the Del Moray department. Carver hoped no one at Nightlinks would look out the window.

Two men in brown suits who should have had PLAINCLOTHES COP flashing in neon on their foreheads came out of the Aero Lounge and strolled along the length of the strip shopping center, passed Nightlinks without pausing, then stopped and stood as if carrying on a conversation.

One of them walked around the back of the building as a man and woman climbed from an unmarked police car and moved toward Nightlinks. Carver was impressed by the number of players here. McGregor had dipped deep into the department's limited labor pool to put on a spectacle for the TV cameras.

A police cruiser arrived, driving fast and leaning hard as it turned into the lot. Its red and blue roofbar lights were flashing but its siren was silent. The only sound was its tires whining like a frantic plea on the hot pavement. Simultaneously, another unmarked Pontiac arrived, braking to a rocking halt in front of Nightlinks with its driver's-side door already opening, and the long form of McGregor unfolded up from it. He glanced around, striking what he must have fancied a heroic pose, then hitched up his wrinkled pants and strode directly to Nightlinks as van and car doors opened and shoulder-held TV minicams appeared along with cables and well-coiffed, attractive people who looked as if they should be employed at Nightlinks.

In front of Nightlinks' door, McGregor paused to make sure everyone had a photo opportunity, then he barged in, followed by two plainclothes cops. The two uniforms who'd gotten out of the squad car trailed respectfully behind, then took positions near the entrance to keep the media at bay, spread their stances, and appeared immovable as stone sculptures outside a public building.

Carver got out of the Olds and headed toward the scene.

When he got near, he was held back along with the media and the rest of the spectators. Nightlinks' door was wide open and there was a lot of activity inside. Loud voices, then silence. A few feet to Carver's left a TV camera with a Channel 6 News logo was set up and an anchorwoman with a Channel 6 News logo on her blazer was speaking into a microphone with a Channel 6 News logo on it, gazing as sincerely into the lens as if she were talking to a lover. One of the uniforms was a man named Geary, who'd been helped by Carver a year ago when his daughter was suspected of manslaughter. Geary was of medium height, but broad, with massive chest and shoulders. He had a face like a bear that had shaved.

"You're a TV star," Carver said to him.

Geary smiled. "If only I had a good side."

"What's going on?" Carver asked.

Geary smiled wider. It wasn't infectious. "Show time," he said softly, mouthing the words more than pronouncing them, so only Carver would be aware of them. Like most of the cops in the Del Moray department, like most of humanity that had come in contact with the crude and amoral lieutenant, Geary hated McGregor. But he had to work for him.

Fifteen minutes passed. Carver was getting tired of leaning on his cane. The media types were getting impatient, milling about and smiling at each other and rolling their eyes. You could take only so much tape footage of cops and cop cars and the outside of a building.

Then the media stirred expectantly on what seemed like instinct and moved closer to the door. Geary and his partner hunkered down as if there might be an assault.

One of the plainclothes detectives led the attractive, skinny receptionist with the thin ankles outside. She was wearing a tight white dress and shoes with silver metal spikes for high heels and was snarling toothily. A sure bet for an appearance on the late news.

The detective deposited her in the back of the squad car, capping the back of her head with his huge hand so she wouldn't bump herself on the car's roof, messing up her fragile and improbable hairdo.

Then a very attractive blond who was probably a baby-faced thirty but was dressed like a naughty sixteen was led outside and placed in the car. She kept her head down, trying to hide her features, as if she might not be recognized on TV or in news photos if she only kept her chin tucked in.

Carver was waiting for Harvey Sincliff, hoping he'd been in

his office and would be taken into custody before his lawyers could be alerted.

But the next thing out the door was a cop carrying a large cardboard box stuffed with file folders. He placed the box in the trunk of one of the unmarked Pontiacs and went back inside for another load. More cops with more boxes emerged. Nightlinks' files would be held at police headquarters and pored over for the kind of black-and-white evidence that would make for high bail and surefire convictions.

Finally Sincliff was led outside. His dark hair had popped loose from where he'd plastered it sideways over his bald spot and was flopping over one ear with each step he took. He was wearing obviously expensive pleated gray slacks shot through with shiny silver thread, a pastel blue shirt, and a yellow and blue tie. Wide red suspenders held up his pants beneath his protruding stomach. He was holding his suit coat in front of him, and when he saw all the media he raised it so it was supported over his head by his forearms and handcuffed wrists like a protective tent.

As the coat draped to the side when he was being placed in the car with the receptionist and the blond, he noticed Carver and his eyes caught fire. He spat in Carver's direction. Would have again, only the cop loading him into the car had gotten spittle on his shoes so he gave Sincliff an extra hard shove and slammed the door. Sincliff glared out through the window at Carver for a few seconds, then lifted his coat again to hide his face.

"That man is not your friend," Geary said.

Carver said, "It's probably my taste in clothes, but it doesn't matter. He's going where everyone dresses alike."

Geary gave his widest smile for the cameras, revealing large yellow canine teeth.

One of the print journalists was trying to get Geary aside for a brief interview as Carver moved away.

"Do you know the man who was arrested?" the woman from Channel 6 News asked, when Carver had reached the fringe of onlookers.

"Nobody really knows anybody else," Carver said, and on through the heat to where his car was parked. Let her ponder *that* one and try to fit her conclusions into a seven-second sound-bite.

He drove to his office and settled in behind his desk, deciding to make himself wait until eight o'clock before calling McGregor.

"SO WHAT do you have from tonight's raid?" he asked, when McGregor had come to the phone.

"One thing I have is you sticking your face in where it don't belong. Don't think I didn't notice you at Nightlinks, piss-head."

"I didn't upstage you. Did you get what you need on Sincliff?"

"It looks good, especially if you and your dark meat come through like you promised. Warrants are being issued for the johns you named. Miami's already arrested Reverend Devine. He's denying everything, calling it a plot against him perpetrated by his enemies in the liberal Hollywood cabal that wants to keep getting rich foisting off its values on the public."

"Sad day for the family. What about Maggie Rourke?"

"She's in custody here now, talking and talking. You were right about her and the way the operation worked, Carver. Some of the escorts would lie down for cash at night. Next day the little gook would make the rounds and collect Nightlinks' percentage of the take and turn it over to Rourke. She'd bank it, then invest it under a phony account at Burnair and Crosley, using the name and social security number of a man who's been dead for twenty years. She keeps saying the dead guy paid all his taxes so she's clean with the IRS."

"Kind of person you'd want to handle your money," Carver said.

"Only thing I'd want her to handle's my dick. I don't trust

anyone with what I stuck my neck out for and stole fair and square."

Carver decided not to comment on that. "So the only link between Sincliff and the prostitution money was when Beni Ho collected it and turned it over to Maggie Rourke. Without that, the most you could prove was that Nightlinks escorts might be engaged in prostitution on their own."

"But we've got that and more. We've got these shit-asses set up for penitentiary time, Carver, so you and Beth better hold up your end of the bargain and help make it stick in court."

"It'll stick," Carver assured him. "You'll be Florida's Eliot Ness."

"I'm that already," McGregor said with apparent seriousness. "I'm figuring to be another Hoover."

"You've got a real chance," Carver told him. "What about Beni Ho?"

"Don't have him yet, but we will. The high-price lawyers are already here quoting the Constitution, so all these people will be out on bail soon, money not being scarce with them."

"What else do you have?" Carver asked.

"Whaddya mean?" McGregor sounded confused. "What else *is* there? You think Nightlinks was into white slavery or treason?"

Carver wasn't sure if McGregor was being devious or if he was actually puzzled. The towering degenerate could play any role the situation required.

"What else did you find when you searched through the Nightlinks files?" Carver asked.

"You mean the names? There were some names that'll surprise people, maybe even more than Reverend Devine's. Believe me, Carver, some of Del Moray's chamber-of-commerce types are gonna be shit-faced when the news breaks. I'm gonna enjoy hell out of that."

"What about state politicians?" Carver asked, laying out an

obvious side road for McGregor to start down. If he didn't humor Carver and take it, his confusion was probably real.

McGregor didn't answer for a long time. His nasal breathing came over the line as a series of muted rasps. Then he said, "You're not asking about any state politicians, dick-face. What do you know that you didn't tell me?"

Carver barely heard him. He was sitting back, his mind searching for where he might have gone wrong. It was still possible McGregor knew everything and was playing it close, but he doubted that. McGregor's voice was full of genuine puzzlement and rage.

"Carver! Carver!"

Then Carver realized that if he was wrong about Nightlinks . . .

"Carver! You asshole! Carv—"

Carver hung up.

The phone rang as soon as he'd replaced the receiver. He snatched it up, knowing it was too soon for McGregor to be calling back.

Beth.

"I saw it on the news," she said. "It looks like Sincliff is going to fall all the way this time. And Reverend Devine can't be happy."

Carver said, "The only one happy is McGregor. Though not without some minor irritation."

"You oughta feel good about this, Fred. I know I do. By the way, Jeff ran down the history of Dredge Industries. It's a shell corporation, used to be one of a number of companies set up for swamp drainage. Incorporated in Delaware in eighty-six, became a subsidiary of the Brightmore Company in eighty-nine, apparently for tax purposes. Brightmore held title to the cottage where Maggie was staying. Then Brightmore, along with Dredge Industries, was acquired in ninety-two by Modelers, Inc. President and CEO of Modelers is Vincent McLain Walton."

It came together in his mind with a click so definite he could almost hear it. He couldn't speak for a moment.

"Fred?"

"We can talk later," he said. He knew Sincliff and the others would soon be back on the street. And the Nightlinks raid had been all over the local news for hours.

"What's going on, Fred?"

"No time to explain."

"Okay," she said, knowing it was futile arguing with him. "But let me in on it first. For *Burrow*. And for us."

"Us first," he said as he replaced the receiver.

The phone was jangling again as he grabbed his cane and made for the door. He let it ring as he burst out into the heat and lowering light of the humid evening. Didn't even pause to see if the caller would leave a message.

His course was as clear to him now as the shining, righteous way to salvation was clear to Reverend Devine.

|42|

THE HOT sunlight was golden in the dusk as Carver parked the Olds in front of the Walton Agency on Sunburst Avenue. The low beige brick building looked like a military bunker that had been converted to civilian use and landscaped with lush bushes and palm trees. There was no sign of activity. The modeling agency might have been closed.

But it wasn't. When Carver pushed on the brass plate of the tinted glass door, it swung open. He stepped inside and stood in sudden coolness on plush brown carpeting. A lamp on an end table next to a small sofa with what looked like an Aztec design on its back was glowing feebly, in anticipation of the night. Verna, the overly made-up receptionist with the candy-red lips, wasn't behind the front desk. The room was unoccupied, and quiet except for the sound of cars swishing past out on Sunburst.

The door marked VINCENT WALTON opened noiselessly and Walton stepped out.

He looked tired and resigned, rather than surprised to see Carver. Today he was wearing designer jeans, baggy and tapered tight at the ankles, and a silky white shirt that was unbuttoned halfway down to reveal his hairy chest and a gold chain with a carved ivory charm on it. With his handsome, weary features and pencil-thin mustache, he reminded Carver of an aged Errol Flynn trying without success to play the swashbuckling leading man one last time.

He said, "I was afraid I'd see you here, Carver. You're the kind of dog that keeps digging till it finds the bone."

"I know why Donna Winship committed suicide, and why Mark Winship and Gretch were killed."

"Well, that's the bone."

"The modeling agency is a front for a much more lucrative business. When someone wants a divorce but knows the price in money or child custody is going to be high, they come to you. You help them."

"Only if they've heard of us and understand our unique service. And if they've been referred to us by a former client. We advertise by word of mouth only and cater to a select clientele, and our price is high because our specialty is in demand." Walton's tone of voice had taken on the quality of a salesman making his pitch, believing in his product.

"You provide someone to seduce the spouse who's going to be served divorce papers but doesn't know it yet," Carver said. "The seduction isn't difficult, considering that your employees are experienced, attractive, and expert seducers, and they have intimate information provided by your clients about their spouses."

"You'd be surprised how easy it is, Carver, when you know everything about a person, from their taste in food and music to their sexual preferences and weaknesses."

"Your employees, like Carl Gretch or Mandy Jamison, accomplish the seduction, then in the course of the affair they arrange to be photographed or videotaped with the victim in a compromising position."

"Preferably one involving sexual deviance," Walton said. "Even a straight arrow like Donna Winship had desires she wasn't aware of until they were awakened in her by Carl. He was good at his work."

Carver felt his anger rise, a pressure pumping through his veins. "The victim usually agrees to any divorce conditions, knowing that if there's a court fight the affair and the tape or photographs will be made public and they'll lose big anyway, as well as suffer loss of reputation. The illicit lover has disappeared by then, run out on them the way Maggie did on Charlie Post. But that only makes the affair seem more tawdry and increases the likelihood of the victim losing even more money, property, or child custody in the divorce."

"You've got it," Walton said, as if Carver were a struggling student who'd finally grasped the lesson.

"But Donna Winship figured something was wrong and hired me to follow her—because she thought someone else might be following her."

"Our private detective and photographer. But he wasn't following her constantly. He's a busy man and spread too thin. You can understand why there's such a need for our services. The world's full of people—male and female—who need the best possible terms of divorce when they want to terminate a bad marriage. I mean, to me, marriage is a valuable institution. Reverend Devine and I agree on that one. He was easy, by the way. Cindy Sue Devine knew about his addiction to sex, so Mandy Jamison became a devout churchgoer and volunteer. It only took a month. She had to wait in line. So now he knows how it feels, huh?" He raised his arms and tilted his head to one side in a parody of the Crucifixion. "It looks now like Cindy Sue is going to control the good reverend's church and the flock that gets shorn regularly."

"In a way, she and you are in the same business," Carver

said. "You both prey on people's misery, offer them paradise, then make your killing."

"I hadn't thought of it that way," Walton said, "but praise the Lord, you're right."

"Speaking of killing," said a voice Carver knew. The other door behind the reception desk had opened and Beni Ho stepped out and leaned on his cane.

"You've placed us in a compromising position of our own, Carver," Walton said. "We're going to have to close shop here, it appears. Make ourselves impossible to find. It's a real shame."

"You'd still be in business if you hadn't gotten greedy," Carver said. "Which of the Winships approached you first?"

"Mark. He wanted the divorce and he wanted the child. So I assigned Enrico Thomas—Carl Gretch—to Donna. Gretch knew she was weak and he could get her to do almost anything with enough time, so he stretched things out. She got kinkier and kinkier, loving every second of it and loving him. Couldn't help herself any more than a woman drowning in the middle of the ocean. One night she told Gretch she'd decided she was going to divorce Mark, and she was worried someone might know about their affair and she might lose child custody." Walton grinned. "Gretch got my okay, then he told her how to avoid that."

"So you accepted both spouses as clients."

"It was the first time we'd done that," Walton said. "It opened a whole new world of opportunity."

"But Donna wasn't as blinded by love and lust as you and Gretch thought. She suspected what was going on and suffered so much guilt that she killed herself, and Beni Ho murdered a remorseful Mark to keep him quiet and made it look like suicide. Then he killed Gretch, after you'd talked him into moving back into his apartment to deflect suspicion after he'd panicked and run. Maggie would have been next. She started out by faking alcoholism, then found it wasn't all an act. Her drinking, and what she knew, posed a problem, even after you left her that dismembered doll as a warning."

"Donna's death was something Mark hadn't figured on," Walton said. "It hit him hard, made him feel responsible. Maggie had managed through Charlie Post to get a position at Burnair and Crosley so she could get next to him after Donna hired us, so she was in a good position to keep an eye on him almost on an hourly basis. And she knew how to get him to talk in bed. She told us he was considering committing suicide and leaving a note explaining why. So we had to prevent that. We simply moved his schedule up and persuaded him to write a note that met with our approval. That zipped everything up neatly. Then you came along," Walton said bitterly, "and it was a matter of time before Gretch would break and talk. So I gave him to Beni."

"And now," Beni Ho said through his ever-present smile, "I get you." He stood up straighter and tossed away his cane. It clattered off the far wall and dropped onto the carpet. "We're not alike anymore, Carver, except on the inside, where it counts most. You understand why I need to kill you."

"And you understand it works in both directions."

"We're more alike than different."

Walton said, "I'll finish packing what we need from here," and went into his office, closing the door with his name on it. In his mind, Carver was finished business.

Beni Ho moved toward Carver in a slight crouch, still favoring the leg Carver had shot. There was intense and glossy concentration in his eyes and anticipation in his smile. Carver could see his tiny, lithe body readying itself, like a cat gathering energy for its spring. The cold fear in Carver's gut was like novocaine, partially paralyzing him, slowing reaction and movement. Ho knew about that and winked at him.

Then he screamed and came at Carver with what martial

arts practitioners call a crescent kick, wheeling his body and leg sideways, his foot arcing with bullet speed toward Carver's head.

But the injured leg slowed him enough for Carver to lean back and away. He felt the *swoosh* of air as Beni Ho's foot flashed past his face. He lashed out with the cane but missed as the little man spun in a complete circle so fast he was a momentary blur.

The sudden action flushed fear from Carver. He thought he might die, but in the fatalistic core of him he wasn't afraid. It had come down to mechanics.

Ho was on him again so fast he could react only by lifting his cane with both hands to try to block the downward chopping blow. The hard walnut cane split in half like balsa wood, doing little other than slowing the edge of Ho's hand before it glanced off Carver's shoulder, probably breaking the collarbone. Carver kicked out with his good leg and felt pain in his toe as it made contact with Ho's shinbone. It was Ho's injured leg, and the little killer's smile was replaced by a look of annoyance as his backhanded elbow blow at Carver missed and he staggered toward him. The mental repose of the trained assassin had momentarily been broken by surprise and pain. Carver kicked the leg again, this time the thigh where the bullet had entered, losing his footing and falling hard onto his back. The unbalanced Ho grunted and stumbled, beginning to fall. So quick and agile was he that he managed to change the direction of his fall so he'd land on top of Carver. In midair he was already drawing back his hand to strike what would be a lethal blow to the throat.

Carver raised the splintered cane and it entered Ho's chest below the sternum. The hand thudded into the carpet near Carver's head. Ho's face was inches from Carver's, grinning with shock, the eyes just beginning to register what had happened. He grunted but couldn't rise. Tried a straight blow with his knuckles that bounced off Carver's forehead and didn't hurt much. Carver twisted the cane and shoved on it at an angle to the heart, letting Ho's weight help drive it deeper. He felt the warm blood on his fists and between their bodies spread.

The little man thrashed wildly and ineffectually, then made a deep, animal sound in his throat and went limp. He sighed, blood frothing at the corners of his grin, and lay in the stillness and silence of death.

The rhythmic hissing sound Carver heard was his own breathing as he came back from the primitive place where he'd been, where all creatures think only of survival.

Ho seemed as light and small and harmless as a child as Carver lifted and rolled him to the side. The countless eight-by-ten glossy head shots of models on the wall smiled down at the scene of mayhem and death as if it were a setting requiring them to register confidence and glee. Carver propped himself up on his elbows, then struggled to a sitting position. He was aware now of a ringing in his ears.

Then its pitch changed and he recognized the distant warbling of sirens. He realized what had happened. Beth had figured it out, too. Or McGregor. Probably Beth, who'd then called McGregor.

Walton had heard the sirens, too. The door with his name on it opened and he came out in a hurry. He said, "Beni, you hear—"

Then he saw what had happened and he stared down at Carver. His lips worked, making his thin, bristly gray mustache writhe like a caterpillar dying in the sun. "I've got a gun in my desk drawer," he said. "I oughta kill you."

Carver said, "Murder's more serious than seduction."

Walton stood thinking about that. The kind of legal help he could afford wouldn't be able to let him walk, but with Ho dead and unable to testify, Walton almost certainly could avoid a homicide charge. The dead could be a convenience in court.

The sirens grew louder and were now obviously heading in the direction of the agency.

Walton stared at Carver for almost a full minute, turning it all over. There were possibilities, even with time running out fast, but none of them were good ones.

Then his broad shoulders slumped and he went to the reception desk and sat down in the chair behind it. He picked up the phone.

Carver thought he was going to call the police, maybe dream up a story about how Carver had barged into the agency and tried to kill him.

But he called his attorney instead.

43

CARVER WATCHED the ocean and let his thoughts roll with the waves. Beth was revising her final installment on the Walton Agency story for *Burrow* on her laptop. They were sitting on the cottage porch, side by side in the webbed aluminum chairs. It occurred to Carver that old married folks sat like that on their porches, though not usually with a computer.

A sailboat banked gracefully into the wind near shore. Beyond it the low profile of an oil tanker, its scooplike hull long and low on the horizon, its superstructure well back on the bow, moved almost imperceptibly through the morning haze like a mirage. A gull soared in close to the cottage, screamed, and glided to the beach to touch down near foam fingers of surf. The warm breeze carried the fetid and fishlike smell of the sea, a reminder of life and death and forever.

"I write this stuff," Beth said, looking up from the computer, "and I get mad all over again at Walton."

Carver knew what she meant. Marriages that might still be

intact, people who might still be alive, had fallen victim to Walton and his experienced and skillful employees. He said, "There's something particularly unfair about the business he was in. Husbands and wives who might never have strayed didn't stand much chance under the pressure of expert seducers who knew the most intimate details about them."

"I don't exactly buy into that, Fred. The spouses have gotta share the blame."

"Kind of an uneven match, though," Carver said, thinking for a moment of Maggie Rourke. Beautiful, almost irresistible Maggie. "I feel sorry for them."

"So do I. But the forbidden fruit was rolled their way, and they're the ones who picked it up and bit into it. Their gamble, their loss, their responsibility."

"Even Donna Winship?"

"Even Donna."

Carver glanced over at her impassive dark features. She amazed him sometimes by being even more uncompromising than he was. But then she'd survived by not compromising about certain things, by keeping a part of herself whole at the center of the damage.

It was surprising how often uncompromising people, if they were discriminative in their choice of battle, were ultimately proved right.

It was called character.

We were here and then gone in this world, and character was the thing that made a difference, that made it all mean something.

"Anyway," she said, "Walton's doing time, and most of the spouses are going back to court and setting their divorces right, sometimes filing criminal charges for fraud."

Carver watched the sailboat tack out to sea, toward silver spokes of sunlight angling down through breaks in mountainous white clouds. Sometimes Florida could be a postcard.

"Speaking of wronged spouses," Beth said, "Charlie Post phoned here yesterday asking for you."

"Am I supposed to call him back?"

"No, he'll call you. He wants to sell you a yacht."

Carver grinned. The sailboat appeared to enter the radiant columns of sunlight and shimmered in the distance as if transformed inside a brilliant cathedral of light.

He watched it until it disappeared in the bright haze.

Here and then gone.